THE L...
MARK T...
in Pet...
acclaimed ...

Praise for

The Mysterious Strangler

"[A] well-drawn mystery . . . an interesting amateur sleuth . . . As with the previous novels, this tale retains a freshness that will please historical mystery readers and Mark Twain fans "
—Harriet Klausner

The Guilty Abroad

"Wonderful . . . Peter Heck introduces readers to the Twain family . . . provid[ing] an incredible degree of freshness to the story line . . . pleasurable . . . an enjoyable historical mystery that will garner him new fans as well as receiving accolades from old readers too."
—*Midwest Book Reviews*

The Prince and the Prosecutor

"Meaty fare for fans of the quasi-historical with nicely done period detail and atmosphere." —*Kirkus Reviews*

"Very entertaining." —*Library Journal*

continued . . .

A Connecticut Yankee in Criminal Court

"An enjoyable tour of 1890's New Orleans . . . Twain can take a bow for his performance. Heck takes a colorful city (New Orleans) and a colorful character (Mark Twain), adds a murder, a duel, some voodoo, and period detail, and conjures up an entertaining sequel to *Death on the Mississippi.*"   —*Publishers Weekly*

Death on the Mississippi

"Lovers of historical mysteries should rush out for a copy of *Death on the Mississippi*, the delightfully droll debut of Wentworth Cabot, newly hired secretary to the celebrated author Mark Twain. Twain lights up the pages as he gives his lectures, mourns his impecunious state with disarming honesty, tells a fantastic tale of hidden gold to his young clerk, and generally suffers fools none too gladly. There's a good plot, a bevy of suspects, lots of Twain lore, and even a travelogue of life on the Mississippi in the 1890's. *Death on the Mississippi* is thoroughly entertaining."   —*Alfred Hitchcock's Mystery Magazine*

"Exciting . . . deftly dovetails flavorsome riverboat lore, unobtrusive period detail, and a hidden treasure with an intricate mystery—all to give peppery, lovable Sam Clemens a starring role in a case worthy of the old inimitable."   —*Kirkus Reviews*

Tom's Lawyer

A Mark Twain Mystery

Peter J. Heck

BERKLEY PRIME CRIME, NEW YORK

This is a work of fiction. Names, characters, places, and incidents either are the product of the author's imagination or are used fictitiously, and any resemblance to actual persons, living or dead, business establishments, events, or locales is entirely coincidental.

TOM'S LAWYER

A Berkley Prime Crime Book / published by arrangement with the author

PRINTING HISTORY
Berkley Prime Crime mass-market edition / November 2001

All rights reserved.
Copyright © 2001 by Peter J. Heck.
Cover design by Ann Manca.
Cover art by Teresa Fasolino.

This book, or parts thereof, may not be reproduced in any form without permission.
For information address: The Berkley Publishing Group,
a division of Penguin Putnam Inc.,
375 Hudson Street, New York, New York 10014.

Visit our website at
www.penguinputnam.com

ISBN: 0-425-18205-3

Berkley Prime Crime Books are published
by The Berkley Publishing Group,
a division of Penguin Putnam Inc.,
375 Hudson Street, New York, New York 10014.
The name BERKLEY PRIME CRIME and the BERKLEY PRIME CRIME
design are trademarks belonging to Penguin Putnam Inc.

PRINTED IN THE UNITED STATES OF AMERICA

10 9 8 7 6 5 4 3 2 1

To CHS
In fond memory

Acknowledgments and Historical Note

The historical model for Huckleberry Finn, as has been known for many years, was Tom Blankenship, the son of the town drunk in Hannibal, Missouri. In 1906, Clemens returned to his boyhood home and visited Tom's sister, who told him that his old friend Tom was now living in Montana, had become a justice of the peace, and was greatly respected. So when my brother Sam, a lawyer here in my home town, suggested *Tom's Lawyer* as a title for a book in my series, I not only liked the title, I knew almost instantly who Tom had to be. After all, the concept of Judge Huck is so rich in possibilities—especially for a mystery—that I found it irresistible.

I made some attempt to uncover what might be known of the historical Tom Blankenship's career after his boyhood days, and turned up a few details of his life before leaving Missouri. But except for Clemens's mention of the meeting with Tom's sister, I learned nothing useful about his Montana days. Eventually I decided simply to extrapolate from the fictional character. As with others who have attempted to continue Huck's career past the conclusion of his own book, I suspect I have fallen far short of my model. But some things are worth the attempt even when the odds are stacked against complete success.

Other historical characters included here are of course Theodore Roosevelt (whom Clemens liked personally, although he disagreed strenuously with his politics); Buffalo Bill, Annie Oakley, and Frank Butler. Clemens signed Annie's autograph book, so it makes sense to assume that he met not only her but her husband and her famous employer. Colonel Burt was the commandant of Fort Missoula, and he did invite Clemens to inspect the troops during his visit to the area.

I learned a good deal of this thanks to Twain collector extraordinaire Robert B. Slotta (AKA "the Twainiac"). He pointed me toward James B. Pond's OVERLAND WITH MARK TWAIN when I asked on the Mark Twain listserv for accounts of the author's visit to Montana and Fort Missoula in 1895. The photos and incidents of that tour provided a mother lode of material for the book I eventually wrote: Clara's piano recital, Twain's attempt to buy a kitten, the visit to Fort Missoula. And I was particularly pleased to learn of the bicycle-mounted 27th Infantry Regiment—a military unit that seemed perfect for a book about Mark Twain.

As always, I have altered and adapted the source material for my own purposes; for example, Clemens's family stayed only a single day in Missoula, which for purposes of my plot I have extended to nearly a week. There is no record that Clemens and Blankenship met at any point after their youthful Missouri days. And neither Theodore Roosevelt, William F. Cody, nor Annie Oakley were in Missoula that summer—although all of them met Clemens at other times.

My wife, Jane Jewell, has been a pillar of support and an invaluable first reader throughout the course of this series. Once again I owe her thanks for numerous corrections and many valuable suggestions that have made the finished manuscript far better than my early drafts. Thanks also to the many friends and readers who have forwarded materials and comments on the books. If the Mark Twain series is long enough, I may eventually manage to work all of their suggestions in! As always, whatever errors and infelicities remain in these pages are my own responsibility.

1

Travel is a bother. I had reached that conclusion after more than a year of employment as secretary to Samuel L. Clemens, who had published a number of books under his pen name, "Mark Twain." And it was being amply reinforced here in Great Falls, Montana, where I found myself arguing with the local theater owner, who refused to pay us.

"You people have a nerve," Luke Broadbent said. He was a skinny fellow with a straight nose and close-cropped gray hair. He wore a beard on his chin, with the upper lip and cheeks clean-shaven. "From all you told me when you booked the place, I expected a sell-out," he said. "And what do I get? Fifty-five people in a hall that holds three-fifty. That doesn't even pay me to open the doors."

"Perhaps you'd have gotten more audience if you'd done some advance publicity," I said. "I walked the whole length of your main street before dinner, and didn't see even one poster."

Broadbent scoffed. "Mark's name's on my marquee, ain't it? Ever'body in town drives past that. Best advertising there is."

I refused to budge. "Then how come there were no advance ticket sales? Did you bother to put notices in the newspapers?"

"Cuts into the profits," was his reply. The fellow had apparently never thought of spending two or three cents to make a dollar. How he managed to stay in the theater business was beyond me. I supposed the local hotel—which he also owned, and where he put us up at what I considered an exorbitant rate—was making enough to cover his losses. That didn't bother me, at least not until he attempted to default on his contract.

Discouraged, I went to give my employer the bad news. I found him in his hotel room sitting up in bed with a book—a position I had learned to recognize as typical. Today, however, it was easy to see that his mind was not on the book—in fact, the book lay spine up in his lap, and his face had a decidedly weary expression. "I'm sorry to disturb you, sir," I said. "How are you feeling?"

"Middling," he said. "The cold's no worse, is about the best I can say. I'll be damned glad to get to Missoula and take a few days to rest up. But you look about as bad as I feel—what's the matter?"

"I'm afraid there's bad news," I said. "Mr. Broadbent says he can't pay us for last night's lecture. I'm considering calling the police to have him arrested."

"Damnation!" he said. He put the book on the bedside table and swung his legs over to assume a sitting position. "Let me get my shoes and my coat on," he said. "I'll see if I can talk some sense into the rascal. How much does he owe us?"

"He signed a contract guaranteeing us seventy percent of the door, with a minimum of two hundred fifty dollars," I said. "But he didn't spend a nickel on publicity, and you saw the size of the house last night. I doubt he took in a hundred fifty dollars all told."

"So he'd have to dig in his own pocket for another hundred bucks to pay me," said Mr. Clemens.

"That's about right, sir," I said. "I haven't done the math."

"It don't matter," he said. "Let's go find him."

Luke Broadbent was in the hotel lobby, standing behind the desk. He saw us coming, of course, and pulled himself up straight as if to increase his importance.

But Mr. Clemens strode right up to him and said, "Broadbent, we need to talk, and unless you've got more brass than you've shown so far, I reckon you'll want to do it behind closed doors somewhere."

Broadbent frowned and said, "Come on in my office." He led us through a door behind the counter and sat us down facing him, in front of a large desk with two or three dozen pigeonholes overflowing with papers. On the wall behind him was the mounted head of a mule deer. "Very well, gentlemen, what's your difficulty?" he said, with the air of a man much put upon.

"For starters, you ought to offer us a drink," said Mr. Clemens. He pointed to a large decanter atop the desk. "Where I come from, it's customary to give a man something to wet his throat when you're talking about money."

Broadbent scowled, and was obviously about to object, but then he reached over to a cabinet behind him, took out three tumblers, and poured a splash of liquor in each. Mine looked to be about one finger; his appeared to be even less. "There you go," he said, handing us the glasses. We all took a sip. To my surprise, after seeing the stingy portions, I found it to be a very smooth rye whiskey.

"Good," said Mr. Clemens. "Now, about the house last night. Cabot tells me you aren't going to give us our share."

"Now, Mr. Twain, that's not exactly what I said," Broadbent began.

"That don't matter, it's what you meant," said Mr. Clemens. "Here's what I'm going to offer you. You can keep your wallet closed, and you can be sure that your name, and the name of your hotel, will become the laughingstock of five continents over the next year. Or we can strike a deal."

"You don't dare," said Broadbent. "There are libel laws in this country—I'll sue you for your last cent."

"Somebody else already has it," said Mr. Clemens. "You can't sue a penniless man. And you'd lose, anyway. I'm a professional, and I can do you more damage with the plain truth than an amateur could with a whole suitcase full of exaggerations. The truth ain't libelous. Ask your lawyer."

Broadbent hemmed and hawed, but Mr. Clemens stuck to his guns. Finally, after half an hour—and another finger of whiskey all around—Broadbent opened his office safe and counted out eighty-two dollars and fifty cents: half the actual box office take. We shook hands all around, and went back upstairs to pack for our train, which was set to leave in less than an hour, now.

At the door to his hotel room, Mr. Clemens turned to me and said, with a shrug, "Well, that's settled. Let's hope the next town treats us better."

I wasn't happy, but I saw no point in berating my employer for a decision regarding his own compensation. Still, privately I hoped this episode was not to be repeated elsewhere on our journey. We were barely breaking even, by my calculations. And when I went to settle up our hotel bill, I saw that he had charged us for the whiskey in his office. As I said before, travel is a bother.

Not that I object to seeing the world beyond my own doorstep, mind you—indeed, it was the lure of unfamiliar cities and distant landscapes that first lured me away from my home town of New London, Connecticut. And my job with Mr. Clemens had amply rewarded me in that regard. Our first tour had taken me on a steamboat ride down the Mississippi from Minneapolis to New Orleans; since then we had taken ship to Europe, with visits to no less than five countries (including extended stays in England and Italy). My eyes had been opened wider, and I could look back with amusement on the callow young man from Yale who had stared with such fascination at the foothills of the Alleghenys on his first trip outside New England.

For one thing, I felt more aware than ever of what it meant to be an American. The food, the language, the money, the way people dressed, and even the way they walked— all these, and a hundred other things that once I took for granted now took on a new significance. A Yankee bred and born, I had not understood my real birthright until I saw how different the rest of the world was. It was as if someone had suddenly lit a lamp in a dark room.

Now Mr. Clemens, accompanied by his wife Olivia and his daughter Clara, was on the initial leg of what he projected as a circumnavigation of the globe. We had sailed home from Europe on the steamer *Pomerania*, which brought my employer and his family to New York at the end of the summer of 189–. There he had stopped off to attend to various business matters, and to settle two of his daughters, Suzy (the oldest) and Jean (the youngest), with friends in Elmira for the duration of our journey.

The plan was to travel westward, first through the United States and Canada, then across the Pacific to the Sandwich Islands, New Zealand, Australia, India, Africa, and Europe. In each of the major cities we reached, my employer would stay awhile to give a series of lectures, and he would do research for a book on his journey. Between the book and the lectures, he hoped to raise enough money not only to defray the costs of the world tour, but to put himself on a sound financial footing once more. It was a grand undertaking! Best of all, I was being paid to accompany him the whole way.

On the other hand, traveling with Mr. Clemens was unquestionably work. His schedule was always busy— when he was not lecturing or traveling from one city to the next, my employer would be visiting old friends or working on the book about his journey. And our hurried routine of travel, getting ourselves and our luggage from hotel to train station and on to the next town and hotel, left little chance to really enjoy the journey. We were carrying along an enormous manifest of valises, trunks, crates, and barrels, as well as a typewriter, paper, blank books for journals, pens and bottles of ink, a small library of references, and a liberal supply of pipe tobacco and cigars. (Mr. Clemens insisted that the latter were an essential component of his office equipment.)   It was my job to keep all this baggage from going astray, and to keep track of all the minutiae of our itinerary: hotel reservations, train and ship departures, and the schedule of lectures and official functions. Luckily for me, the two ladies took charge of their own wardrobes; I was nearly swamped as it was.

And things were not going well. For the first time since I had been with Mr. Clemens, his ability to summon up his energy for a lecture seemed to have deserted him, partly because of a lingering cold. Luckily, his thorough preparation and rehearsal (with Mrs. Clemens as his prompter and severest critic) allowed him to give an acceptable performance—or so one would have surmised from the enthusiastic audiences that greeted him along the way. But he, fully aware of how much better each night's presentation ought to have been, sank into depression.

This was not helped by the shrinking of his audiences as we moved west. In Cleveland and Toronto he had a full house both nights, and Mr. Clemens rose to the occasion with sparkling performances. But in northern Minnesota and North Dakota, the houses diminished, culminating in the debacle in Great Falls. And as the number of unoccupied seats grew, my employer's disposition darkened—although he was enough of a trouper not to let it show in his onstage demeanor.

I think the landscape had an effect on him, as well.

While the first part of our journey was along familiar
eastern railways, with green rolling hills and pleasant
farmland, at Cleveland we switched to a steamer across
the Great Lakes—Mr. Clemens had decided to take as
much as possible of the journey by water, and had even
decked himself out in a kind of steamboat pilot's cap.
Alas, the accommodations on this route were a far cry
from the luxury of an Atlantic crossing, and the lake
crossing was soon more an annoyance than a novelty.
Worse, when we finally did return to land, it was in the
flat territory of Minnesota and North Dakota—a landscape that soon grew dreary to my eyes. It did nothing
to improve Mr. Clemens's mood, either.

I had hopes that things would improve as we came
into the mountains. But the tour continued to go badly.
In one Minnesota town, the driver we had hired to take
us to the train was nowhere to be found on the morning
of our departure, and I had to race around town until I
finally found a milk wagon willing to take four passengers and their baggage to the station. We made that train
with only minutes to spare, after a hell-for-leather ride
past seemingly endless wheat fields, with milk bottles
clinking in the back of the wagon.

So, when (after a stunning ride through mountainous
scenery) we pulled into the Missoula, Montana station, I
was glad that our schedule had a few days' slack built
into it at just that point. The single performance scheduled for this town would probably generate just enough
revenue to cover our expenses, but I thought that a week
of rest and relaxation would be welcome at that point of
the tour. Now it looked like a better idea than the tour
itself. If nothing else, I looked forward to staying in one
place long enough to shake the dust of travel off my
clothes, and to sleep in the same bed for more than a
single night.

We got out on the platform, glad as always to stretch
our legs after a long day's ride. As it happened, an east-
bound train had come into the station only fifteen minutes

before ours, so all the baggage porters were busy unloading it. We would have to wait until they were free before our luggage could be unloaded for shipment to the hotel—possibly another half hour's wait. Seeing my employer's frown when he learned of the delay, I offered to stay behind and supervise the unloading while Mr. Clemens took himself and the two ladies to the hotel, and my employer quickly agreed. But we soon discovered that passengers on the earlier train had already hired all the available transportation. Had it not been for the presence of his wife and daughter, I think my employer's language might have turned sulfurous at that news; even with them present, he let out a few choice epithets.

"I say," came a man's high-pitched voice from a short distance away. "I know that voice. What are you doing here, Clemens?"

I turned to look at the speaker: a robust-looking fellow in his thirties, with a thick mustache and round, wire-framed glasses, incongruously topped with a western-style hat. His precise enunciation indicated an education in one of the better eastern schools, which (to my ears, at least) somewhat ameliorated the voice's harshness.

"Roosevelt!" Mr. Clemens exclaimed. "What in the world are you doing out here?"

"Well, I'm between jobs," said the other man, showing a toothy grin. "I resigned my government position, and I decided to come out here and refresh myself in the wide open spaces before going back to New York City for my next job. It's already lined up—I probably shouldn't talk about it just yet, but if you look at the news in a few weeks' time, you'll see the announcement. Suffice it to say I expect it to be an absolutely bully challenge."

Mr. Clemens introduced me to the man; Theodore Roosevelt was his full name. He was a Harvard man who had lived several years in the west before returning to New York and running as Republican candidate for mayor of that city—unsuccessfully, needless to say. "Did you ever follow up on that book idea I gave you?" asked Mr. Clemens. "I've quit the publishing business myself, but I still think you'd have a valuable property on your hands."

"You may be right," said Roosevelt. "Certainly there seems to be plenty of interest in the west—Colonel Cody's show proves that, along with all the wretched dime novels. Perhaps there is a market for another book about the *real* west. I'm afraid I've had no chance to write it, though—setting the Civil Service Commission to rights has kept me busy the last few years. And I fear my new job will be every bit as demanding."

"Well, I reckon the material will keep," said Mr. Clemens. "But I wouldn't wait forever on it—you may never do anything else in your life as interesting as running a cattle ranch in Wyoming. If you tell the story right, the book could be bringing you money for as long as you live."

"Oh, I don't plan on settling into a dull routine if I can help it," said Roosevelt. "A vigorous life's the only kind worth living; sit still too long, and you're likely to get rusty."

"Couldn't prove it by me," said Mr. Clemens, with a chuckle. "My most vigorous exercise nowadays is lighting cigars—unless you count swearing—and I reckon I've got a ways to go before I call myself rusty."

"Oh, I hear tell you've been doing a bit more than that," said Roosevelt, grinning even wider; he seemed to have more than the normal quota of teeth. "Chasing down malefactors at home and abroad. There's a bully occupation for an old rascal like you!"

"I've helped the police catch a few, but I leave chasing 'em to younger rascals like you," said my employer. He reached over and put his hand on my shoulder. "Cabot here used to play football at Yale, so he's my man when there's running to be done—or fistfighting."

"Cabot—Wentworth Cabot, you say?" Roosevelt looked at me more closely. "I remember you, now. I was at the game a couple of years ago when you smothered a fumble right on the Harvard goal line . . . a very alert play, young fellow. Too bad the wrong team won the game."

"Oh, I was just lucky enough to be there when the ball came loose," I said, modestly. Then I looked him in the eye and ventured, "But I'm afraid you must not have paid very close attention to the game, because the right team *did* win."

Roosevelt laughed heartily, and clapped me on the back. "Well, Harvard's time will come," he said. "Our fellows know what it takes to win, and Yale better not take them for granted."

We spent a few minutes talking about football. Roosevelt was clearly an enthusiast, more so than I. Besides, having spent the last nine months abroad, I would have had a difficult time keeping up with the game. Europeans had little interest in American college sports, as far as I could tell. Still, it was enjoyable to remember the old days on the gridiron—once a player, always a player, it seemed.

Roosevelt was describing with considerable enthusiasm Harvard's latest formation, in which a number of players locked arms and advanced in unison to form a screen for the ball carrier. Mr. Clemens, whom I knew to be no follower of football, broke in. I had been wondering how long it would be before he found something to say; he seemed to consider it a point of honor to express an opinion on any subject at issue, whether or not anyone had solicited one from him.

"Well, I don't see where football's much use beyond giving a few young fellows a chance to break their necks where a crowd can enjoy it," he said. "On the other hand, it doesn't appear to have hurt Wentworth much, so I reckon there's no real harm to it."

"There's where you're wide of the target, Clemens," said Mr. Roosevelt, peering through his round glasses. "Football builds character. Waterloo was won on the playing fields of Eton. I think we can expect similar results from the playing fields of Harvard and Yale."

"I'd think the playing fields would be a lot more use to the country if they kept it *out* of battles," said Mr. Clemens. "Show me the school that builds that kind of character—that's the school I'd want my country's leaders to come from."

Roosevelt shook his head. "The world's not what it used to be, Clemens," he said gravely. "America's going be pushed around by Europe if we aren't ready to take our rightful place and hold it. We can't afford to be weak. Sooner or later, someone's going to test us, and if we're not ready, we're going to be shoved aside like a weakling on the football field. I don't want America to be a weakling among nations, Clemens. And I don't think you do, either."

"Don't be so sure you know what I think," said Mr. Clemens. "I'm going to tell you one thing I'm worried about—and I'd bet a dollar it's never crossed your mind. You're one of a whole generation of Americans who don't know what war's really like. And because you think it's like football, or something else just as silly, one of these days you're going to get a hell of a lot of people killed for no good reason."

"No good reason?" Roosevelt scoffed. "Perhaps you ought to let the people who're going to fight a war decide what's a good enough reason to start it. That's always been one of the problems—old men make the decisions, and young men die because of them. There's a new century just around the corner, and it's high time to let a new generation take the helm."

"Oh, I'm glad to let the new generation take the helm," said Mr. Clemens. "I'm even gladder to let them carry my luggage, and fetch me cigars, and chase away salesmen, so I can get some work done in peace. It's the perfect division of labor."

"If I didn't know better, I'd think you were referring to me," I said, raising an eyebrow.

"Or to me," said Clara Clemens, who had been listening to our conversation. "Hello, Mr. Roosevelt. You may recall that we met a few years ago, when I was much younger."

He peered at her through his round glasses. "My goodness, yes, I remember you, Miss Clemens," he said. "You were quite the musician back then. I trust you've kept up with your lessons?"

"You should hear her," said her father. "If there's a piano at the hotel, I'll get her to play something for you. That is, if you're going to be in town overnight."

Roosevelt smiled broadly, and said, "Why, as it happens, I am—for several days, in fact. And if you all are free, it'd be my pleasure—after you're settled in—to take you all to dinner. I know a place that serves the best beefsteak in Montana . . ."

"You've got yourself a deal," said Mr. Clemens with a smile. For the first time since we'd left New York, I began to think he was finally on the way to recovering from his cold.

2

Having been to Boston, New York, London, Paris, and several other large cities of Europe and America, I was amused to see that my Baedeker described Missoula, Montana as a "rising little *city* of 3,426." The word seemed rather overblown for someplace barely a third the size of my Connecticut home town, New London.

But as we rode the horse-drawn bus to the Florence House, where we would be lodging during our stay, I had to admit that Missoula was conspicuously on the rise. It boasted two very respectable modern hotels and an impressive bank, and there were trolleys running regularly along the main street, Higgins Avenue. Still, I think the most remarkable sight our first day in town was a fellow we came across leading his horse down the street to the blacksmith shop—while riding a bicycle. The rider's straw boater was the final absurd touch.

"There's the surest sign of the decadence of the horse," said my employer, with a broad grin. "If I were that poor animal, I think I'd rather die than be led around by a damned bicycle!"

"Perhaps you would, father," said Clara Clemens. "But I'd hardly compare you to a horse. There's another creature that seems to fit your nature better."

"Perhaps I'd better not ask which one," said her father, a mock frown on his face.

"Oh, I don't think you'll be able to put off finding out indefinitely," said Clara with an enigmatic smile. "Sooner or later you'll want to know, and then you'll ask me."

"And what will you tell me when I ask?" said Mr. Clemens.

"Perhaps I should let you stew a bit longer," said his daughter smugly.

"As long as you don't call me a Missouri jackass," muttered Mr. Clemens.

Now it was Mrs. Clemens's turn to wear an enigmatic smile. "Oh, Youth, I can't *imagine* why you'd think Clara could possibly have that comparison in mind," she said. After a pause, she added, "But perhaps you're the best judge of your own character."

Mr. Clemens's mouth fell open, and for once he seemed to be speechless. Just as I thought he might have found a reply, the bus lurched to a stop, and the driver called out, "Florence House, everybody off!"

I was nearest the door, and so I opened it and alighted first, then turned around to offer my arm to the ladies as they dismounted from the bus.

As I dismounted, I noticed a small group of uniformed soldiers standing in the street a short distance away. That was somewhat unusual in my experience, but I remembered that the Baedeker had mentioned an Army post a few miles from Missoula. Evidently they were in town on some errand. Then, a second glance showed me that most of them were negroes—and that did surprise me. I had noticed, in fact, that colored people were few and far between in most of the towns along the northern route we were traveling. Except for the porters on our trains, I had hardly seen a dark face since leaving Cleveland.

I turned to assist first Mrs. Clemens, then her daughter, down from the bus. Mr. Clemens got down on his own, and stood for a moment in the street as I started off to alert one of the hotel porters that we had arrived, and that our baggage was coming on a separate wagon.

I had scarcely taken three steps when one of the soldiers came over to me and asked in a resonant baritone, "Excuse me, sir, but are you Mr. Mark Twain?"

"No, I'm his secretary," I told the man, who I now saw was wearing sergeant's stripes. "That's Mr. Twain over there."

"Thank you, sir," said the colored sergeant, and he marched over to my employer. Now my curiosity was piqued, and I turned to see what was about to transpire.

"Mr. Mark Twain?" said the sergeant, stopping in front of my employer.

"That's what I call myself," said Mr. Clemens, noticing the soldier for the first time. "What can I do for you, sergeant?"

The sergeant came to attention. "Sir, I have orders to place you under arrest," he said firmly, and reached out to take my employer by the arm.

I don't think I have ever seen my employer so surprised. Considering what I had been through with him in over a year of employment, that covers a great deal of territory. In any case, the sergeant's announcement rendered him speechless.

After a long moment, it was Mrs. Clemens who broke the silence. "Why, Youth," she said, using her pet name for her husband, "what have you done now?"

Mr. Clemens shook his head. "I don't know, Livy," he said, mild as a kitten. "I didn't know I'd done anything particularly illegal since I'd been in these parts, but some people have long memories for small offenses. Maybe the Army remembers some of the stories about me being a southern spy that got spread around during the war— not a word of truth in them, of course. But if the sergeant says he has orders, I reckon he does, and there's no point arguing with him. I'll just have to go along with him and find out what it's all about."

"Perhaps he will tell us," suggested Clara Clemens, looking at the sergeant. She walked up to him and looked him in the eye—not easy, for he was a six-footer with the physique of a blacksmith. "Please, sir, could you explain why my father is being arrested? We have just arrived in town, so he can hardly have broken any of your laws."

"I've got my orders, ma'am," said the sergeant, mildly. I thought he was slightly disconcerted to be questioned by a well-dressed young woman, though he maintained his military bearing and calm expression.

"See, there's nothing to do about it but go along with him," said Mr. Clemens, still puzzled. "If it's that old spy nonsense, I don't know what I can do except tell them the truth and hope they believe me. Wentworth, I'll leave it to you to see that Clara and the Madam (meaning his wife) are settled into the hotel, and the luggage is taken care of. Then come see if you can bail me out, if this fellow will tell you where he's taking me."

"I'll do it, sir," I said, somewhat nonplussed. Mr. Clemens had rescued me from incarceration on at least one occasion; now it looked as if the tables were going to be turned. Then I realized that I didn't know whether the soldiers would take my employer to the local jail, or to their base at Fort Missoula, which I understood to be some little distance from town. I turned to the sergeant and asked, "Sergeant, would it be possible for you to wait until I get these ladies settled into their rooms, so I can go with my employer to wherever you're taking him?"

The sergeant turned very slightly toward me and began, "Sir, I have my orders . . ."

"At ease, Sergeant Johnson, I'll take it from here," said a new voice. I turned to see an officer, a white man I judged to be about my age, who had previously been mingling with the colored troops, and thus escaped my notice. "Mr. Clemens, I am Captain Kerr of the 27th Infantry Regiment. I have been instructed by Colonel Burt, the Commandant of Fort Missoula, to allow you your freedom until tomorrow noon, at which point you are ordered to attend him for luncheon in the officers' mess. If you will accept parole on these terms, he will send transportation for you and your party tomorrow at eleven o'clock sharp."

Mr. Clemens chuckled and said, "Captain, I hope you'll tell your colonel he has a mighty eccentric way of delivering a luncheon invitation. But I won't hold it against him—or against the sergeant, here. Tell your colonel we'll be there, and I hope he doesn't take the notion to clap me in irons before feeding me."

"Colonel Burt will be looking forward to it, I can assure you," said the captain with a little bow. "And if the way the invitation was delivered has caused any offense, I certainly hope you won't hold it against anyone but me, Mr. Twain. That was my little joke, not the sergeant's—and certainly not the colonel's."

"I'd be the last to hold a joke against anybody," said Mr. Clemens. "As I said, you can tell Colonel Burt we'll be there—and if past experience is any guide, I reckon we'll all have a fine time."

"Thank you, sir," said Captain Kerr. "I'll give him your acceptance directly, and we'll be looking forward to your visit." He gave another bow and returned to the soldiers in his detail. They quickly mounted onto a pair of mule-drawn wagons, which I later learned were military ambulances, and took their departure. I briefly wondered whether they had come to town specifically to invite Mr. Clemens out to lunch, or whether delivering the invitation had been tacked on to some other business. And then a pair of porters arrived to transport our luggage inside, and I turned to more immediate matters.

We settled into the hotel, which was quite modern and comfortable inside. Mr. Clemens retired to his bed for a few hours of reading and rest, while the ladies busied themselves with their baggage—three weeks on boats and trains had left a great pile of dirty laundry to be sorted out and delivered to the local washerwomen. About five o'clock, my employer dressed for dinner and his lecture, which we had scheduled for our first night in town. I took dinner with him—an excellent cut of beef, with roasted potatoes and gravy—and afterward we walked downhill together to the lecture hall, an Odd Fellows' Hall a few blocks distant along the main street. It was a relief to me to see how Mr. Clemens's strength was returning; a few days earlier, he would almost certainly have taken a coach for that short walk.

We arrived perhaps twenty minutes before eight, and the lecture hall was already full. There had been a time when I would have been pleasantly surprised at this, and another (a bit later) when I would have taken it for granted as my employer's due. Now, given the spotty turnout in several towns along our route, I was actively relieved to see a long line of local citizenry threading its way through the doors into the Odd Fellows' Hall. This was the largest auditorium in town, although it would have been considered rather puny in a city of any size.

Still, as was usually true of Mr. Clemens's audiences, every degree and sort of local humanity was in attendance. There were prosperous-looking businessmen, looking as fat and contented as their eastern counterparts. There was the usual turnout of literary ladies, a breed recognizable not so much by dress as by attitude. There were working men, which in this part of the country meant cowboys and miners, many of them wearing their work clothes. In the balcony, there was even a small group of colored soldiers, all in uniform, from Fort Missoula, whom I saw ride up on their bicycles as I was talking to the ticket-taker a short while before Mr. Clemens took the stage. In short, the local populace had come in considerable numbers to see what my employer had to offer in the way of entertainment. Having watched Mr.

Clemens perform on stages all over our country and in several European nations, I was confident that they would not be disappointed.

It was my practice, once Mr. Clemens was onstage, to spend the next hour or so taking in whatever sights there might be in the neighborhood of the theater, and return at the end of the show. Having already heard his stories several times, I had no particular reason to sit through them again. But in a town the size of Missoula, there were few attractions in the evening hours, unless I wanted to go drinking in the local saloons—a pastime that held little appeal for me, particularly since I had no congenial company to join me. And, having made good use of my time during the train ride, for once I was caught up with my paperwork. So I decided to stand in the back of the room—I was pleased to see that every seat was full—and see how my employer's monologue fared with this Montana audience.

As usual, he came on stage with no introduction, so quietly, in fact, that one would have had to be paying attention to notice him before he reached center stage—except, of course, that those audience members who *did* notice him immediately broke into applause, and the rest followed suit. He stood there calmly, a sober expression on his face, exactly as if he were about to embark upon a learned discussion of the geology of the local mineral deposits, or the fossil remains of the mastodon, or some other subject of serious import. As I well knew at this point, that expression was completely at odds with what was really about to follow.

Finally, when the applause had mostly subsided, he said, "I'm pleased to be here in Montana."

"You lie!" came a raucous shout from somewhere in the audience—I could not tell where. There was a shocked silence, and I leaned forward, craning my neck to see if I could locate the person who had shouted.

My employer raised an eyebrow. "Of course I lie," he said. "It's how I earn my daily bread, and a good bit of butter, too. I'm not quite good enough at it to get elected to Congress, but I do what I can despite that little inadequacy." He paused and pointed in the direction from which the shout had come. "Did you have anything else to tell these folks, or can I go ahead with my own lies?" he asked.

The audience was laughing, clearly on Mr. Clemens's side. I relaxed now; I knew that when it came to verbal sparring he was the equal of anyone I'd ever seen him matched against. What worried me was the possibility that he might stumble when someone caught him off his guard, breaking into his prepared monologue—and I knew how carefully it was prepared. For all his seeming spontaneity on stage, Mr. Clemens had scripted his monologue down to the last pregnant pause and rehearsed it as rigorously as any actor preparing a role. Any unexpected deviation from the script had the potential for disaster, or so I feared. But my employer had regained the upper hand, and with any luck he would be able to continue his presentation with no further interruption.

After a moment's silence, he nodded and began again. "As I was saying, I'm mighty pleased to be here in Montana. This is the first time I've been in the state . . ."

To my horror, a voice from the audience called out, "That's a damned lie. What about the time you were kicked out of that mining camp for theft?" It was a different voice, and came from another portion of the audience.

Mr. Clemens leaned his jaw on his right fist, with his left hand just touching his right elbow as if to support it. "It's been a long time since I heard that story," he said. "It's not a bad one, all told. Although I probably shouldn't say so, because I made it up myself. At the time, I was trying to get into New York politics, and after studying the incumbents, it seemed to me that a criminal record was a prerequisite for the position I was after." The audience laughed, and Mr. Clemens continued, "So I invented something I thought would suit. But I was in over my head, as I've already told you—the other fellows were a good bit better at it than I was."

"I didn't pay my money to sit here and listen to a damned liar," came another shout—this was the first voice again, I thought. This was beginning to look like a concerted attempt to break up Mr. Clemens's talk—and if the two were not stopped, they might succeed in doing just that. I stepped down into the aisle, trying to identify the hecklers. If worse came to worst, I might have to eject them—although I was all too aware that it might create a worse disturbance than if I left them alone.

"Oh, you're wrong about that," said Mr. Clemens. "You knew what kind of show you were coming to see long before you paid for your ticket—it's been advertised all over the country. If you didn't know I was going to get up on stage and tell a bunch of lies, you have only yourself to blame. But don't get upset about it. I do have one advantage over most of the liars you'll see. They're trying to make themselves look like something other than complete fools, and so they put out dreary, self-serving lies, duller than dishwater. They'd be better off keeping quiet and hoping nobody notices. I have no such hope, so I'm free to tell you the most remarkable lies I can contrive. And I can promise you full value for your money. After all, the truth is our most valuable possession. We need to economize it."

The audience laughed heartily, and many of its members stood and applauded. Mr. Clemens stood there quietly, waiting for the applause to die down. I was impressed; it took more self-control than I could have mustered to handle the heckling as well as he did. With any luck, the incident was now over.

But the hecklers weren't about to give up. Once again, as soon as silence fell, a voice called out: "You're a damned liar!"

This time the answer came not from the stage but from the audience. "And you're a damned fool. Either shut up or go home." Now the applause was deafening, and it became clear that the rest of the audience was unanimous in its desire to silence the catcalls. "Go home, go home!" a chant began, and it built until a man stood up toward the back of the auditorium, shoved his wide-brimmed hat down over his head, and stormed out. I got a good look at him as he went past me. There was a flash of light from the lobby, and then the door swung shut behind him. The applause stopped as Mr. Clemens raised a hand.

"You better be careful," said my employer. "If you want all the fools in the place to shut up, you're likely to end up with no show at all."

There was another round of laughter, and somebody called out, "Oh, go ahead and talk. We've already paid for it, so we might as well find out how bad we've been stung."

This sentiment was greeted with more applause, and Mr. Clemens bowed. "All right, then, don't say you didn't ask for it," he said, and went back to his monologue. The rest of the evening he had the audience in the palm of his hand, and gave them every bit of their money's worth. It may have been the best performance I'd ever seen him give.

3

As always after Mr. Clemens's lectures, a small crowd gathered to greet him outside his dressing room. Many of these were minor local dignitaries, would-be authors seeking advice, and panhandlers of one variety or another. Part of my job was to gently steer away anyone who became really persistent or annoying. This night everything went smoothly, but I kept an eye on one gray-haired man in an old but respectable suit who waited on the fringe of the crowd until most of the others had met my employer and taken their leave. Then the fellow stepped forward and extended a big hand toward my employer.

"Sam Clemens," said the man, with a crooked grin. "I reckon you don't remember me . . ."

Mr. Clemens frowned, but he shook the proffered hand and said, "You're from Missouri, if I know the accent, and I ought to." He peered closely at the old fellow's weather-beaten face.

"Well, that's right," said the man. "Long time since I been there, but I s'pose it's still in the voice. Not too much of Missouri in your voice, anymore—you sound like a big city dude, Sam."

"You ought to hear this young rascal talk, if you think I sound like a dude," said Mr. Clemens, pointing at me. "Damn if I don't think I *do* know you, but I'm not putting the face together with a name."

"You sure ought to know me, Sam," said the fellow, tucking his thumbs into his pants pockets. "You done put me in a book, and as if that warn't enough, you went and done it again."

"No—it can't be!" said Mr. Clemens, his mouth wide open in astonishment. "Tom Blankenship—is that you, Tom?"

"I can't deny it," said the man. He clasped Mr. Clemens's proffered hand, and the two pumped their arms up and down vigorously. Blankenship added, with a grin, "Unless you want to call me the same name as in those books you wrote—Huckleberry Finn, though I like my own name well enough."

"No, Huck's Huck, and you're yourself, Tom," said Mr. Clemens. "You never did half the things he does in those books . . ."

"Oh, I reckon I *did* do close to half," said Blankenship. "You told a few stretchers, but not so many that I couldn't recognize myself. And some of the things I didn't do, I wish I *had* done. Those were two pretty good books, Sam, and I'm glad I got the chance to say so to you. Boy, you done all right for yourself."

"I guess I have, Tom," said Mr. Clemens. "But what about you, Tom? What are you doing way out here in Montana?"

"Well, Sam, I come out here right after the war," said Blankenship. "I got in a bit of trouble back in Hannibal—nothin' too serious, but enough to make me think I'd do better someplace where I didn't have a reputation and a bad name handed down from my old Pap hangin' over my head. It was a time when a lot of folks needed a fresh start, so didn't too many people take much notice. Not that there was too many people here to begin with."

"I know what you mean," said Mr. Clemens. "I did pretty much the same thing in Nevada and California. It made me what I am today—well, it gave me the chance to become what I am, and I managed to make the most of it. But what are we doing standing around gabbing when we could be sitting down with something cool to wet our whistles? Can I buy you a drink, Tom?"

"It won't cost you much, Sam," said the other man, with a serious expression. "I'll take a cup of coffee, and that's all. I stay away from anything harder—after I seen what a mess it made of my old Pap, I'd be a fool to meddle with it. But drink or no drink, I'd surely love the chance for a good long talk with you."

"It's a deal, then," said Mr. Clemens. "Let's go find someplace we can sit and gab. We've got over thirty years to catch up on. Where's a good place in this town?"

"I don't know anyplace hereabouts," said Blankenship. "Least not if you're more interested in talkin' than fist-fightin' and raisin' Cain. There's some nicer spots downtown, near the big hotels . . . let's see what we can find in there."

"Sure," said my employer. "In fact, let's go to my hotel. If my wife and daughter are still awake, I bet they'd like to meet you. They've read all about you in my books."

"Then I reckon they don't more than half know me," said Mr. Blankenship with a chuckle. "But I'll do my best to fix that."

So we climbed into the rented carriage and drove back together. On the way, Mr. Clemens (realizing that he had been acting as if I were not present) introduced me to his friend. Blankenship told us that he had made quite a name for himself in Montana, and had served for some years as justice of the peace in his little town, a rural community some distance from Missoula. "Justice of the peace!" said my employer, slapping his hand on his knee.

"I should've known—it's the perfect job for you. Why, Solomon wouldn't be any better at it."

"I reckon not," said Blankenship, with a chuckle. "At least I've never tried to cut any babies in half."

Mr. Clemens laughed. "You hear that, Wentworth? Now that Tom's a judge, all the precedents are up for grabs. If we can just get him appointed to the Supreme Court, the millennium can't be far off."

"That'll be the day," said Blankenship. "But even if you got me past the President and the Senate, there's eight hard-headed fellows on the court who'd be sure to outvote me. I reckon I'll stay here in Montana."

"And they're damn lucky to have you," said Mr. Clemens. Just then our driver reined in his horse, and my employer looked out the window. "Here we are, boys," he said. "Let's see if the hotel bar's open—that's probably our best shot at getting me a drink and Tom a coffee. Wentworth, you'll join us, won't you?"

In fact, I had assumed that these two men, both at least thirty years older than I, would prefer to reminisce about old tales and old times without my presence. But I did have a degree of curiosity about my employer's boyhood. Tonight's stories might be even better than usual. "If you gentlemen don't feel a young pup like me will cramp your style, I'd be delighted to join you," I said.

"Great, come along," said Mr. Clemens, and he made a beeline for the barroom. Blankenship and I looked at each other, shrugged, and fell in line behind him.

The hotel bar was, in most externals, little different from many I had seen on our journeys into the interior of the country. The owner's taste in decorations was somewhat gaudier than one would have found in a similar establishment back east; I was particularly struck by a grizzly bear's head over the bar itself. Still, for sheer vulgar display, the place was considerably outdone by Tom Anderson's saloon in New Orleans. But the dress of the habitues was rather more varied, with impeccably dressed men who might have fit in comfortably in the Yale Club in New York rubbing elbows with others who might easily have stepped out of an album of Civil War battlefield photographs. The latter— booted, sombreroed, pistol-carrying specimens with extravagant facial hair and "chaws" of tobacco firmly planted in their cheeks—were as far as I could tell every bit as affluent and (at least by local standards) respectable as their more conventional-looking counterparts.

We commandeered an empty table in a back corner of the room. As often happened when my employer entered a public place, several of the patrons already present recognized him, either nodding a greeting as he passed or leaning over to inform their neighbors that "Mark Twain" was in their presence. I knew from experience that, sooner or later, our conversation was likely to be interrupted by locals eager to meet the eminent visitor, and possibly to buy a drink for him—or to cadge one for themselves. But for now, they kept their distance, though there seemed to be one or two watching us every time I looked around the room.

The bartender brought our drinks—whiskey and soda for Mr. Clemens, a coffee for his old friend, and a cold beer for me—and my two companions returned to the conversation they'd begun on the ride home. Much of this had been along the lines of "Whatever happened to good old Jimmy Tucker?" and the like, of little or no interest to those not acquainted with the person in question, who as far as either of them knew might have been dead a quarter century or more. But now, with the more mundane details out of the way, they began to warm to their subject.

"Remember the time about five of us played hooky and took a canoe out to Glasscock's Island?" Mr. Clemens asked. "We were all going to be pirates."

"Sure, and the biggest thing we ever pirated was that there canoe," said Blankenship. "Not that I minded missin' school back then, but it was a mighty considerable letdown from what you led us to expect, Sam."

"Why, you can't expect me to take all the blame for that, Tom," said Mr. Clemens. "If you'd just used your imagination . . ."

"There you go again, Sam," said Blankenship, shaking his head. "That's jes' exactly the way you used to talk when we was kids. Didn't anything come of it back then, and I don't see how there's much of anything goin' to come of it now."

"I wouldn't say that," said my employer. With an expansive gesture, he added, "Why, almost everything I have I owe to my imagination."

"Well, if you say so, Sam, I suppose it must *be* so," said Blankenship, but the expression on his face was the epitome of skepticism. Mr. Clemens himself could scarcely have improved on it.

Seeing his old friend's evident disbelief, my employer leaned back in his seat and said, "I can see you haven't changed much, Tom. You always were a real Missouri mule when it came to buying any bill of goods you couldn't inspect with your own eyeballs."

"And I owe what *I* am today to that, Sam," said Blankenship. "You ever sit in a courtroom trying to fish out the truth of a matter, when both parties to the case is perjuring theirselves to beat the band and their lawyers is sweating like hogs trying to compound the offense, you'll see what I mean."

Mr. Clemens laughed. "I reckon I do know what you mean," he said. "And I'd lay pretty good odds there's not a lawyer in Montana who can get a lie past you— hell, I'd back you against most New York lawyers, if it came to that."

"Don't lay it on too thick, Sam—you're like to make me afraid you've got another parcel of nonsense to peddle," said Blankenship, but I could see he was flattered.

"Tall tales are my stock in trade," said Mr. Clemens. He drained his glass and continued, "But there's got to be a kernel of truth in 'em, or they aren't worth a rap.

Any fool can sit down and tell stretchers—there is probably a couple dozen of 'em in any bar in town, going at
it better than most lawyers could manage. What makes a
writer—well, a pretty big part of it, anyhow—is being
able to tell a lie that, when you hold it up and look at it
in the daylight, turns out to be the truth after all."

Blankenship rubbed his chin, pondering that statement.
"If you can do that, you're smarter than I thought," he
said at last. "A lie's a lie, as far as I can tell—and I've
heard enough of 'em to fill all the books you've written
and a few more, I reckon."

"It's not that simple," said Mr. Clemens, fiddling with
his empty glass. "Think about it. Lies come in more
styles and flavors than cigars, once you start looking at
'em. There's the lie you tell your wife when she asks you
whether she's gained weight—and you *better* lie, if you
want to get out of that question in one piece. There's the
lie you tell somebody when he invites you to a dinner
where you know you won't like the company. There's a
whole wagonload of lies somebody tells you when he's
trying to get out of paying back money he owes you.
Why, there are liars who make any writer who ever lived,
even Sir Walter Scott, look like an amateur. I could introduce you to some people who never tell the truth at
all, except by accident."

"Thanks, but I know plenty of them myself," said
Blankenship with a wry grin. "That's almost the only
kind you meet when you're dealing with lawyers as much
as I do. If it weren't for having to make a living, I'd just
as soon have nothing to do with lawyers ever again."

"I'll drink to that," said Mr. Clemens. Then he looked
at his empty glass. "No, I guess I can't," he said. He
glanced in the general direction of the bartender, then
frowned. "Wentworth, go get me a refill, will you? Get
yourself another one, too, and see if that fellow will bring
the coffee pot over to fill up Tom's cup again."

"Yes, sir," I said. I pushed back my chair and walked
over to the crowded bar. The bartender was in the middle

of attaching a fresh beer keg to one of the taps, but after a moment I caught his eye and he nodded, and held up his finger to indicate that he'd take my order as soon as he finished. I nodded back, and turned to signal to my employer and his friend that it would be a few moments before I could complete my errand.

But as soon as I turned around, there was a short, grizzled fellow staring fiercely up at me. "I don't like the company you keep," he said, fixing me with his one good eye. My mouth fell open with surprise, but before I could reply to his abrupt statement, he added, "I don't like you, either."

"I'm sorry to hear that," I said, doing my best to keep my voice even and unprovocative. "If it would change your mind, I'll be glad to buy you another of whatever you're drinking, and then I'll be out of your way directly."

To my surprise, the man squinted at me and growled, "What the hell—if you're buying drinks, make mine a whiskey."

"Done," I said warily. To be honest, I had not really expected the offer of a drink to mollify the fellow; a man who opens a barroom conversation with a flat statement of his dislike of the other party is not likely to respond to attempts to buy him off. Still, there was a small chance that the fellow had taken the cut of my clothing as a sign of affluence, and decided to try to frighten a drink out of me. If buying the drink kept him out of the way, it would cost Mr. Clemens some small change; if not, I was no worse off than before.

I turned back to see how the bartender was doing, just in time to see him ambling toward me, wiping his hands with a towel. He leaned over toward me, and before I could place my order, he whispered, "Watch yer back— that's Jed Harrington, and he's pure pizen."

"Excuse me?" I said, but before he could add another word, a sharp blow landed on the back of my head, and for an instant I saw stars.

Almost instinctively I whirled to defend myself. There stood Harrington, grinning crookedly. He was holding an empty beer bottle by the neck; presumably, that was the weapon he had struck me with. "*Told* you I didn't like you," he said.

"Put that bottle down," I said, uncomfortably aware that nearby conversations had stopped, and that people had turned to look at Harrington and me.

"What you fixin' to do if I don't put it down?" said Harrington. He slapped the bottle into the palm of his other hand. I noted, absently, that he was left-handed. The grin turned into a pout, and he continued, "Reckon I oughta keep it, case you get frisky."

I was speechless. To me, it was incredible that Harrington would attack me after I had just agreed to buy him a drink. But Harrington had still another surprise up his sleeve. He slapped the bottle into his palm again and said in a matter-of-fact tone, "Ain't you going to buy me that drink? And while I think about it, you can spring for my pals here." He gestured over his shoulder, where two seedy-looking fellows stood leering at me. The two of them looked, if possible, even less respectable than the fellow who had hit me.

"I hardly think so," I said icily. "You attacked me the minute I turned my back on you. Why should I give you another chance, let alone start buying for everyone you call your friend?"

Harrington drew himself up straight and sneered. "See, I knew you was the kind to renege on a promise," he said. "That's why I didn't like you to start with." He spat on the floor, very close to my boots, and raised the bottle like a hammer, saying, "Let's see what kind of stuff you've got in you."

Despite his obvious attempts to provoke me, I had no desire whatever to get into a brawl with the fellow. For one thing, his aim with the bottle might improve; for another, his two friends looked ready to wade in the minute the action started. Even unarmed and drunk, he was likely to be dangerous—short as he was, he might weigh two hundred pounds, and it did not look like fat. I had already been told he was "poison," and nothing I had seen contradicted that assessment. "Go find another victim," I told him. "I'm not going to fight you." But I did not turn my back on him.

He grinned. "Then I reckon I'll just have to beat the tar out of you," he said, brandishing the bottle and taking a step forward. One of his sidekicks giggled and nudged the other with an elbow. I glanced around, looking for an easy escape route, but the bar was behind me, and a ring of spectators had gathered, drawn by the promise of mayhem. None of them seemed interested in preventing the confrontation. I could try to break through them, but not without giving Harrington a clear chance to land another blow before I was out of his range. With a sigh, I balled my fists, ready to defend myself.

There was a strange moment of total silence, and then suddenly a voice rang out: "Don't move a muscle, Jed— I've got you in my sights. You and your two pals."

Both Harrington and I turned to look at the speaker, and there we saw Tom Blankenship with a revolver aimed at my assailant's midsection. I am no expert on weapons, but the hole in the end of the barrel looked very large from where I stood. Harrington visibly blanched at the sight of the firearm. "Damn it, Blankenship, this ain't got nothin' to do with you," he said. "Just a little bit of fun, is all."

"I know what your idea of fun is, and we don't want any part of it around here," said Blankenship, perfectly calmly. "Now, put that bottle down, nice and easy, and skedaddle while you've got the chance. I don't want to have to pull the trigger on this thing—I might miss and bust up some of the hotel's fancy glassware."

"Damn you, you ain't seen the last of me," said Harrington, but he dropped the bottle and turned toward the door. The crowd parted, and just that quickly, he was gone, and his two friends with him.

"I sure hope I *have* seen the last of him," said Blankenship, putting the pistol back inside his coat. Then he gestured to the crowd. "All right, folks, the show's all over. You can go back to whatever you was doing." Then he patted me on the back and said, "Well, son, let's go get Sam that drink he wants. I reckon he's even thirstier, now."

"I don't know about him, but I can surely use it," I said, following him to the bar.

Back at the table, Mr. Clemens said, "That's the damnedest show I ever saw, Tom. When you stood up from the table, the last thing I expected was for you to come out with a six-gun."

"In my line of business, it's just common sense to have one handy," said Blankenship soberly. "These are mighty rough parts, Sam—pretty near as rough as Missouri back when we were growing up. I'm glad to say I've never yet shot anybody, and I hope the day don't come that I have to, but if I have to do it to keep the peace, I'm not going to be without the means."

"Well, I reckon it did the job," said Mr. Clemens, shaking his head. I noticed that association with his boyhood friend had made his Missouri drawl a bit more pronounced, and that his grammar had fallen off from its usual standard. The exact opposite effects were evident when he had spent time with his wife. "Still, I don't like it—you pull one of those things out, and you're opening a door for the devil. I don't know if that other fellow was carrying a gun, but if he'd had one and tried to go for it . . ."

"I know," said Blankenship. "Believe me, I know. But I've had doings with Jed Harrington before. He used to have a little spread up in the hills outside of Dillon, a run-down place with maybe fifty head of cattle, didn't ever amount to much. He moved away about a year ago—I didn't know he'd come up here. Down there, he used to come into town every now and then to blow off steam, and sometimes it came to the sheriff's attention, and next thing anybody knew, it had turned into my business. I had to fine him two–three times, and found against him in a lawsuit, once. One time he busted up the general store, and I had to put him in the can for ten days. From the way he acted tonight, he didn't learn much from any of it. So we know each other, Jed and me. He knows better than to mess with me, but I don't think he likes me any more than he likes Mr. Cabot here." He paused. "I don't reckon Jed likes much of anybody."

"Sometimes I feel that way myself," said Mr. Clemens. "But Livy usually talks me out of it. I want you to meet her, Tom. I think you'll like her, and Lord knows she's heard enough stories about you."

"Mostly fibs, I reckon," said Blankenship. "Not that the truth's all that much to be proud of, at least what you must remember about me from the old days. You remember when that old slave back in Hannibal used a hairball to tell our fortunes, and said I was bound for trouble, and was going to end up being hung. Well, for a long time I feared he was right, I tell you. He said I ought to keep away from water—that's why I come here to Montana. I figure there ain't enough here to worry about."

"He was just making wild guesses, same as every other fortune teller," Mr. Clemens scoffed. "I've seen a few in my time, some of 'em pretty good, but they all turned out to be shams in the end."

"Maybe, maybe," said Blankenship. "But that old slave was right about some other things, Sam, things nobody could just guess. The hairball told him I was going to get married twice—first to a poor girl, then to a rich one by and by. It was right about that, and about a few other things, too. But I sure hope it was wrong about the gallows. I wake up at night thinking about that, sometimes."

"Well, take my advice, it's nothing to worry about," said Mr. Clemens. "Even a hairball can make a lucky guess, I reckon. But you're in no danger of hanging, Tom—all in all, you're as honest as any man I know.

Hell, unless I learn to keep my mouth shut, I'm more likely to end up on the gallows than you are."

"Well, Sam, maybe we'll both be lucky and die in bed, after all," said Blankenship, chuckling.

"You call that lucky?" said Mr. Clemens. "That's not my idea of luck—my idea of luck is not dying at all. But I'm not about to bet a nickel on it."

The two old friends laughed, and the conversation moved on to less morbid topics. And despite the fact that they spent most of the time talking about events twenty years before I was born, I listened in fascination. When, a good bit after midnight, I finally found my way to my hotel room and bed, I had to admit that, except for my run-in with Harrington, it was one of the most enjoyable evenings I had spent in months.

4

The next morning found me joining my employer at breakfast with his wife Olivia and their second daughter Clara. Mr. Clemens had polished off his beefsteak and eggs, and was reading aloud from the newspaper while finishing his coffee. "Well, well," he said, holding up the paper. "It looks as if Montana's decided to give us the red carpet treatment this summer—look who else is in town." He turned the paper around to show us an article about Buffalo Bill's Wild West Show, which was in Missoula right now.

Clara Clemens clapped her hands. "Oh, Father, can we go to see it?" she asked. "You've told so many stories about the western cowboys, and now that I'm really out here, I want to see everything."

"This isn't quite the real thing, you know," said her father. "It owes as much to Barnum as it does to anything that really went on back then. I reckon it's at least half lies . . ."

"Certainly, and that didn't stop you from taking the girls to see Barnum's circus, did it, Youth?" said Mrs. Clemens, smiling as she used her pet name for her husband. "I think I would like to see the Wild West Show, myself—in spite of some of your stories."

"In spite of my stories?" Mr. Clemens pouted. By now, I had learned to recognize that one of his mock protests was on its way. "Why, Livy, I'll have you know that every one of those stories is absolutely authentic . . ."

"That's precisely what worries me, Youth," said Mrs. Clemens, cutting him off in mid-sentence. "But I suppose that Clara has already been exposed to them, as well as to a number of other influences most refined families would consider quite unsuitable to a young lady of her age and station."

"What do you mean?" my employer sputtered. He looked from his wife to his daughter and back, frowning.

Clara answered him with a twinkle in her eye. "Why, Father, you've made so much of a point of telling us just how wild the west was in your day, and now that we're out here, you claim it's nowhere near what it used to be and that Buffalo Bill's show is all trickery. Well, we're not going to let you spoil it for us. We're going to see it and enjoy it in spite of you and your stories."

Mr. Clemens looked at her, then at me. "Wentworth, do you have any idea what she's talking about?"

"I think she's pulling your leg, sir," I said. "In any case, I think you're going to have to bite the bullet and take the ladies to the show. And if it's not any great imposition, I should like to see it myself."

Mr. Clemens glared around at the three of us, a suspicious expression on his face. Finally he shrugged and said, "Somebody's pulling my leg here, but I'm not sure just who it is. But if you all want to see Buffalo Bill's show, I don't see why not—we've got nearly a week in town. Wentworth, why don't you go see if you can get us tickets? If they're sold out, give the boss my name and see if that'll spring a few loose."

"Yes, sir, I'll do it directly," I said. I knocked back the half inch of coffee remaining in my cup—it had been one of my greatest pleasures to get back to real American coffee after a steady diet of the European product—retrieved my hat from a peg next to the door, and went out to find the Wild West Show.

The newspaper article had given the location of the Wild West Show as a property on the western edge of town, so I engaged a cab in front of the hotel and told the driver where I wanted to go.

He turned around and sized me up. "Goin' to the Wild West Show, eh?" he said, in a flat, nasal voice. "From the way you talk, you're from back east. That right?"

I admitted as much.

"Ever been to Montana before?"

"This is the first time," I confessed.

"That's what I figured," he said. He snapped the reins and clicked his tongue. The horse gave him a look over its shoulder, then (without particularly hurrying) began to move forward.

The driver guided it onto Higgins Avenue and, once it was moving in the right direction, turned back to me. "I don't understand it," he said. "Man comes all the way out here from—where, New York?"

"Connecticut," I said.

The driver grunted. "Close enough," he said. "Here you are in Montana, and what do you go see? A make-believe show about cowboys. Real thing's right in front of your nose, and you go spending your money on a sham."

"To tell the truth, I haven't seen much of the real thing," I said. "Take away the mountains and Missoula doesn't look very different from the town I grew up in." This was not quite true. For one thing, New London had a seaport, which shaped its character as much as the mountains did Missoula's. The trees along the river were cottonwoods instead of the elms and maples I was used to. However, I thought my bald statement might encourage the driver to expound upon the differences between

east and west, a subject in which I had a certain amount
of interest.

"Well, it's changed a lot," the driver admitted. "Durn
near a city, nowadays. Electric lights and telephones all
over town, people wearing those little skinny-brim hats
and patent-leather shoes like you have on . . ." He turned
around and looked at me. "I bet you've never even rode
a horse. Tell the truth, have you?"

"Yes, I have," I said, remembering summers on my
Aunt Esther's farm up near the Massachusetts border.
"It's been a while, but I have."

His expression turned skeptical. "Ever shot a gun?"

"Yes," I said. A spirit of mischief came over me. "In
fact, I fought a duel with pistols not that long ago. The
other man died." It wasn't exactly a lie, although it left
the driver free to draw a conclusion that was a considerable distance from the truth.

The driver whistled. "Maybe you dudes ain't all that
soft, after all," he said.

"Soft?" I echoed. "No, I don't think so." I cast my
mind back over all I had been through the last couple of
years, and chuckled. Perhaps it had not been quite as
active a life as a Montana cowboy's—or a Naragansett
Bay fisherman's, if it came to that. But it had hardly been
what I had expected when I signed on as traveling secretary to a famous writer, either.

The cab had reached the fringes of town—whatever
the driver's opinion, Missoula was hardly a sprawling
metropolis—and turned onto a side road. Ahead I could
see tents, a large corral with horses in it, and a wooden
grandstand of the sort I was used to seeing at football
fields. The Wild West Show, I assumed. Sure enough,
the driver pulled up into a driveway that let out at a little
shed. "Here we are, Mister," he said. "You want me to
wait?"

"Yes, I shouldn't be very long," I said, handing him a
dollar. "Here's for the ride out, and something for your
waiting time."

"Good," said the driver. "Jack Briscoe's the name. You ever need a good driver, I'm your man." It may have been no more than my imagination, but he seemed to look at me with a sort of respect, now that he thought I'd shot a man in a duel. For a moment I felt ashamed of myself for the deception. What did I think I was gaining by encouraging a small-town cab driver to think I was a killer? Shouldn't I set the story to rights, before it was too late?

Then I shrugged. Most likely I'd never set eyes on Briscoe again. And if it turned out I needed his help for any reason, I might as well have what little advantage I could get. I gave him a nod, got out of the cab, and went looking for the ticket office.

To my surprise, there was nothing in the way of a business office visible. I investigated a couple of temporary-looking buildings, which upon closer examination appeared to be storage sheds and which in any case were tightly padlocked. Nor was anyone visible in the circus-style tent at one side of the pathway where we had pulled up. This went against all logic; surely the proprietors were interested in making money. But if they were, they had neglected to erect any sort of sign enabling the public to find someone from whom to purchase tickets. The few workmen on the premises—men carrying tools, or pushing wheelbarrows of feed for the horses—were apparently too busy to talk to me, and the few I did manage to question seemed to have no idea what I was looking for.

I was about to give up and take the cab back into town when two people came around the corner of the wooden grandstand: a man and a young girl, both wearing western hats. The man was carrying an oblong wooden case, and the woman had something over her shoulder—perhaps a parasol, I thought. Perhaps they could direct me to someone who would take my money. "Hello," I called. "Can you help me find the business office?"

They stopped and looked at me. At closer look, I could see that the person I had taken for a young girl was a woman perhaps thirty years old, with dark hair and bright eyes. She wore a short skirt, just below the knees, over leather leggings—a costume that indicated that she must be part of the show. And, instead of a parasol, the object she was carrying turned out to be a rifle. "I'm sorry, what did you want?" she said in a flat midwestern voice.

"I'm looking for the ticket office," I said. "My employer and his family want to see the show, and he sent me to get some tickets. We'll be leaving town at the end of the week, so we'd want something before then."

"Oh, that's a shame," said the man, setting down the case, which was evidently of considerable weight. He was a bit older than the woman, and wore a well-trimmed dark mustache. I thought I detected a touch of an Irish brogue in his voice. "The show's still in rehearsal, and won't open until next week. Where are you going to be afterward? We've got shows scheduled all over the country—perhaps we'll be playing close by where you live."

"I'm afraid not, unless you're headed for California—or Australia," I said. "Mr. Clemens is on a world tour, and we don't expect to be back in the United States until some time next summer."

"Mr. Clemens!" said the woman. "Do you mean Mark Twain? Is he in town? I met him a few years ago—he signed my autograph book."

"Yes, that's the name he writes and performs under," I said, only slightly surprised that the woman had met him—at some point or another, he seemed to have met everyone of any interest in the world. Then I shrugged, and said, "Well, if the show is still in rehearsal, I suppose we won't be able to see it. Thanks for telling me, even though the news was bad."

"What a shame," said the woman. Then she turned to the man and said, "Frank, do you think Mr. Cody would allow Mr. Clemens to attend one of the rehearsals? I would hate for him to go away disappointed, especially since he's going to be away so long."

"Sure, and that's up to Cody," said Frank. "But I'd be surprised if he couldn't arrange something for Mark Twain. Where are you staying? We'll ask the boss and send word to him. And possibly Annie and I can get to see him before you all leave town. It'd be a pure delight to share a meal with him, if such a thing can be arranged."

"We're at the Florence House," I said. "I'm Wentworth Cabot, his secretary, and if you leave a message there for me, I'll see it gets to Mr. Clemens. I appreciate your offering to ask Mr. Cody, and I'll tell Mr. Clemens about it. If he has an open date, I'm sure he'd love to dine with you. Whom shall I tell him I spoke with?"

"Frank Butler," said the man, smiling. "Frank Butler and Annie Oakley, at your service. And our compliments to Mr. Mark Twain."

"Thank you," I said. "Perhaps we'll see each other again."

"Oh, I'm sure we will," said Miss Oakley with a pleasant smile. She put the rifle back over her shoulder, Butler lifted up the wooden case, and they continued about their business while I returned to my cab. I hadn't accomplished what I had come for, but at least I had something to tell my employer. And, not at all to my surprise, the cab driver was every bit as impressed that I had met Mr. Butler and Miss Oakley as he was when he thought I had killed a man—although I was not quite sure why.

I arrived at the hotel to find an Army ambulance waiting outside the door, with a squad of black soldiers in attendance, standing near their bicycles. The current commandant of Fort Missoula was evidently a great advocate of modernizing the army, and saw the bicycle as a quick and efficient way of getting his men into combat without reliance on railways and without the expense of keeping a large number of horses. While at first glance it was an incongruous picture, I well remembered how easily I had gotten around on my bicycle when we were in Italy, and thought it a clever answer to the problem of moving troops—although I suspected the cycles might be less than useful in a heavy snowstorm or deep mud.

Mrs. Clemens and Clara were sitting in rocking chairs on the veranda, wearing their traveling outfits. "Hello, Mr. Cabot," said my employer's wife. "Are you ready to go to the fort? These soldiers have come to take us there."

"Yes, of course," I said. Then I looked around again. "Where is Mr. Clemens?" I asked.

Mrs. Clemens answered with a sigh, "He's walking out to the fort." I remembered that she suffered from a weak heart that prohibited strenuous exercise, and realized it must also make her worry about her husband unduly exerting himself. I could understand her concern; after all, he was nearly sixty years old, and did little in the way of physical work.

"What?" I said. "Didn't he know the soldiers were coming?"

"He said something about wanting to stretch his legs after being cooped up in the train so long," said Clara. "I suspect we'll find him halfway there, sitting on a stump and out of breath. It will be amusing to stop and offer him a ride in an ambulance."

"I suppose so," I said. "In that case, I'm ready—as long as the soldiers are, that is."

"Yes, sir, we're ready whenever all you folks are," said one of the soldiers, whom upon a second look I recognized as Sergeant Johnson, who had "arrested" my employer the day before. It took me a moment to recognize him because today he was smiling.

The sergeant and I helped the two ladies into the ambulance, and he gestured for me to join him on the driver's seat. When we were both seated, he picked up the reins and gee'd up the pair of mules hitched to the wagon; in a moment we were turned around and headed along Higgins Avenue toward the south end of town, with the balance of the squad following along on their bicycles.

I had learned from my Baedeker that Fort Missoula was situated perhaps four miles south of the town of Missoula. This outpost, I learned, had for some years been the home of the 27th Infantry, a regiment of colored soldiers commanded by white officers. According to Sergeant Johnson, the fort had been built in 1877 to protect the new city from the Indian tribes of the region, a threat that had dissipated as the aborigines learned that trade with their civilized neighbors brought more benefits than the warpath. Indeed, I had so far been a bit disappointed that the few Indians I had seen during my time in the west were, except for the occasional feather in the hat or string of beads around the neck, dressed in much the same fashion as the white inhabitants of the region.

Mrs. Clemens and Clara were disappointed when I told them that the Wild West Show was still in rehearsal. But when they learned that the two performers I had met would try to arrange for Mr. Clemens and his family to see a rehearsal, they seemed satisfied with that alternative. "After all," said Clara, "in a rehearsal we might have a chance to see behind-the-scenes things that a regular audience wouldn't see. Perhaps we'll even get a chance to meet the performers."

"I think you would have that chance in any case," said her mother. "Your father's name opens many doors, Clara. Not all of them are necessarily ones you'd wish to go through, of course."

She paused, putting a hand to her brow and scanning the road ahead. "Where can he be?" she asked. "I can't imagine that he has walked all the way to the fort by himself."

"If he started out early enough, he may be there," I said. "It isn't really that great a distance, and so far the road is clear and level."

"I reckon we'll find him at the fort, gabbing with the

colonel," said Sergeant Johnson with a chuckle. Then his expression became apprehensive, and he said, "He isn't goin' to hold it against me that I played that joke on him yesterday, is he? I'd hate to get in trouble for that . . ."

"You don't need to worry about that," I assured him. "Mr. Clemens has always taken jokes in good humor. In fact, he's a bit of a joker himself."

"That's good, that's good," said the sergeant. "I'd hate to have somebody who was friends with the colonel mad at me."

We were interrupted by Clara. "Look! I told you so," she said. I turned to see where she was pointing, and there, sure enough, was Mr. Clemens, walking along the road toward us. While the entire region of western Montana is considerably elevated above sea level, and there are mountain ranges in every direction, the road was level and clear at this point. Except for a few stands of cottonwoods in the distance, we had a good view in every direction. And of course my employer's white suit and pilot's cap made it impossible to mistake him.

In a few minutes we pulled up next to him and Sergeant Johnson stopped the ambulance. I jumped down to give him a hand. "Have you been to the fort already?" I asked.

"No, damn it," he muttered. "I got to a fork in the road a ways out, and couldn't decide which way to go. Some damn farmer came along and sent me the wrong way. I must've gone fifty or sixty miles before I realized there wasn't any fort there. So I turned around and came back—but I guess I must have missed the turn again."

"Don't worry, we'll get you there now," I said, giving him a boost up into the ambulance next to his wife, who was rolling her eyes. "Meanwhile, I've got news." I told him about meeting Miss Oakley and Mr. Butler, and relayed their offer to ask Mr. Cody to let us watch a rehearsal of the Wild West Show.

"Well, that sounds like Annie Oakley. She's the damnedest little lady I ever saw," my employer said with genuine awe in his voice. "She can all but write her name with that little rifle of hers. If she ever got really mad at somebody, there wouldn't be a safe place in America to hide. Her husband's not a bad shot, either, but she beats the band."

"Her husband?" I asked. "Is she married to Butler?"

"Has been since she was barely out of school, I hear tell," said Mr. Clemens. "Love at first sight, or so I heard the story. He was a trick sharpshooter who traveled the theater circuit, and when he came to her home town the local people set up a match between them. She beat him all hollow, and next thing anybody knew, they were getting married. Or something like that. You can ask them when we have dinner. If we can get the two of them and Bill Cody, and maybe Roosevelt, too, we'll have a party to remember."

"Yes, sir," I said. "Would you like me to see if we can arrange it?"

"Sure," said Mr. Clemens. "See if they're all free tomorrow, and reserve a table for eight in the best restaurant in town."

"I'll get busy on it as soon as we're back in town," I said. It did sound like an interesting dinner group, although I was not entirely sure how much common ground I would have with a woman whose main interest was shooting a rifle. But Mr. Clemens's taste in dinner guests had never to my knowledge resulted in a dull evening, and I decided to trust it once again. If nothing else, Mr. Clemens would steer the conversation in some interesting direction.

As it turned out, events would provide us with a topic for conversation that none of us had managed to foresee.

❧ 5

After a few more miles, Fort Missoula came into view. At first sight, our destination had almost none of the features the word "fort" is likely to conjure up: no parapets, no ranks of cannon—no *fortifications,* to put it in a word. I was told that many of the western military establishments were designed as "forts without walls," relying for defense on active patrol by their men. Considering that the enemy they had been erected to defend against was in general lightly armed and highly mobile, even a civilian such as I could recognize that there was little point to erecting a large stone building to keep out someone who had no interest in getting inside it. Instead, there was a low fence that was built up to a modest gate flanked by two sentry boxes at the point where the road entered.

Our ambulance drove up to the gates, where a pair of tall negro soldiers stood on guard, with neat uniforms and gleaming equipment. Sergeant Johnson brought his team to a halt, and the soldiers behind us dismounted from their bicycles with impressive precision. Behind the sentries, a narrow door opened, about the size one would see in a home, and a white man in an officer's uniform appeared. "Permission to enter the fort with civilian visitors, sir," said the sergeant, saluting the officer.

"Permission granted, Sergeant," said the officer, whom I now recognized as the captain who'd ordered Sergeant Johnson to "arrest" Mr. Clemens the day before. The wooden gate behind him swung open; evidently there had been someone awaiting the command, and Sergeant Johnson flipped his reins and the mules moved forward. A few moments later, we were inside Fort Missoula.

Directly inside the entrance there was a large level field, perhaps two hundred yards on a side, with a bit of woods beyond it. Along the near side ran a walkway of wooden planks leading to little houses with white picket fences around front yards and flower beds as immaculately landscaped as any home in the better sections of one of our cities. Officers' quarters, I surmised. Along an adjacent side of the parade ground were whitewashed single-story wooden buildings that, from their size and shape, were almost certainly barracks.

A short, white-haired man in an officer's uniform stood in front of a small group as our ambulance came to a halt again. "Mr. Clemens, welcome to Fort Missoula," he said heartily.

"Colonel Burt?" asked my employer, giving a hand to the sergeant who helped him down from the ambulance. I stood on the other side and helped first Mrs. Clemens, then Clara, to alight.

"At your service, Mr. Clemens," said the colonel. "It's a pleasure to see you here. We get our share of visitors from the military and government, but we're always glad to welcome a man who's made his fortune by his own wits."

"Thank you, Colonel," said Mr. Clemens. "I'm afraid I've gone and lost it by my own stupidity, but I'm doing my best to get it back—which is what brings me to these parts." He introduced his wife and daughter, then me, and the commandant in his turn introduced the other officers with him: his adjutant, Major Lewis, and the fort's medical officer, Major Hyland.

We shook hands and exchanged the normal pleasantries, and then the colonel invited us to review the troops—of course, Mr. Clemens accepted. We followed our hosts to an elevated wooden stand, painted white and shaded by a canopy, overlooking the parade ground. A thirty-piece military band, all colored, struck up a lively march, and for the next half hour we watched the 27th Infantry Regiment demonstrate its prowess at marching and drilling, both on their bicycles and on foot.

"I can't claim to be any kind of military expert," said Mr. Clemens, after a while. "But these men are about as sharp as any troops I've seen—and that includes the British and the Prussians. Your officers have done a fine job here."

"Thank you, Mr. Clemens, but it's as much to the soldiers' credit as to the officers'," said Colonel Burt with a broad gesture toward the men in question. "In fact, I find that these colored troops take discipline far more readily than white. And I'm proud to say that this regiment has the lowest desertion rate in the entire Army. In a pinch, I'd put them up against the best troops in the world. I wish the top men in the War Department shared your opinion, but they don't often get out this way."

"It's their loss," said Mr. Clemens. "That band's damn fine, too; I'm not sure they play those marches quite the way Sousa wrote 'em, but I like what they do even better than the Marine Band."

"That ought to go without saying," said Major Lewis, with a chuckle. "The marines are all right in their proper place, mind you, but they ought to leave music and other such refinements to the more intelligent segments of the population."

"Which in this case is colored," said Mr. Clemens. "I'm glad to hear you say that, Major Lewis. The day may yet come in this country when a man can get credit for his accomplishments without the color of his skin being held against him. I reckon it may have to wait until the generation that remembers slavery is dead and buried, but I'm glad to see signs of it coming. Watching these men has done my heart good, Colonel Burt, and if I'm ever in a position to commend your work here to somebody in authority, it'll be my pleasure to do it."

Colonel Burt's smile got even wider. "That would be a great service, Mr. Clemens. I can't begin to tell you how grateful I'd be. But perhaps—as a first step—I can give you and your party the best luncheon you'll have between here and San Francisco!" And with that, he signaled his officers to dismiss the troops, and our little group accompanied him to the officers' mess hall, where the Army cooks did their best to fulfill his promise. I can testify that the officers, at least, are well fed; a roast leg of lamb with mashed potatoes, several green vegetables, fresh bread, and a choice of wines and other beverages to wash it down left me more than satisfied.

After luncheon, Colonel Burt said, "Now, Mr. Clemens, I've got a special treat—or so I hope you'll find it. When we heard that Mark Twain was coming to Montana, one of my officers suggested that this would be a perfect opportunity to bring together some of our old-timers for a story-telling party."

"Well, that sounds like something I'd like to hear," said Mr. Clemens, elevating his bushy eyebrows perhaps half an inch. "Maybe I'll even toss in a yarn of my own, if you don't mind."

"Bully," said the colonel, rising from his chair. "Why don't we freshen up our drinks, and take a walk over to the main mess hall, and see if the boys are ready to start talking."

"If my experience is any guide, you're going to have a lot more trouble stopping them talking than getting them started," said Mr. Clemens with a smile.

As we rose to join the colonel, Mrs. Burt turned to Mrs. Clemens and Clara and said, "And while all the boys are telling each other yarns, why don't we girls go into the parlor? We have a rather nice pianoforte, Miss Clemens. Would you be willing to play a little for us?"

"Certainly, Mrs. Burt," said Clara with a pleasant smile. But the way her eyes flicked in her father's direction, I got the distinct impression she would not have been at all averse to following her father over to the mess hall for a round of story-telling.

I followed my employer and the colonel out of the officers' mess across a corner of the compound to a large, squat, whitewashed building. Several colored soldiers who were lounging outside jumped to their feet and came to attention as their commanding officer came into view, and the colonel said, genially, "As you were, men. Any of you who have a mind, come along inside—we're having a story-telling contest here."

"A contest?" said Mr. Clemens, a bit of amusement in his voice. "Is there a prize, then? I'd like to know what I'm working for, if I'm in competition with your local boys."

"Oh, not really a contest," said the colonel. "That was merely a manner of speech. It's really just a friendly little pow-wow, that's all."

"I bet that's what the Sioux told Custer about Little Big Horn," said Mr. Clemens, grimacing. "Well, lead on, Colonel. But mind you, if I see some old trapper testing the edge on his skinning knife in there, I'm likely to duck out the door. I didn't raise this full head of white hair to be a trophy for one of your local boys."

"It would look damn good hanging in my tepee," said a gravelly voice. I turned to see a lean, copper-skinned man with a hawkish countenance leaning against the outside of the building. His clothes were at first glance the same as those of the cowboys I had seen, but on closer inspection I saw that his wide-brimmed hat had a feather in the band, and there was a string of beads around his neck. His long iron-gray hair was done up in braids. *An Indian*, I thought.

"Now, we know you better than that, Joe," said the colonel, chuckling. "Mr. Clemens, this is Joe Fox; one of our best Indian scouts. Don't pay him any mind; he thinks it's a great joke to scare easterners, but he's really pretty tame—why, he doesn't even have a tepee. Lives in the barracks."

"Well, I'm relieved to hear that," said Mr. Clemens, looking the scout up and down. He patted himself on the crown of the head and said, "As pretty as you think my hair might look hanging over your mantelpiece, I happen to think it looks even better right where it is. So I guess I'll wait awhile before volunteering it as an ornament."

"No accounting for taste," said the Indian, with an expression that might have won him thousands at a poker table. "But don't you wait for me, Mark Twain—you got stories to tell, and I want to hear 'em."

"Well, come along, then," said the colonel. "There's plenty of standing room in the back."

The scout nodded, and then Mr. Clemens and I followed the colonel into the building.

A murmur of voices arose as Mr. Clemens ambled through the door, but (in contrast with the audiences at his lecture appearances) this assembly did not greet him with a round of applause. Instead, I was reminded of the way I had seen my comrades on the Yale football team react to our opponents as they made their first appearance on the playing field. Now I understood my employer's apprehension about this story-telling contest. Far from being the star of the show, with the others as his audience, he was being treated as just one of a whole field of competitors. And, as one might expect in such a situation, his opponents were reserving their opinion until he showed them what he could do.

My evaluation of the circumstances was confirmed when a glance around the room showed me that there was no podium or stage for my employer. Instead, there were chairs drawn up in a circle, most of them already

occupied by grizzled cowboys, miners, or Army officers.
The range of costume ran to extremes: sharp blue Army
uniforms mixed with plaid shirts, red flannel, overalls,
buckskins, and chaps, and there was a fantastic variety
of hats, from sombreros and slouches and workingmen's
caps to a bedraggled stovepipe at least twenty years old,
and at least one honest-to-god coonskin complete with
tail hanging down the wearer's back.

Colonel Burt showed my employer to one of two vacant chairs in the center of the circle, and took the one
next to him. "Well, it looks as if we're all here," said the
colonel. "Why don't we get started?"

He looked toward Mr. Clemens, who nodded and began, "Well, thank you, Colonel Burt. I . . ."

He was cut off in mid-sentence by a deep-voiced man
with a bald head and a long, forked white beard. "I'm
Bill Cannon," said the old-timer. He spit on the floor,
then continued, "*Old Man* Cannon they calls me, and I
reckon I been in this part of Montana long as any white
man alive. I seen a hell of a lot in my day, and it ain't
done yet. I bet there ain't a one of you recalls the winter
of '52, when all the cricks done froze. I was trapping
with Malachi Wells back then, and if you know him you
know he wasn't one to take no guff."

"Now, Bill," began one of the other men, but Cannon
roared ahead like a locomotive through a cloud of gnats.

"Malachi and me, we was up the Swan River, by the
Kootenai Mountains. This was in November, mind you—
early November, but it was already mighty cold. You live
here in Montana, you know about cold. And in '54, it
was *god*-a-mighty cold."

"Cannon, I thought it was '52 you was telling about,"
said one of the Army officers, rubbing his chin.

The old man turned a fierce cross-eyed glare on his
questioner. "Gol-durn it, are you telling this durn story,
or am I?" he rumbled. Without waiting for an answer, he
plowed on. "Yessir, mighty cold it was, and looking more
like it might snow every minute. Well, after the sun went

down, it just kept gettin' colder and colder. Malachi and me, we'd throwed up a right solid lean-to against the wind, and we had us a fire going, but it wasn't any use. I'd taken off my mittens, and I was rubbing my hands right next to the fire, and they wouldn't hardly get any warmer. Finally, ol' Malachi turns to me and says, 'What the hell's wrong with this fire? It's cold as a well-digger's ass, and that's no lie.' It was true, too—there were big icicles starting to grow off his mustache, no more'n a couple feet from the fire.

"Well, right then I noticed that the flames weren't even flickering—they were just sort of staying in one place. I stuck out my hand into the flame, and durn if that fire wasn't frozen solid. We had to wait till the sun come up next morning before we could thaw it out . . ."

Mr. Clemens chuckled and said, "Well, you boys might think that's cold, but . . ."

He'd barely gotten that much out of his mouth before a wild-haired man stood up and roared out, "Damn me, that don't hold a *candle* to the time back in '67 when I went prospecting up in the Rattlesnake Mountains. Jackie Pierce was there. He'll swear to every *word* of this . . ."

"Or would if he warn't three years dead and gone," drawled one of the other locals. He winked and nudged his neighbor, who started as if awakened from a sound sleep. This fellow scratched himself, looked around, then dozed back off almost at once.

The speaker ignored the interruption. "We was climbing up a narrow trail that run alongside a cliff that must've been a couple thousand feet *straight* down," he said, pointing in that direction with a crooked forefinger. "I was in front, and Jackie was behind me, leadin' the pack mule with all our supplies. Well, it went smooth enough until I come around a bend in the trail, and there right smack in front of me is the biggest gol-durn grizzly bear you *ever* did see . . ."

"I don't know, Les, I seen some pizen big bears," chimed in another listener, a large chaw in one cheek.

"This one whups 'em *all*," bellowed the story-teller, and launched back into his tale, which was nearly as absurd as the one his predecessor had told, and accompanied by wild gestures. As soon as his story was done, Mr. Clemens again made an attempt to get in a word of his own, but this time he was cut off in mid-syllable by Gunnar, a burly lumberjack with a thick Swedish accent, and so it went for story after story, with each of the old Montana hands taking the floor for round after round of prevarication. And at every apparent lull in the filibuster, my employer tried to get his hand in, invariably without success. After each attempt to get a word in edgewise, I saw him glance at Colonel Burt, with a mute plea for assistance in his eye, but the commander of Fort Missoula paid him no heed.

Finally the frustration became too much for my poor employer to bear. He rose to his feet, his hands raised in supplication, and cried out, "I beg you, boys, just give me one chance! That's all I ask, just one chance."

At this there was a general round of laughter, and Colonel Burt smiled. "Why, Mr. Clemens, you ought to know the old saying—always save the best for last! You'll get your chance, I promise you."

Mollified at last, Mr. Clemens sat back and listened. And even though I could see him still champing at the bit, I think that, all things considered, he really did enjoy himself—and he finally got to tell a story of his own. When he was done, Colonel Burt stood up and said, "Now, I promised you old-timers a prize for the best story, and I'm as good as my word. I've got twenty dollars and a barrel of good whiskey for the winner. And our honored guest, Mr. Clemens, will choose!"

My employer sat up with a look of surprise on his face. "Why Colonel, I didn't know you were going to make me choose—all these fellows had damned good stories. I reckon that barrel's big enough. I'd say give all of 'em a drink, with my professional congratulations."

The men cheered, and the colonel smiled, but he said,

"That's fine with me, but the best story-teller ought to take home what's left—and there's the twenty dollars, too." He held up the gold piece for all of us to see. "Captain Kerr, why don't you serve the boys their drinks, and while you're doing that, Mr. Clemens can decide on a winner for the twenty dollars and the left-over whiskey."

There was another cheer, and the men lined up to get their drinks while Mr. Clemens cogitated. I could see that my employer was reluctant to crown any one of the storytellers as the best, but finally he stood up and said, "All right, where's the fellow who told that story about the jumping frog full of buckshot?"

"That was me," said a little man, excitedly. He stood about five foot three, and wore dungarees over a red woolen union suit. This was matched by a red nose so out of proportion to his face that it gave him the appearance of some kind of tropical bird. The story—about a miner with a pet frog that became a jumping champion—had seemed familiar to me, but I had thought it particularly well told.

"Congratulations," said Mr. Clemens. "You're the winner! Colonel Burt, give this man his twenty dollars." The colonel looked somewhat confused, but he did as Mr. Clemens said, and there was another round of cheering, and more drinks—in which my employer enthusiastically joined.

Finally, it was time to go, and Colonel Burt escorted us out to the ambulances for the ride back into town. He seemed to have something he wanted to say, and I wondered what it was. At last, Mr. Clemens looked at him and said, "I bet you're wondering why I gave that little fellow the prize for his frog story, aren't you?"

"I certainly am," said the colonel. "You must know as well as I do, Mr. Clemens, that the story Peewee told was identical to "The Celebrated Jumping Frog of Calaveras County," your most famous story. You gave the prize to a man who stole your story!"

"Well, it was the best story I heard all afternoon," said

Mr. Clemens, with a twinkle in his eye. "Besides, he wasn't the first one who ever stole that story, Colonel. Where do you think *I* got it from?"

When we returned to our hotel, I found a message waiting at the desk for us. Mr. Clemens had already gone up to his room to rest and change clothes before dinner, so (as he had authorized except in the case of personal correspondence from immediate family) I opened it. To my considerable pleasure, it was a note from Colonel William F. Cody, suggesting that Mr. Clemens and his family join him tomorrow afternoon for a special performance at the Wild West Show, to be followed by dinner with him and his leading performers. According to my calendar, my employer and his family were free to accept.

I went upstairs and tapped softly on my employer's door, after a moment I heard him say, "Come in," and I opened the door and entered.

He was sitting propped up in bed again, with an open book in one hand and a pipe in the other. On a stand beside him were (in addition to his tobacco jar, matches, and an ashtray) a small stack of other books, a sheaf of manuscript to be edited, a handful of pencils, and a pocket knife. Mrs. Clemens was sitting in a comfortable-looking armchair by the window, with her own book in hand and a cool glass of lemonade on an adjacent table.

I handed my employer the note, and he quickly scanned it. "Great news, Livy," he said, and read the invitation aloud to his wife.

"That's very generous of Colonel Cody," said Mrs. Clemens, putting her book on her lap, with a finger between the pages to hold her place. "I'm certain Clara will be pleased, too. But I hope you'll write back to him and ask to have Mr. Cabot included." She looked at me and smiled, then added, "It would be a shame for him to miss a special performance, when it may be a year or more before he has another chance to see Colonel Cody's exhibition."

"Thank you very much, Mrs. Clemens," I said. "By all means, if you don't think it would be presumptuous. I would certainly enjoy seeing the show, especially now that I've met two of the performers."

"Good, I'll ask for a spot for you, then," he said. "And I reckon I'll add on Roosevelt and Tom Blankenship, too—they'd both be good company at a dinner party, and I reckon Cody won't mind giving them a free ticket. Besides, I'm going to insist on paying for the dinner myself. I don't mind Cody's giving us a free show, but the meal's going to be on me. Although if Cody's not making more money than I am nowadays, he's a bigger sham than I think he is."

"Youth!" said Mrs. Clemens, using her pet name for her husband, although her tone was gently chiding. "It's hardly gracious to accuse someone who's just sent you an invitation of being a sham. Especially in front of poor Cabot, who has never met Colonel Cody. He is likely to have the entirely wrong impression."

"No worse impression than he'd get if he read those awful dime novels by Ned Buntline," said Mr. Clemens. He peered at me through a cloud of pipe smoke. "Or have you read them, after all? You don't seem quite the type . . ."

"I know the books you mean," I said, remembering how some of my boyhood friends had hoarded their pennies to purchase the lurid-looking books purporting to relate the exploits of "Buffalo Bill," with front covers decorated with sensational pictures of cowboys firing their guns from horseback, usually at pursuing Indians. "I remember seeing one or two of them, although they were never my sort of reading. But I assure you, I know better than to believe everything they say about Colonel Cody."

"If you haven't read them, how do you know what

they say?" asked Mr. Clemens, an impish expression on his face.

"Working, as I do, for a man who claims to tell lies for a living, I believe I have had ample opportunity to learn the difference between reality and fiction," I said quietly. "Would you like me to send a return message to Colonel Cody?"

Mr. Clemens sat there with his pipe in his mouth, staring at me. I was just beginning to wonder whether I might have gone too far in response to his gibes when he blew out a huge cloud of smoke and shook his head. "It's the curse of growing old," he said. "Mark my words, Livy, between Clara and Wentworth, I'm getting such a dose of my own medicine that if I had any sense at all I'd reform my ways."

Mrs. Clemens looked at him with raised brows. A tiny smile came over her lips as she said, "But as we already know, Youth, you haven't any sense whatsoever, or you would have reformed many years ago." And before my employer could recover from his astonishment, she turned to me and said, "And Mr. Cabot, by all means send a reply to Colonel Cody, telling him that we will gladly accept his kind invitation, and asking his permission to add yourself as well as Mr. Roosevelt and Mr. Blankenship to the party. And of course you will convey Mr. Clemens's insistence on returning the favor by asking Colonel Cody and his performers to dine with us."

"Do what the Madame says," said Mr. Clemens, with a nod. By this time he had abandoned his pose of wounded dignity and reverted to his pattern of having the last word in every discussion.

"Yes, sir," I said, with as little emphasis as possible, and left to send the message. As I went down the stairs to the lobby, I passed Clara Clemens on the way up, and she looked at me with puzzlement on her face as I passed. It wasn't until I came to a mirror on the next landing that I could see that I was grinning from ear to ear.

6 ⌒

The next morning went quickly. Our forwarded mail had caught up with us, and so Mr. Clemens and I had a pile of correspondence to go through. Meanwhile, the two ladies (with the assistance of a maid supplied by the hotel) busied themselves with the luggage. I could not fathom why, but Mrs. Clemens and Clara actually seemed to enjoy the prospect of unpacking and repacking the large trunks full of clothing—enough, it seemed to me, to fill half a railroad baggage car. At intervals, Mrs. Clemens would come into the room where her husband and I were working to ask his advice on some article of clothing—whether it was appropriate for California's climate, or whether it still fit. Mr. Clemens bore all this with good humor, although at the third or fourth such interruption, he looked at me and rolled his eyes.

In any case, it was early afternoon when our little group assembled in front of the Florence House to take a cab out to the grounds of the Wild West Show. Mr. Blankenship had given his regrets; apparently he had made some previous appointment that he could not break.

But Mr. Roosevelt had accepted with enthusiasm—I had yet to see him do anything *without* enthusiasm—and came walking up just before the cab arrived, wearing his western sombrero, which was undoubtedly more appropriate for the occasion than the riverboat pilot's hat Mr. Clemens had adopted as his headgear for this excursion. A few moments later the cab arrived, driven by Jack Briscoe, the same driver who had taken me to the Show before. A fifteen minute drive put us at the gates of the arena where the show was in rehearsal.

I had seen pictures of Colonel Cody, not only on the covers of those dime novels my boyhood friends (and I, to tell the truth) had devoured, but also on advertisements for the Wild West Show. I recognized him immediately when he strode out to greet our cab. The pictures did him justice; he was tall and athletic-looking, with flowing dark hair and a well-trimmed goatee. He wore a modified cavalry officer's dress uniform, with stylish knee-high boots and a ten-gallon hat pitched at a rakish angle.

He shook Mr. Clemens's hand vigorously, saying "Welcome! Wonderful to see you again!" Mr. Clemens introduced his family, then Mr. Roosevelt, and finally me. Cody's handshake was firm, his gaze level; he looked every inch a leader of men. If I had been constructing a western hero from whole cloth, I suspect I would have ended up with someone much like "Buffalo Bill."

The introductions over, Colonel Cody led us into a nearby tent, where there was a table of refreshments laid out. "I wouldn't be much of a host if I made you sit through the show with an empty stomach or a dry throat," he said.

I thought it a bit early in the day for anything stronger than lemonade, of which there was a large pitcher. I poured large glasses of lemonade for Mrs. Clemens and Clara, then helped myself. For his part, my employer joined Colonel Cody in a bumper of whiskey and soda, and everyone helped themselves to the platter of cold meat, which turned out to be thinly-sliced buffalo steak—

a dish I had not tasted before. It was somewhere between beef and venison, I thought, with a distinct gamy flavor that added savor without being overpowering.

Mr. Roosevelt wiped his mustache and said, "I haven't had a taste of buffalo since I was ranching in Wyoming, nearly ten years ago. A fine meat—but I understand the creatures are much reduced in numbers nowadays."

"I guess I had a bit to do with that," said Colonel Cody, swirling his whisky glass. "These days the herds are pretty well thinned out. I won't deny that I miss the day when any clever fellow could go out with a Springfield rifle and bring down a couple hundred of the beasts between sunup and sundown."

"Those days may never come back," said Mr. Roosevelt, shaking his head. "A shame—we may be the last generation to enjoy the prairies and the mountains in their pristine glory."

"The prairie's being turned to wheat and corn fields," said Colonel Cody. "The wild country I grew up in is gone forever. But that's the price of progress—and a price I'm willing to pay. I worked my whole life to bring it about."

Roosevelt spread his hands. "I'm as much for progress as any man alive, but not if it comes at the expense of something irreplaceable. The day is coming when the only buffalo will be in zoos, pitiful remnants of a day when their hooves rang like thunder across the great plains."

Cody sipped his drink, then lifted his chin and said, "To tell you the truth, the Army decided to exterminate the buffalo more or less out of policy, to reduce the Indians' ability to live off the land. And it pretty much worked, I'm proud to say. Don't get me wrong, Mr. Roosevelt. I'd be surprised if you could find a white man who's spent more time with the Indians than I have—or got along as well with them, when they gave him the chance. But even the Indians know that the future belongs to civilization. They're planting farms, or moving to the cities, becoming more like the white man. And when the whole story's told, I say that's a good thing."

"And what do the Indians say, Colonel Cody?" asked Clara Clemens, eyeing him curiously.

"A good question, young lady," said Colonel Cody, nodding to Miss Clemens. "As it happens, I've got a couple dozen Indians—some Sioux, some Cheyenne, a few Crow—all riding in the show for me. Now, I can't claim to speak for all of 'em, but I don't think there's a single one that would give up regular work—drawing a salary, eating a white man's food, sleeping in a regular bed—and go back to the old ways. And the way I know that is, once they sign on with me, they stay with me."

"What about Sitting Bull?" asked Clara, not backing off an inch. "He went back to the old ways after being with your show and was killed out on the prairie."

"And a shame it was," said Cody, a wistful look in his eye. "I could have brought him in peaceful as a lamb, but the Army withdrew my orders. He'd likely be alive today if they'd let me go after him, instead of sending out a whole posse of hotheads."

I could see Mr. Clemens muttering to himself, and I wondered whether it was because he was annoyed at his daughter's quizzing Cody on Indian affairs. It took very little knowledge of history to know that my race had often treated the Indians shamefully, but it was equally clear that, left to their traditional ways, the Indian tribes would have been a permanent barrier to the settlement of the west.

I was trying to formulate my thoughts into a question when Colonel Cody drained his glass and said, "Now, I'll ask you all to excuse me while I go saddle up and get the boys ready for the performance. I'll apologize in advance for any slips—this is still really a rehearsal, but of course we'll do our best to make it as sharp as possible. And please feel free to refill your glasses before you go out to the grandstand—we don't want anybody getting thirsty. Mr. Warner will show you the way in a few minutes."

With a bow to the ladies, he swept out of the tent and left us in the care of his assistant.

After a brief interval, allowing us to freshen up our drinks, Mr. Warner led us out to the grandstand, which overlooked a level area about the size of a football field, surrounded by a rough fence on two of the remaining sides and a large unbleached canvas curtain on the last side. There was a red-, white-, and blue-striped canopy over the stands roughly where the fifty-yard line would be, and (the early August sun being hot even here in the mountains) we settled under it to take advantage of the shade. Our party being small, we all sat in the front row. I was at one end, next to Mrs. Clemens.

Almost as soon as we were seated, a loud cacophony broke out behind the canvas curtain, and we all turned to look. Almost at once, the curtain parted, and through the opening careened a stagecoach drawn by four horses that ran as if they were being pursued by the devil himself. A moment later, that image almost came to life, as the curtain parted again to admit a party of the wildest-looking horsemen I had ever laid eyes on: Indians, in full feathered regalia and warpaint, whooping and brandishing rifles and bows and arrows, in hot pursuit of the stagecoach.

Atop the stagecoach two men rode precariously. One struggled to control the pounding horses, while another aimed a rifle at the pursuing savages and squeezed off shot after shot. At this, the Indians returned the fire, ducking low behind the necks of their steeds so as to expose themselves as little as possible to the defenders' fire. For now we saw that the passengers in the coach were also armed, and doing their best to repel the attack; the barrels of rifles and pistols protruded from the windows, and more shots were fired on both sides.

Clara Clemens squealed and ducked low as the first

shots rang out. Her father laughed. "Don't worry, Clara—they won't be using real bullets for this part of the show."

"I know," she replied, blushing. "It's just so vivid that I can't help jumping."

Twice around the arena went the coach, with the Indians drawing near, then falling back, as the driver struggled to control his horses. Finally one Indian drew up to the coach and leaped onto the back of one of the horses in the team. In a trice, he had seized the reins and began pulling the horses to a halt. The rifleman atop the coach turned and aimed at him, but held his fire, no doubt afraid of hitting his own animals. At last, at the far end of the arena from the curtain, the stage came to a halt, the horses panting after their exertion. The band of Indians swooped upon the stage like a wolf pack on a fallen deer. All seemed lost for the poor passengers.

But now from behind the curtain came another group of riders, cowboys armed with rifles and pistols, and at their head rode Colonel Cody on a stunning white charger! A silver plated revolver in his hand, he rode directly at the disabled coach, firing at the Indians—some of whom had now dismounted, the better to plunder the coach and its helpless passengers.

The Indians scattered, leaping to the backs of their horses and dashing madly away from the pursuit. Colonel Cody and his men were hot on their trail, firing shot after shot at the fleeing marauders, until at last the Indians disappeared behind the canvas curtain and Colonel Cody brought his magnificent steed to a halt. He turned to us and swept off his hat, bowing deeply.

And then, as the light breeze slowly began to disperse the acrid gunsmoke, I remembered this was all a show, put on for our benefit, and along with the rest of Mr. Clemens's party, I stood and applauded wildly. It was the most stirring performance I had seen, made all the more dramatic by the remarkable horsemanship of both the Indians and the cowboy "rescuers"—not to mention the coach driver, who had obviously been in complete control of his apparently runaway team the entire time.

The stagecoach took another circle of the arena, followed by the cowboys, all waving their hats and performing every kind of acrobatics imaginable on horseback, and exited through the curtain to the enthusiastic applause of our small group.

Then, out of an entryway under the stands came the figure of a young woman, skipping out onto the field and blowing kisses to the audience. Her skirts were short, worn over buckskin leggings, and her long hair was crowned by a broad-brimmed cowboy hat. It was none other than Annie Oakley.

While she acknowledged our applause, Frank Butler and two assistants were setting up a table with half a dozen shotguns and laying various other pieces of equipment about the field. As soon as they were done, Miss Oakley darted over to the table, picked up one of the weapons, and shouted, "Pull!"

At her signal, one of the assistants yanked on a cord, and into the air flew a pair of clay pigeons. Before they could reach the peak of their trajectory, the shotgun fired twice and they were blown to dust. She skipped back to the table, picked up another gun, and gave the signal again. This time four clay pigeons went into the air. The gun spoke twice, two pigeons broke, and before one could wink an eye, she had picked up another gun and broken the other two.

Now Frank Butler stood down the field, a clay pipe in his mouth, and she took a rifle from the table. In the other hand she took a small mirror, and stood with her back to her husband, the rifle across her shoulder as if she were a soldier, looking in the mirror. Suddenly I realized what she was about to do, and wondered at Butler's courage. But he did not flinch as she leveled the barrel of the gun, her gaze fixed on the mirror, and then a shot rang out. Fifty yards distant, the bowl of the pipe shattered—leaving six inches of the pipestem in Butler's mouth. My mouth was open at the seeming ease with which she had performed the feat. But she was already darting over to the table to get another gun, and the exhibition continued.

There was more riding and shooting, with Colonel Cody excelling at both, although at the end of the day I thought that Annie Oakley had outshone her famous employer in her cool command of her firearms. Finally, the entire cast of the show rode into the arena, accompanied by a brass band dressed in cowboy garb, and drew up in a line in front of us to take a bow. All of us in the grandstand stood and applauded wildly, trying our best to make up for the thousand or more empty seats around us. It was the most exhilarating outdoor show in my experience—and while Mr. Roosevelt would probably have contested the point, that definitely included the three Yale–Harvard football games I had played in.

"That was one hell of a show, Colonel," said Mr. Clemens, back in the tent. He raised his glass to toast the old buffalo hunter. "If I'd paid for it, I'd say it was worth every cent."

"I wish it had been better," said Colonel Cody, raising his glass in return. "That was just a rough rehearsal—too rough, I'm afraid. We've barely begun to put the whole thing together. Why, the band missed half its cues, and—"

"Don't apologize too much," said Mr. Clemens. "I've stood in front of my share of audiences before now, though maybe I haven't made as regular a thing of it as you have. But one thing I've learned: You never tell the paying customers anything they don't need to know. If there were problems, I sure didn't see them. It was a fine show, and you can be sure I'll put out the word."

"That's much appreciated," said Colonel Cody, with a little bow. "And I'll be sure to return the favor by telling folks about your lecture tours."

Mr. Clemens nodded. Then a wry smile came to his face, and he said, "That would be almost a perfect arrangement, except for the fact that you're headed east and I'm going west. We'll both be advertising to exactly the wrong customers!"

Colonel Cody laughed. "There's only one answer for it," he said. "I'll just have to turn around and follow your route. It should be easy—all I'll have to do is cancel six months' worth of bookings and start from scratch." He hooked his thumbs into his belt and grinned.

"A brilliant stratagem," said Mr. Roosevelt, grinning back at the Colonel. "I'm sure the Wild West Show will be an unprecedented sensation in Australia and India."

"Maybe not in India," said Mr. Clemens, deadpan again. "I hear tell they've already got Indians there. Unless Kipling's been pulling my leg, anyhow."

"Well, that ruins the whole scheme," said the colonel. "We'll just have to think up another one. I'm sure the three of us can manage it."

"I reckon so," said Mr. Clemens. "But why don't we adjourn to town so we can talk about it over dinner? I wouldn't be surprised if you worked up a pretty good appetite after all that riding and shooting."

"It would be my pleasure," said Colonel Cody. "Let me just call Annie and Frank, and get the stagecoach ready . . ."

"The stagecoach?" said Mrs. Clemens. "What do we need that for?"

"Why, Mr. Clemens is buying me dinner," said the colonel. "It's the least I can do to give you a ride into town, and in the best accommodations I can provide. I think the Deadwood Stage will just fit the party."

"And get you a bit of free publicity in addition," said Mr. Roosevelt with a chuckle. "Excellent planning, Colonel Cody."

"We'd be glad to accept," said Mrs. Clemens, with her forefinger on her chin. "But I do hope you will instruct your coachman to drive a bit more carefully than he did in the arena today. And I would certainly hope that we won't be pursued by wild Indians."

"Ma'am, I will promise you as smooth a ride as you

ever had," said Colonel Cody, bowing low. He continued
in a serious tone, "But as far as the Indians, please understand that I can only speak for the ones in my employment. I hear tell there are still quite a few wild ones
hereabouts." He turned and winked at my employer.
"Why, just last week . . ."

"Thank you, Colonel Cody. I think that will quite suffice," said Mrs. Clemens with a broad smile.

The colonel left to see to the details while we finished
our drinks. In a short while, Frank Butler and Annie Oakley joined us, and my employer introduced them to his
family and to Mr. Roosevelt. I had already made their
acquaintance, but I made it a point to compliment Miss
Oakley on her exceptional marksmanship. "You must
have put in long hours of practice to be so accurate," I
said.

"Long hours, and I had a strong incentive," she said
quietly. "I hunted to support our family from the time I
was a little girl in Ohio. If I missed a shot, it cost us
food on the table or money we couldn't do without. So
I learned not to miss."

"You've come up in the world," said Mr. Roosevelt.
"At least now a missed shot won't cost you a meal."

"No, but it could cost me something I'd miss even
more," she said with a glance at Frank Butler. There was
a moment of silence. Then she raised her chin and added,
"But I won't miss that shot." She smiled again at her
husband, and a special look passed between them.

"Sure, and it gives me every reason to treat the little
lady like a queen," said Butler in his broad Irish brogue.
He put his arm over her shoulder and gave her a squeeze.
Everyone laughed, but I think we were all aware of the
implication of his statement. I wondered what it was like
to be able to trust another with your life, and put it to
the test day after day. I wondered if I would ever find
someone I felt that way about. At least once, I had
thought I had—but it had not turned out as I had hoped.
Perhaps it might happen again . . .

These musings were interrupted by the return of the colonel. "All right, ladies and gentlemen, we're ready to ride," he said. "The Deadwood Stage has carried its share of celebrated men and women, including the crowned heads of Europe—so come aboard! Who knows when you'll have another chance?" We all moved toward the waiting stage.

"Why, if I learned to shoot and joined the show, I could ride it every day," said Mr. Clemens. His wife and his daughter Clara stared at him as if he'd gone mad, and I understood why—he was the last person I could imagine wielding a firearm with any competence. But after a moment he winked at me and continued, "And if I learned to spit gold pieces, I'd never have to work again. Lead the way, Colonel."

We all climbed into the coach, except for Colonel Cody and two of his "cowboys," who escorted us on horseback. And although no wild Indians or stagecoach robbers approached us, we still managed to have a wonderful trip back to Missoula, with a good view of the western scenery. The afternoon sun shone brightly on the semi-arid countryside, and I was reminded again of how much the colors of the landscape in this part of the country differed from those of my home town in Connecticut. The greens were not as dark, and the rocks displayed a wild variety of reds, browns, blacks, and tans; even the sky seemed a distinctive shade of blue. A jackrabbit burst from behind a stand of pines and sprinted alongside the road for a moment before dodging crazily into the underbrush again. It was a fitting symbol of this rugged country, I thought.

The stagecoach pulled up at the hotel, where we found Tom Blankenship waiting in a rocking chair on the veranda. He had pled a previous engagement when Mr. Clemens invited him to come view the Wild West Show rehearsal, but told us he would be free to join us for supper.

The arrival of the coach caused no little flurry among the locals. A group of small boys, accompanied by a skinny brown dog with feet at least three sizes too big for its body, followed us the last few blocks, whooping like the Indians that had chased the vehicle during the rehearsal, and their noise drew a crowd of spectators to watch us alight in front of the hotel. Colonel Cody, who had ridden alongside us on his handsome white horse, waved his hat to the crowd, then dismounted athletically in time to help the ladies out of the coach. The children applauded as he helped Clara and Mrs. Clemens alight, and he rewarded their applause by sweeping his hat off and giving a theatrical bow. They giggled and nudged each other.

My employer and Mr. Roosevelt obviously enjoyed the attention as much as the colonel. But I thought Mr. Blankenship was somewhat sheepish as Mr. Clemens waved at him and called, "Hey, Tom! Ain't this the style? Don't you wish you could've ridden into town on the Deadwood Stage?"

"I guess not," Blankenship said, standing up and putting his hands into his pockets. "My good old buggy gets me anywhere I want to go just fine."

"That's what's always been wrong with you," said Mr. Clemens, feigning grumpiness. "Never had any sense of style. It's a wonder you aren't still wearing a tow shirt and dungarees."

"It's about what I do wear, when I'm not dressed up for folks," said Blankenship calmly. "Don't tell me you go out chopping wood and feeding the horses in your going-to-town suit?"

Never having seen Mr. Clemens chop a stick of wood or feed even one horse, I was interested in hearing his answer. But no sooner had Blankenship asked, than a loud commotion arose on the other side of the street. My first thought was that the pack of urchins who had run after the coach had started some kind of mischief. But when I turned to see what the young scamps were up to, my eyes narrowed and my heart began to pound. The cause of the commotion was hardly as innocent as I had thought.

One of the blue-clad soldiers of the 27th Regiment sprawled on the ground next to his bicycle. Even as I watched, the rider tried to rise from the ground, only to be pushed back by a trio of leering bullies. In the middle was the barrel-shaped figure of Jed Harrington, the man who had picked a fight with me in the barroom the night before. His two cronies laughed raucously. Without a word, I balled my fists and sprinted across the street, ready for action. Behind me I heard Mr. Clemens exclaim, "What the hell?" and someone else's footsteps hurrying after me. I didn't turn to see who it was. Either they were coming to help me or not.

I was perhaps halfway across the street when Harrington noticed me. He pointed and said something to his two partners, and the cowboys looked up from the negro infantryman they had been taunting. Harrington grimaced; then the three of them, as if at some signal, spread out in a line abreast and stepped forward to confront me.

Their challenging stance made it clear they weren't going to abandon their game at the first sign of interference. Realizing that I was probably facing a fight, I slowed down and changed my direction, moving around the three men to see if there was any way I could help the soldier. He had sat up in the dusty street, trying to catch his breath. Having taken a few falls off a bicycle in my time, I hoped he hadn't landed on the handlebar. "Are you all right?" I asked.

He looked up at me, wide-eyed, and I thought I recognized one of the men who'd come with the ambulance to take us to Fort Missoula the other day. He nodded, panting, but said nothing.

"Damn blackies ought to learn to ride them things right, 'fore they bring 'em into town," said Harrington, grinning evilly. He and his companions had turned together and were looming over me and the fallen negro soldier.

"Hell, Jed, give 'em a break," said C. D. He spit a stream of tobacco juice on the street, barely missing the soldier. He continued. "Army can't give 'em horses, 'cause you gotta be smarter than a horse to ride one."

"That ain't true," said Zach'ry. "You seen Injuns riding horses all the time, so smart don't have nothing to do with it."

This remark obviously struck both his companions as a rare witticism, and I heard snickers from the other bystanders, who had turned to observe the new attraction now that Cody and his men had dismounted. But at the same time, I saw that the men of our party—Mr. Blankenship, Mr. Roosevelt, and Mr. Clemens—had come across the street. At least the bullies were now outnumbered, although they seemed not to realize it yet.

"How is he?" asked Mr. Roosevelt, kneeling down next to me.

"I think it's just the wind knocked out of him," I said. "If his bike isn't damaged too badly, he may be able to get back out to the fort on his own power once he's got his breath back."

"No such luck," said Roosevelt, pointing to the front wheel of the vehicle in question. Even at a glance it was clear that a third of the spokes were hopelessly bent and snapped. A thick length of dowel—a broom handle?— was still lying within the rim, the obvious instrument of destruction.

"You three—you did this," I said, straightening up. Now I wasn't so sure I wanted to avoid fighting them. It was as clear as anything that they had brought the bike and rider down as a prank, and cared nothing that they might have hurt a man—a U.S. *soldier*.

"What if we did?" said C. D. He spit another stream of tobacco juice, in the general direction of my shoes, although it fell a couple of feet short. "It's a free country, last I heard tell." He looked to his two companions and the growing crowd of bystanders for support. There was a buzz of voices, some in agreement and some not. There might be no fighting now, but there was still a moral victory to be won.

"That don't mean you can treat a man like a dog," said another voice. I looked up; it was Tom Blankenship. "No, that ain't right. I wouldn't go out of my way to harm a dog, or any other kind of critter, just to see him fall down so's you could laugh at him and mock him. And we ain't even talking about destroying gov'ment property, which is a crime. You're going to pay for that bike, Jed Harrington."

"You can go whistle, Blankenship," said Harrington. "You don't have no jurisdiction here in Missoula. Here you ain't nothing but a country bumpkin." He spit again.

"Here's my jurisdiction," said Blankenship, slapping his coat pocket and taking a step forward. I remembered now what he carried there. "I don't want to pull this iron out in front of the ladies and all these polite folks, but I'll do it if you make me—and if I do, I'll march you three out to the fort and let *them* take care of you for a while. I guess they can figure out some way to make you boys sorry you ever messed with one of their soldiers. Or you can save everybody time and aggravation if you dig into your pocket for enough money to fix this man's wheel and give it to him right now. Your call."

Harrington scowled. "Ain't much of a selection, with four of you here to beat up on me if I say no."

"Make that five," came a new voice. It was Colonel Cody. "Any man who wants to pick fights with the U.S. Army, he's going to have to explain himself to William F. Cody." He let his hand rest on the pearl handle of his revolver. The three bullies exchanged worried glances.

"And if something did start up, don't go pretending your two buddies wouldn't be in it thick as flies, either," said Blankenship, pointing at Harrington. "You three jumped on this here soldier for no cause. I think ten bucks would probably pay to replace an Army bike. But let's make it twenty, just to pay this poor man for knocking him down and making a mock of him—not that I think it's enough, but I'll let it go at that. Now, are you going to go in your pocket, or are we going to take you out to the fort to talk to the U.S. Army?"

Harrington bit off a foul word, but he dug into his pocket. He pulled out his hand and picked out two coins, then flung them in the dirt near the soldier. I could see the gleam of gold as they flew through the air. "There's the damn money," he said. "Twenty dollars—that's all this coon's getting from me, Blankenship. And I'll remember the high-handed thief that took it from me—don't you have any doubt about it." He glared at the soldier, who had recovered enough to sit up, and growled, "You won't always have your friends with you. Remember that."

"I'll remember you," said Blankenship, staring Harrington dead in the eye. I would not have liked to have that look turned on me. Neither did Harrington, evidently. He held it for perhaps five seconds, then turned to his cronies. "Let's go, boys," he said. "This place is startin' to smell bad."

"Yeah, it stinks," said Zach'ry, looking significantly at the soldier. The three of them stalked off.

I paid them no mind; the soldier had gotten to his feet at last and was gingerly checking out his hurts. I picked up the money and gave it to him. "Here, take this," I said. "It won't make up for what they did, but maybe it'll make them think twice about attacking the Army again."

"Thank you, sir," said the soldier, still breathing somewhat heavily. "They caught me off guard. I think I'll be all right. And I surely do thank you all."

"No, we're the ones who ought to thank you," said Colonel Cody. "I've fought for my country, and I know what that uniform means. Any man who'd play that kind of prank on the soldiers who protect him ought to be horsewhipped. When I was a younger man, I did it to his kind more than once. If need be, I'll do it to him and his sidekicks both."

"Amen," said Mr. Roosevelt. "I'm just glad we got here in time to keep any more from happening."

"Yes, let's hope this is the end of it," I said. I had an uneasy feeling that it wouldn't be, though.

7

Dinner that night was a treat—excellent food, and conversation to match. But the incident of Harrington and the black soldier had cast a shadow over the mood of the company, which lifted during the meal itself, but returned after the ladies had left the table and we men sat there over brandy and cigars—those of us who indulged in those pastimes, at least. Mr. Blankenship had taken the pledge against liquor, although he clearly enjoyed a smoke—a habit I had never found in the least appealing, although I helped myself to the brandy.

As a former Army scout, Colonel Cody was especially incensed that a civilian would attack an American soldier for nothing but malicious sport. "That fellow wouldn't own enough land to set both his bootheels on if it hadn't been for the Army making this country safe," he said, shaking his head. "A mongrel dog has more gratitude than that, sir. A rattlesnake has more."

"That's the natural truth," said Tom Blankenship, who was sitting opposite Mr. Clemens and the Colonel. "In fact, if I had my choice between Harrington's crowd and a hornet's nest for next-door neighbors, I'd take the hornets every day—and maybe throw in a passel of copperheads, and a wildcat or two for luck. At least them critters won't come looking to start a fight. But Harrington and his kind will, every single time."

Mr. Roosevelt leaned back in his chair, swirling his brandy snifter. "It's surprising that nobody has taught the fellow manners before now," he said. "The west may seem uncouth to those who've never lived here, but that's a misconception based on ignorance. Living in the society of men armed to the teeth goes a remarkably long way to promote good manners."

"Or to put it more bluntly, it gets rid of bad manners except when they're connected with a quick trigger finger," said Mr. Clemens. "Which I suspect is how Harrington's lived so long without getting ventilated. Is that about right, Tom?"

"You hit it dead on, Sam," said Blankenship. He chewed on his cigar a moment, then went on. "Well, there's another point, too. Out here, you don't bump into your neighbor anywhere near as much as back in a settled place like Missouri. I reckon my old pap would've liked Montana, as much as he could like anyplace. Pap was always pretty much a loner, 'cept when he wanted to buy some whiskey or lose his money at Seven-Up. Come to think of it, he was pretty much as mean as Jed Harrington."

Mr. Clemens blew out a long puff of smoke. "And he didn't live very long, either," he said.

"No, he didn't," said Blankenship soberly. "I'm already ten years past him, and hope to live a few more, Lord willin'. There was an old slave back home told me I was born to be hanged, and I was afraid of that for a long time. But now sometimes I think I might even make it to my three score and ten."

Frank Butler laughed. "Now, there's a worthy ambition," he said. "I think I might even have a chance at it myself, as long as little Annie's aim holds true."

"I'll drink to that," said Colonel Cody. "Damnation, I'll drink to us all living to a hundred."

"If that depends on Annie Oakley's hitting every shot, you can bet on it," said Mr. Roosevelt, grinning broadly. "I thought I was pretty good with a rifle, but I'd give anybody at the table even money she's the best there is."

"She's among the finest wing and target shooters I've ever seen, no question," said Colonel Cody. "But I think Frank will agree with me that at least two of this company might match her on a given day—and possibly three, if you're as good as you say, Mr. Roosevelt."

"Sure, and I'm a big enough man to admit she's better than I," said Frank Butler. "And if any of you want to question that, would you be willin' to stand with a pipe in your mouth and choose which of us you want to shoot it out?" All of us laughed at that.

"I'll let somebody else try that experiment," said Mr. Clemens, tapping the ash off his cigar. "In fact, if you give me my choice, I'd just as soon not have anybody shoot my pipe out. Waste of good tobacco."

"Sure, and you don't think I'd put the good stuff in for little Annie to shoot at, do you?" said Frank Butler with a sly grin. That set off another round of laughter, and calls for another round of brandy.

"There's a fellow after my own heart," said Tom Blankenship, puffing on his own cigar. "There's nothing like having to smoke the rattiest old tobacco that nobody else would have—Sam knows what I'm talking about, we grew up together—to make you appreciate something good when you can get it. This is mighty good stuff, Sam, and mighty good company to smoke it in."

Mr. Clemens beamed. "The best company I've been with in a long time, Tom," he said. "I sure wish we'd been closer together all those years—imagine the grand times we'd have had!"

"We'll just have to make up for it tonight," said Colonel Cody. "That's all any of us can do—enjoy the good times while we have them. And hope they keep coming back."

"Now that's something I'll drink to," said Mr. Clemens, and we all raised our glasses. "To the good times—may they last forever!"

"To the good times," we all echoed. But even as I said it, I couldn't help remembering that just a few short minutes ago we had been speaking of far less pleasant subjects. And I wondered, even as I drained the toast, just how long it would be before we were forced to deal with the harsh side of life again.

The party broke up just before eleven o'clock, when Colonel Cody stood and announced in a voice that was remarkably clear, considering the amount of brandy he had taken on board, that he and his performers had an early rehearsal the next day. So the colonel, Mr. Butler, and Annie Oakley returned to the Wild West Show encampment, a few miles outside Missoula. After saying their own good-nights to our group, Mr. Roosevelt and Mr. Blankenship walked together to their separate accommodations a few blocks away. The ladies of our party having gone upstairs right after the Wild West group departed, that left me and Mr. Clemens to while away the tail end of the evening.

The day had been seasonably hot, but here in the mountains the evening air cooled down quickly. Mr. Clemens said, "Let's walk out onto the veranda—those rocking chairs out there looked comfortable. There's nothing like setting and rocking a spell to settle your mind after a busy day."

That sounded congenial to me, and so I followed him out the door onto the long front porch of the Florence House. This time of night, the street was nearly empty, with the glow of a gibbous moon punctuated by brighter pools of light cast by gas lights stretching at intervals off into the distance. I could see mountain peaks reflecting the moonlight—the Bitterroot Range, I thought.

We sat and rocked quietly for several minutes, Mr. Clemens puffing on his cigar. The night sounds—the songs of night birds in the distance, the low whirring drone of locusts—were audible in between the rhythmic creaks of the chairs on the wooden porch. At last he said, "Lovely evening, isn't it? There's nothing like getting away from the big cities to remind you how pretty the world must have been before the damned human race took it over."

"Before the human race?" I asked. "According to the best geologists, that was an age of monsters—dinosaurs with teeth like carving knives, and other huge creatures designed for slaughter. That seems the opposite of pretty to me." I had seen some of Professor Marsh's specimens at Yale, and had an excellent notion of the dimensions of those monsters, and of their fearsome armament.

As I had surmised, he was in the mood for a bit of argument. "Sure, I've read a fair amount of geology," he said. "Some of the ugliest critters you ever saw were dug out of the ground not too far from here—or their bones were, anyhow. And you know what? Not a single one of 'em ever told a lie, or swindled a widow, or knocked another critter down because he was the wrong color, or strung him from a tree for believing in the wrong religion. They just did what they had to, to make a living—that's all. No worse than you and me eating that fine fresh brook trout earlier tonight. And far better than the likes of Jed Harrington."

"You're judging humanity by its worst, not its best," I said. "No dinosaur ever wrote a book, or built a cathedral." I smiled in the darkness; I thought I had scored a point.

"As if that made any difference," replied Mr. Clemens. He snorted, then rocked a couple of times before continuing. "Some of the worst specimens of humanity I know have written books—it's no recommendation at all. Cathedrals are worse because the way they get built is that rich people decide they can make up for all the evil they've done by ordering a few thousand poor people to slave away their lives building a cold, drafty, stone monstrosity. They'd have done better to build decent houses, or even a few good barns, for all those people to get some use out of."

"Perhaps," I said. It seemed to me he was missing some central point, but I wasn't quite able to articulate it. After a moment's thought, I countered with, "If you don't feel that literature and art justify Man's existence, how do you justify making your own living by writing books?"

"I wouldn't claim it justifies my existence," he said. "It's what I do for a living, the same way that an allosaur made his living chewing on brontosaurs. What justifies my existence is that I tell the truth about what goes on in the world, even if I have to disguise it as a pretty story sometimes. And when I can, I stand up to the bullies— not just the Jed Harringtons, but the fancier ones, the Rockefellers and Carnegies and Vanderbilts and Morgans, who bully with money and power—and I do my level best to make them sweat." The end of his cigar seemed to glow in the night.

"I still sense a contradiction there," I said. I stretched my legs out and propped my feet on the porch railing, enjoying the night sky. Then I pointed out, "You rail against the rich and powerful, but what makes them any worse than the dinosaurs that ruled the earth before them?"

"Hypocrisy," he said. "The dinosaur that ate another one for supper didn't pretend it was eating it in the name of progress, or religion, or civilization. It didn't claim it was entitled to eat it because it was from a better class of society than the other one, or because the other one was a foreigner who didn't have any rights not to be eaten. And it didn't claim to be the other's best friend one minute and turn around and eat it first time it got hungry. But if you stand in the middle of any town big enough to have two named streets and heave a brick over your shoulder, you're like to hit a man who claims he has the right to lord it over somebody else for one of those reasons."

"Perhaps you're right," I said, standing up. "In any case, I'll agree with your original premise—it *is* a lovely night. I'm thinking about taking a walk to work off some of that dinner and brandy. Would you like to join me?"

"I reckon I'll pass," he said. "Climbing upstairs is about all the work I can muster energy for right now. That, and turning the pages of a book—I've just started Howells's new one. It's called *A Traveler from Alturia*. You ought to read it when I'm done, or maybe I'll give it to Roosevelt. You youngsters need to be shaken up now and then, and this is just the stuff to do it."

"If Roosevelt doesn't want it, perhaps I'll look into it," I said, somewhat amused at being patronized. "I think I will take that walk—I'll see you in the morning."

"All right," he said. "Steer clear of the dinosaurs." He stood and headed back toward the hotel's front door.

"I shan't worry on that score," I said, and stepped out onto the sidewalk and, after a moment's indecision, set off toward the riverfront.

The Florence House was just far enough from the river to make a pleasant stroll. I started out briskly, humming a little tune to myself—"Daisy Bell," which had been so popular the summer before. The air had a crisp edge to it even though we were still in August, but as long as I kept up a steady pace, there was no danger of getting chilled. Back in New London, I had more than once gone swimming in weather no warmer than this.

But I was not interested in a dip in the river tonight, or any other boyish pleasure. Mr. Clemens's dark mood had rekindled memories of our stay in Florence, Italy, and the mere mention of the place called forth all too many ghosts of "might have been." I had thought that half a year, and the return to my native land, might have erased them more thoroughly. But no—here they were again, and once more I was overcome with brooding over the vicious snuffing out of an innocent life. Standing between the railroad tracks and the riverside, looking out at the swift-flowing moonlit water, I could almost believe his bitter assertion that the human race had less dignity and virtue than the ferocious carnivores that roamed the earth millions of years ago.

But then I thought back to this afternoon. Jed Harrington was a fair specimen of mankind's worst instincts, and yet he had been thwarted in his mischief. The worst part of our nature did not always have a free hand. When good men acted together, they could turn back the darkness. It might never go away entirely, and evil once done could never be reversed. There were no final victories. But good men could join forces to oppose the darkness, and win from time to time. Not every time, but often enough to give life some meaning. I think, deep in his heart, my employer believed this, too.

I picked up a small stone and threw it into the water, watching the ripples spread in the moonlight. Somewhere off in the distance a dog barked, and after a few moments another answered him. I shivered; there were clouds gathering now, and the night had suddenly gotten cold. It was time to turn my steps back toward the hotel. I took one last look at the river, and headed back toward the Florence House.

I had turned the final corner and come halfway down the block when I realized there was someone in the street ahead of me. There in the middle of the street, directly in front of the hotel entrance, stood a heavy-set man. Even at this distance I knew who it was: Jed Harrington. Drunk, from the way he staggered and pointed an arm. A moment later I heard his voice, and I knew that I had walked into trouble.

"Blankenship!" Harrington bawled. "Come on out here. I want my money back, Blankenship!"

He obviously thought that Blankenship was staying in our hotel—not an implausible deduction, since that was where he had seen him twice before. My first instinct was simply to tell Harrington that he was wrong, and hope he would go away. But even if he believed me, that might only send him looking for his quarry—and if he found him, that might mean even more trouble. I decided to see if I could get inside without drawing his notice. Then I could try to telephone the police, if no one else had already done so.

I edged toward the porch, hoping to get into the shadow before he could see me. No such luck. He pointed directly at me before I was halfway to my goal, and stepped forward to block me.

"You!" said Harrington, fixing me with a malevolent glare. "Don't you move a peg, if you know what's good for you. Hey there, Judge Blankenship! You get your stinking carcass down here or I'll make this dude pay for you!"

"I wouldn't plan on it," I said as calmly as I could manage. I didn't want to give Harrington any reason to think I was offering to fight him. I didn't think he could beat me in any fair fight, but I didn't think he was likely to adhere to any gentlemanly notion of fairness, either. More likely, he'd come at me with a knife, or get one of his cronies to sneak up behind me and cudgel me down. Better not to challenge him. On the other hand, I didn't want him to think I was an easy mark.

"Wouldn't plan on it?" Harrington sneered. "Oh, don't the dude talk pretty! Wouldn't plan on it, he says. Well, here's what I think of your plans." He spit into the dust of the street, then looked up at me. "Maybe I'll make you lick that up, dude."

At that, I realized I was going to have no luck in pacifying the man. I would have to try to get away from him and either enter the hotel by a back door or find a policeman. I glanced quickly over my shoulder to make certain I had a clear escape route. To my dismay, a bulky figure loomed in the shadows just outside the reach of the street light—one of Harrington's cronies, no doubt.

"Hey, Mr. Dude, look me in the face when I'm talking to you," said Harrington. My head snapped back to face the rancher, whom I still had to consider my main threat. He would no doubt call the tune for his henchman—whatever he had in mind. Meanwhile, I would just have to keep my ears open for anyone attempting to sneak up on me. I had no desire to have someone club me from behind or throw a stranglehold around my neck.

I decided it was better to end the confrontation before Harrington could make it any more unpleasant. "I don't think we have anything else to say to one another," I said in a level tone. "Good night, Mr. Harrington." I turned as if to go away down the street. Perhaps he wouldn't follow me.

"Hold on, sonny, it ain't your bedtime yet," said Harrington. " 'Fore you go to sleep, you're goin' to do a little dance for me." He gestured significantly toward the holster on his hip. Now a chill went up the nape of my neck. I hadn't noticed him wearing a gun before. The fact that he had it now meant that he was probably ready to use it—and I was a convenient target.

"I'm afraid that'll have to wait for another time," I said, beginning to back slowly away. I had heard that a pistol was a short-range weapon, the accuracy of which diminished rapidly beyond fifteen or twenty yards. Harrington might be a good enough shot to hit a fleeing man in the dark at that distance, but that risk struck me as preferable to standing still. On the other hand, some of the members of the Wild West Show had demonstrated an amazing degree of marksmanship with the weapon . . . and anybody might get off a lucky shot.

"Not so fast, sonny," said Harrington, reaching for the pistol.

"I'd keep my hand away from that, if I were you," came a voice from behind me. Even before I turned to look, I knew who it had to be. The flat Missouri accent was as good as a signature: Tom Blankenship. As he stepped out into the street light's glare, I could see that he was holding a rifle at the ready. "Jed, if you're lookin' for me, here I am. No need to bring the boy into it."

"You don't scare me, you stinking coward," snarled Harrington. "I can draw and put the dude down before you get a shot off. And I just might do it if I don't get my money."

"My first shot will be straight through your heart," said Blankenship, raising the rifle to his shoulder. "Don't think I can't do it—I've been shooting since I was a boy, and I can still hit a squirrel halfway across the county. You might get a shot off at Mr. Cabot, or at me, 'fore I pull the trigger. But I promise you right now that if you make a move for your iron, I *will* kill you. So keep your hands away from it."

"You'd hang for it," said Harrington, but his voice wavered, and his hand stayed well clear of the holster.

"Maybe so," said Blankenship. "It won't do you much good, if I do. But I'm going to be a good sport, and let you walk away quiet-like, instead of calling in the police. If you're smart, you'll keep on walking until you're plumb out of town."

"I'm not going to forget this, Blankenship," said Harrington with a malevolent stare. "This is the third time you've balked me. Sooner or later, you'll cross my path, and I'll be ready for you—you and all your friends, if it comes to that. And then you'll be sorry you treated old Jed this way, I promise *you*."

"You done talking?" asked Blankenship, almost amiably. "Do you still want to argue about the money I made you give that soldier you and your cronies bushwhacked? Or do you want to find out how good I can shoot?"

"Don't get your dander up, I'm going," said Harrington. He shot an evil glance at me, then spat on the ground in my direction before turning around and stalking off—a good bit slower than I might have done it, with a rifle aimed at my chest.

When he was out of sight, I turned to my rescuer and said, "Thank you, Mr. Blankenship. I think you have just saved me from a very unpleasant experience."

"Don't think nothing of it," he said, cradling the rifle under one arm. "Now, son, if I was you, I'd get indoors before that sidewinder decides to try shooting at us from cover."

I glanced back at the corner Harrington had vanished around. "Do you really think he might?"

"I wouldn't put it past him," said Blankenship. "He showed some pluck walking off so cool, but that don't mean he won't turn and try his luck when he thinks he's safe. Best thing is not to tempt him. Good night, Mr. Cabot."

"Good night, Mr. Blankenship," I said. "Thank you. I'm lucky you came along when you did."

"Ain't entirely luck," he said. "I was headin' to pay a late visit to a friend, and it brought me right past here. Once I seen what was happenin', I just done what needed doing. Now get on inside."

With no further ado I made my way inside the hotel. Finding no one else of our party awake, I went directly to bed.

8

I was awakened from a sound sleep by a pounding on my door. I stumbled out of bed and called out, "Coming!" while I threw on a dressing robe. After a bit of fumbling, I lit the lamp and opened the door a crack.

There stood Theodore Roosevelt. "Let me in, so I don't wake the whole floor," he said. "That blackguard Harrington's dead."

"Dead!" I opened the door to admit him. "How did it happen?"

Roosevelt rubbed his mustache between his thumb and forefinger. "Shot," he said. "With a rifle, or so the sheriff tells me. The witness says he was standing out in the open, with nobody else nearby."

"Witness? Who's the witness?" I asked. I sat back down, on the edge of the bed. I could not escape an uncomfortable memory of the events outside the hotel, but for now I decided not to mention them.

"One of Harrington's cronies," said Roosevelt. "But why don't you fetch Clemens so I can tell you both the whole story without having to repeat it. It'll keep that long, I promise."

"Yes, you're right," I said. I stood up and retrieved my trousers from the chair where I'd hung them and began dressing. It was a matter of minutes before, more or less respectable, I knocked on Mr. Clemens's door.

A few moments later I heard his voice groan from inside: "Who is it?"

"Cabot," I said. "I have bad news." Then, after a moment, I amended myself: "Well, bad enough."

Mr. Clemens cracked the door open. "And it can't wait till morning?" He looked at my face, then said, "Hang on a minute. I'll get some clothes on and we'll go to your room. That way we can talk without keeping Livy awake."

The door closed and I stood there for perhaps two minutes before it reopened and my employer appeared in his bathrobe, with one of his pipes in his hand. "OK, let's go. You can tell me the nub of it while we're walking."

"Harrington's been shot," I said. "Roosevelt came to tell me. There's more to the story, but he wanted you to hear it."

"More? I'd think that'd be story enough," said Mr. Clemens. "Not that I'd have shot the son of a bitch myself, but I won't be going into deep mourning, either."

"I doubt anyone will, except his family—assuming he had one," I said, opening the door to my room and ushering him in. I saw Roosevelt sitting in the chair where I'd had my pants hung, the electric light glinting off his spectacles. "Still, it's a terrible way to come to one's end. I hope the killer is found quickly."

"Well, the sheriff thinks he has found him," said Roosevelt, standing. "That's why I came to tell you two. He's already made an arrest—I saw it myself."

"And how did you happen to see that?" asked Mr. Clemens. "It's after two o'clock in the morning—how long ago did this happen?" he added, tapping his right index finger on the palm of his left hand. He sat down on my bed and put his pipe in his mouth, then rummaged through the pockets of his bathrobe and pulled out a matchbox.

Roosevelt shook his head. "An hour, perhaps—as best I can estimate. After our supper party, I rode my horse out to the fort to visit some of my friends among the officers. The conversation got very interesting, and by the time I realized what hour it was, it was late. They offered to put me up for the night, but I have a breakfast meeting tomorrow . . ."

Mr. Clemens looked up from his pipe. "Breakfast meeting? What about?" There was obvious suspicion in his voice.

Roosevelt shrugged. "Politics," he said nonchalantly. "I'm going to be talking to a couple of important local Republican leaders—testing the waters, if you know what I mean. I have an idea what I'd like to do, ten or fifteen years from now, and I'm trying to find out what it may take to get me where I can do it. The talk with the Army people was on the same general subject, if you want to know the truth."

"Politics," said my employer. "I knew you were up to no good, but I didn't think it was that ugly. Well, I'll forgive you this once. But back to the story. You were out at the fort, and it was late . . ."

"Yes," said Roosevelt. "I rode back into town, and had taken the horse back to the livery stable—it was late, as I've already said—and when I got in, it took me about five minutes knocking to get the stableman to answer the door."

"Yes, poor rascal probably wanted to sleep," drawled Mr. Clemens.

Mr. Roosevelt ignored him. "I was walking back toward my hotel. The livery stable is on Hazel Street, about four blocks away, and I was walking back on Third when I heard a commotion. So I went to see what it was."

"Drawn to the sound of trouble," said Mr. Clemens. "That's Roosevelt, all right."

Again Mr. Roosevelt ignored him. "What I found was

three men struggling. At first I thought it was just a fight, and I was about to wade in to help the fellow the other two had ganged up on. But then the moon peeked through the clouds, and I saw that one of them was wearing a badge, and of course that made everything different."

"Not necessarily," growled Mr. Clemens. But he didn't pursue the point, and motioned Roosevelt to continue.

Roosevelt said, "It turned out to be two sheriff's deputies taking your friend Blankenship into custody."

"Tom Blankenship?" barked Mr. Clemens. "That's *hogwash*!" (Actually, he used a term somewhat stronger, although it shared its barnyard etymology with my euphemism.) He glared at Roosevelt, as if expecting him to recant his statement.

"On my honor," said Roosevelt, raising a hand as if swearing an oath. "I asked the deputies what was going on, and they told me they'd found Harrington shot dead a little time before. When they saw your friend walking the street at that hour, they stopped him for questioning."

"Tom wouldn't like that," said Mr. Clemens, frowning. He took a puff on his pipe and said, "He's always come and gone pretty much as he pleased. Still, walking around late at night can't be grounds for arresting him, can it? Or did he do something outright criminal, like spitting on the sidewalk?"

"No," said Roosevelt. "But one of the deputies recognized Blankenship, and knew there'd been bad blood between him and Harrington. In fact, he told me he'd seen him pull a gun on Harrington just a couple of nights ago, in some bar. And last night, Blankenship was carrying a rifle."

"Damnation," said my employer, pounding his fist on the bed next to his leg. "I knew there wasn't any good going to come of that gun."

"One moment," I said, suddenly alert. "You both have to know what happened just before I came to bed." And I told them, briefly, of my encounter with Harrington, and of Blankenship's appearance to rescue me, rifle in hand.

"I'll be damned," said Mr. Clemens. "That looks bad for Tom. What the hell was he doing with a gun?"

"You'll have to ask him," I said. "But first, let's hear the rest of Mr. Roosevelt's story—what happened then?" I asked before Mr. Clemens could say anything more. I wanted Roosevelt to finish his story before my employer went off on a tangent.

"Well, I persuaded the deputies to let me go with them to the jail," he said. "Blankenship calmed down when he recognized me, so when I undertook to vouch for his good conduct, they were willing to let me come along. And of course he was glad to have a friendly face in view."

"If you call it that," said Mr. Clemens, with a wink at me.

Roosevelt went on. "In any case, when we arrived at the jail, the sheriff was questioning one of the dead man's cronies who'd been with him when the fatal shot was fired. That's when the witness said that Harrington had told him he'd had words with Blankenship earlier that night."

"That's no proof he shot him," said Mr. Clemens. "Hell, if I shot every man I had words with, the population would be about half what it is."

"Possibly even smaller," said Roosevelt. "But the upshot is, the sheriff thought that argument, combined with the rifle, was sufficient grounds to hold your friend on suspicion. And that's when Blankenship asked me to come get you."

Mr. Clemens set down his pipe. "All right, then. Give me a few minutes to get dressed. Wentworth, I'd like you to come with me." He stood up.

"Yes, sir," I said. "I'll be ready whenever you are." I stretched my arms and stifled a yawn as Mr. Clemens stumped down the hallway to change into his street clothes. Then I looked at Roosevelt and asked, "You must know—can a fellow get a cup of coffee anywhere around here this time of night?"

Missoula's jail was only a ten-minute walk from our hotel; nothing is very far in a town of three thousand. It was on the first floor of a fairly large brick building in the center of town. We entered to find a lean, leather-faced man in a western hat sitting at a desk under a bare electric bulb. Another man, older and hatless, with a salt-and-pepper mustache, was leaning against the wall next to a telephone. On the other side of the phone was a gun rack displaying an imposing array of carbines and shotguns. Both men wore silver badges in the shape of six-pointed stars.

The man behind the desk looked up as we entered and asked, "What can I do for you, gents?" Then he saw Mr. Roosevelt come in behind me and turned to his partner. "Call the sheriff, Al," he said. "Four-eyes is back, with some friends."

"Yep," said the other man, and went through a doorway directly behind the desk.

Mr. Clemens turned to Roosevelt and said, "Well, I appreciate your telling me the news and bringing me down here. I reckon you can go get yourself some sleep now, if you want—I've at least had a couple of hours, and you've had none at all."

"Oh, I couldn't sleep now for the life of me," said Mr. Roosevelt. "Besides, this situation has piqued my interest. I'll wager I can be of some additional use to you before the night's done."

"All right with me," said Mr. Clemens, though I sensed in his voice that he would prefer to have the field to himself. But before I could pursue the thought, Al returned. With him was a compactly built, dark-haired man with a clean-shaven face and pale grey eyes that gave me a moment of chill when his gaze flicked across my face.

"I'm Henry Williams, sheriff of Missoula County," he said in a level voice. "What's your business, gentlemen?"

Mr. Clemens stepped forward and said, "You've got a friend of mine locked up, and I'd like to talk to him. Better yet, I'd like to get him out of here."

The sheriff looked my employer up and down, then said, "Unless you've got a writ, he's staying right where he is. The man's under suspicion of murder."

"I don't have a writ," said Mr. Clemens. "I'm not a lawyer, anyhow—just a man who hates to see his friend rotting in a jail cell if he didn't do anything. Can we talk to him, at least?"

"Maybe," said the sheriff, rubbing his chin. He stared at my employer for a long beat, then nodded and continued, "I'm going to search you before you get anywhere near my prisoner, and there'll be a deputy watching while you talk. I don't want him breaking out, maybe hurting one of my men because somebody passes him a gun. You understand me, mister?"

"I understand you," said Mr. Clemens. "Now, let's make sure you understand me. The man you're holding isn't some no-account rum-bum who shoots people down when they don't agree with him. I've known him for fifty years, and I can swear he's no killer."

"That might carry some weight if I'd ever laid eyes on either one of you before," said the sheriff. "Seeing as how I haven't, all I've got is your word for it."

Theodore Roosevelt stepped forward and boomed, "Sheriff, do you know to whom you're speaking?" He suddenly seemed much larger than he really was.

The sheriff didn't notice. "No," he said. "And it doesn't matter. You and your friends may be big shots back east, but don't expect that to get you any special treatment in Missoula, Montana. I'm sheriff here, and as long as I'm wearing this badge, what I say goes. Now, do you want to talk to this Blankenship fellow or not?"

I could tell that Mr. Clemens was struggling to hold his temper. He stepped forward, and I braced myself for an outburst, but then he seemed to relax. "Of course I do," he said. "My name's Sam Clemens, by the way, and

Tom Blankenship's one of my oldest friends. I wouldn't have gotten out of a soft hotel bed and come down here in the middle of the night if he weren't. I reckon you aren't in here just for amusement, either."

I relaxed a bit myself. My employer had regained control of his temper, and had decided to work his considerable charm on the sheriff. Formidable as his anger could sometimes be, his friendly side usually got better results—especially when dealing with someone in a powerful position.

"No, the only reason I came in tonight was because there was a killing," said the sheriff. "My deputies could probably have handled it—in fact, I'm pretty pleased about how quick they were to make the arrest—but people expect me to be on the job when something serious happens. That's the way it is."

"Well, I know how that goes," said Mr. Clemens. "I was a steamboat pilot once, so I know about having to jump out of bed when there's work to be done. And I won't keep you any longer than I have to. What do I have to do to talk to Tom?"

The sheriff looked at all three of us. "First let me check to make sure you're not carrying," he said. "Al, cover me while I pat them down."

The deputy stood back, his hand hovering near the butt of a holstered pistol that I now realized he was wearing, while the sheriff patted our pockets, armpits, and pants legs—searching, I assumed, for any concealed weapons. He took his time about it, and was businesslike. Finally he stood up and nodded. "All right, they're clean. You and Charlie take 'em to the cell and let 'em talk."

"Right, sheriff," said Al. "You fellows, follow me." He led us through the door into a short corridor, the second deputy following behind us. On either side were doors, one open to reveal a small office—the sheriff's, I guessed. We stopped at another door at the end of the corridor, this one reinforced with metal bars and secured with a heavy lock. The deputy took a key ring from his belt and opened it, and we went through.

Here we found ourselves in a broad transverse corridor with a large barred enclosure on the other side. At either end were heavy barred doors, presumably leading to smaller cells. It bore a family resemblance to the New Orleans jail where I had spent several hours, except it was a good bit cleaner. A closer look showed three or four men inside, all except one (who was stalking furiously up and down, waving his arms and ranting to whoever might be listening) in attitudes suggesting resignation. Tom Blankenship was not among them.

"Your friend's over here," said Deputy Al, gesturing as he began walking toward the left. He looked back over his shoulder and added, "Don't walk too close to the bars. Sometimes the prisoners grab people."

I kept my distance from the bars.

The deputy stopped in front of the door and took out his key ring again. "I have to lock you in," he said. "I'll give you half an hour. If you want out before then, holler—one of us will hear you. Same if you get in trouble."

"All right, we understand," said Mr. Clemens.

"OK, then, stand clear," said the deputy. He opened a little window in the door and looked through. "OK, you can go in," he said. He pushed the door open and the three of us filed through into the cell.

The cell was illuminated by a small electric bulb in the ceiling, with a wire grill over it, presumably to prevent prisoners from breaking it. It took a moment for my eyes to adjust to the dim light. When they did, I saw that Blankenship was lying on the small cot that was the only piece of furniture in the cell—apparently sound asleep.

"Tom, get up," said Mr. Clemens. "We're here to help you."

Blankenship rolled over and rubbed his eyes. He blinked a couple of times and then his gaze fixed on my employer. "Sam!" he said, then yawned. "You're just the man I want to see."

Mr. Clemens shook his head. "Tom, you're the only man I can think of who'd get arrested for murder and go to sleep in his cell." I was surprised myself; on the two occasions when I had been in police custody, the last thing on my mind was sleep.

"Well, I've been in jail before," said Blankenship, stretching his arms and stifling another yawn. "Been in worse spots than that, if you get down to it. I reckon there ain't much more can happen to me than already has, and if it does, I might as well be rested up for it. But I'm glad you're here, Sam."

"I wish you could've waited for daylight to get arrested," said Mr. Clemens. "I'd give you a piece of my mind about it, except I don't reckon getting arrested was your idea to begin with. But the deputy's only going to give us a little while to talk. Why don't you tell me what happened to make these fellows think you're the one that killed Harrington."

"Well, Sam, I reckon that's easy enough," said Blankenship. "They found me on the street not far from where he was shot, and I happened to have my rifle along as well as my good old forty-four. Good heavens, I'd have wanted to ask me some questions if *I'd* been one of those deputies."

"Hold on, let's backtrack a bit," said Mr. Clemens. "Go back to the start and tell me what you were doing out on the street to begin with. If I understand right, it was pretty late at night."

"Sure was," said Blankenship. "What happened was, after supper I got powerful drowsy—you know what it's like when you start gettin' old, Sam. So I went back to my rooming house and took a little nap. Only thing about that was I got up about ten o'clock, rarin' to go. Except there ain't much place to go in this town unless you like drinkin' and carryin' on, which I don't. I sat there and read the newspapers, but that got dreary after a while—

seems like they mostly had bad news, and all that about folks I didn't even know. And so after a while I said to myself, *Now, Tom, here's a nice summer night, why not go out and have a little stroll around town.* And so I walked on downstairs and walked out to look at the stars and listen to the birds singing."

"And you took along a rifle," said Mr. Clemens. "Cabot told us what happened outside our hotel. Why'd you take the gun, Tom?"

"I reckon force of habit," said Blankenship. "Ever since I was a boy, if I go out walking, I take along my rifle. You might see a rabbit or a squirrel and get yourself some dinner, you know? You remember growing up in the country, Sam. A fellow feels almost naked without that rifle on his arm."

"It's been a long time since I carried one, Tom," said Mr. Clemens. "For Cabot's sake, I'm glad you had it last night. But for your own sake, it looks pretty bad."

"Mr. Cabot told us that part," said Roosevelt. "But that was a couple of hours before the shooting. How did you manage to get caught up in that?"

"I just wandered around a bit more," said Blankenship. "And finally, I decided to head back to my place. I was walking along, not paying anything much mind, and all of a sudden I heard something that snapped me out of my thoughts. It was a gunshot—and believe me, gentlemen, I know that sound all too well, and what it means in the middle of a town late at night. It's been my business to deal with it more often than I'd like to remember. But there's no way to escape responsibility, and so I roused myself out of my thoughts and went in the direction I'd heard the shots from."

"That's the spirit," boomed Roosevelt.

"That's a damn good way to get yourself shot," said my employer, at the same time. The two men stopped and glared at each other.

Blankenship laughed, and they both looked back at him. "I reckon you're both right," he said, with a crooked grin. "Anyhow, it was a distance off, and when I got there, what should I see but Jed Harrington lying on his back, with one of his cronies kneeling next to him, with a great big pistol in his hand. If that fellow looked up and seen me, Sam, next thing I knew that gun would be pointed at me and like to go off. I didn't want no part of that argument."

"Can't say I blame you," said Mr. Clemens. "So you made yourself scarce, and then the deputies found you?"

"Pretty much," said Blankenship.

"One question," said Roosevelt. "It seems to me you had plenty of time to return to your rooming house. But the deputies found you still on the street over half an hour later. Why were you out there, instead of someplace safe?"

Blankenship's grin evaporated. "I can't tell you that," he said. "It's the first thing the sheriff wanted to know, and I wouldn't tell him, either. That's why I asked you to bring Sam here. He's the only one can help, right now. Though—" he nodded at Mr. Clemens—"it didn't have to be in the middle of the night. It could've waited till morning."

"How do you think I can help, if you won't give any reason why you were acting suspicious?" asked Mr. Clemens.

An earnest expression came over Blankenship's face as he said, "You're the smartest man I know, Sam. I know it looks bad for me. Goodness, I've sat as judge in a lot of cases where I sent a fellow off to jail because his only story was something that didn't look as bad as this must. Sometimes I wonder if those fellows got a fair shake from me, but I got to do the best I can by the law."

"I'm not following you, Tom," said Mr. Clemens. "You know it looks bad for you, and this is a murder case, not some petty argument. But you won't tell us what you were doing out there just a short distance away from the scene of the crime. What do you expect me to do?"

"I want you to be my lawyer, Sam," said Blankenship. "If you can't figure out a way to get me out of this, there ain't nobody in Montana that can."

"Lawyer?" Mr. Clemens fairly spat the word out. "You want me to be your lawyer? Tom, I don't have any training in the law, and I'm too damned old to take it up at my age. Besides, I have to leave town on the Saturday morning train, unless I'm going to cancel my whole lecture tour and lose thousands of dollars. I'll find out who the best local lawyer is, and pay him whatever he wants to charge to take your case, but there's no way in hell I can do it myself."

"Well, Sam, I reckon I best make my will, because if you won't help me they'll hang me sure," said Blankenship. "Look, you don't have to prove I didn't kill Jed Harrington. All you got to do is prove somebody else did—which shouldn't be too hard, because somebody else *did* kill him. When you show them that, they'll have to let me loose, and that's all I can ask. Will you give it a try?"

"Jesus," said Mr. Clemens, rolling his eyes. "Tom, you always were a hard-headed one, you know that?"

Blankenship answered mildly, "Sure, and you were always the best liar and conniver I ever did see. If that don't make you a natural-born lawyer, I don't know what does. 'Sides, I know you've done this before, for other people. I read it in the papers. Come on, Sam, do it for me. If you ain't found the killer before you need to leave town, you can get me somebody else—but it's you I want on my side, not some Missoula shyster. I've seen most of them in action, and you beat 'em all hollow."

Mr. Clemens shrugged. "Well, maybe I do tell lies for a living, but there's got to be more than that to being a lawyer. But I'll tell you what. I'll do what I can to find who did kill Harrington, and failing that to spring you loose some other way. Are you sure you don't want to tell me why you were out there in the street instead of safe home? It won't go any further, I promise you."

Blankenship looked at Roosevelt, and then at me, and finally at Mr. Clemens, and then he shook his head. "Nope," he said earnestly. "Maybe when this whole mess is over I can tell you, but not until then."

I could see Mr. Clemens holding back his temper. But after a long pause he said, "All right, then. What can you tell me that might help me find the real killer? I've got to start somewhere, and you're the only witness I've got, so far."

"Well, I already told you most of what I know," said Blankenship. "I heard the shot, went to see what it was all about, saw Harrington dead, and then after a while the deputies came and arrested me. Mr. Roosevelt was with me for that part, and he can tell you what happened after that. I was mostly paying attention to keeping the deputies from acting any more zealous than they already were. That's how it is, you know, when you're in the middle of a situation like that."

"Hmmm . . ." said Mr. Clemens, rubbing his chin. "You said you saw a man next to him with a pistol. Did you recognize that man? He's an obvious suspect."

"Nope," said Blankenship. "He was facing half away. Most likely it was one of his two buddies, C. D. or Zach'ry. You ask the sheriff's men—they'll tell you."

"I'll do that," said Mr. Clemens. He looked at Roosevelt, then back at Blankenship. "Do you have any idea who Harrington's enemies were?"

"Most everybody that knew him, I reckon," said Blankenship. "But you'll find that out, I know, Sam. If there's anybody that could find it out, you're the one. I reckon I can rest a lot easier with you looking after me."

"Rest? How the hell are you going to rest when you're in jail on a murder charge?" Mr. Clemens exploded.

"Ain't much opportunity for anything else, far as I can see," said Blankenship. "In fact, I hear that deputy coming down the hall, and that means he's going to ask you fellows to leave. I'll let the deputies know you're my lawyer, so they'll let you come see me any time, I guess.

But you probably need some sleep now, Sam. I want you to rest up real good. In the morning you can get started on finding some way to prove I'm not guilty. I'm sure you can do it."

"All right, but there's no reason you have to stay here in jail," said Mr. Clemens. "Why don't we just tell them you're a magistrate down in your home town. They can telegraph down there for verification, and once they see it's true, they'll probably let you out until we can clear you. It's bound to be a lot more comfortable . . ."

"No, Sam, I don't want that," said Blankenship. "I'd just as soon stay here as let word get back home what kind of trouble I'm in. We won't raise that point at all."

Mr. Clemens's mouth hung open, and I don't know whether he would have managed to find some reply to Blankenship or not. But just then the deputy's knock came on the cell door, followed by the announcement, "Time's up, gentlemen. I want the prisoner to set on the bed, put his hands on top of his head. The rest of you stand to one side while I open the door. Everybody keep your hands where I can see 'em, now, so I don't get nervous."

And a few moments later we were out of the cell, and Tom Blankenship was lying on his cot again, looking as peaceful as a baby.

9 ⤳

Before we left the sheriff's office, the sheriff told us that the man found with Harrington was his side-kick, C. D. The gun he'd been holding hadn't been fired. That, along with the fact that he'd stayed with his wounded friend instead of fleeing, had been sufficient in the sheriff's eyes to exonerate him—although he'd been asked to stay in town pending a full investigation.

Sheriff Williams also told us there would be a hearing in the morning, before a local judge, who would attempt to determine whether there was sufficient reason to hold Blankenship for a formal trial. At that point, the judge would consider motions to grant bail or to release the prisoner on his own recognizance.

"That'll be our best chance of getting him out," said Mr. Roosevelt as we rode back to the hotel. "Normally, it would be sufficient to show that your friend has some standing in the community, and as a magistrate, he surely does. Since he doesn't want you to bring that fact out, you'll have to try another tack. I'd say we need to establish that there's reasonable doubt as to his having committed the crime, which in my opinion there is. A moderately bright first year law student should be able to get him released on bail."

"Well, I reckon I'm up to that, then," said Mr. Clemens. He took a long puff on his pipe and said, "Come to think of it, I've already got some experience at bailing out accused murderers—remember when I got you out of that New Orleans jail, Wentworth?"

"All too well, sir," I said. "Although I don't usually think of myself as an accused murderer."

"Oh, people can accuse you of anything," said my employer. "That don't make it true, especially when you can prove it ain't. Of course, that last part's likely to be the hardest part."

"Don't worry, Clemens," said Mr. Roosevelt. "I'll be glad to add my weight to the cause. I haven't told you what my new job is because the mayor had asked me to wait for the official announcement. But I think I can trust you not to tell anyone who doesn't need to know. You're riding with the next Police Commissioner of New York City."

"Not tell anybody?" Mr. Clemens looked over at Roosevelt, and I thought I detected a sly grin. "I'll guarantee you that—in fact, I hope you'll keep your mouth shut about it until I've got poor Tom out of jail. We're in Montana, remember? You'd be better off telling them you were a second assistant devil from West Hell than that you had anything at all to do with New York City."

Roosevelt's jaw dropped, but then he let out a great hearty laugh and said, "Clemens, you're a complete original! I'd best measure my legs when I get back to the room and make sure you haven't pulled one of them six or eight inches longer than the other!"

"If there's any problem, you can always apply to me and I'll be glad to operate on the other one," said Mr. Clemens, puffing contentedly on his pipe. "But here we are back at the Florence House. I don't know about you boys, but I'm going to see if I can catch another couple of hours in bed before I have to get up and play lawyer.

You youngsters may enjoy this jumping out of bed in the middle of the night, but I don't mind telling you I need my sleep. And that's what I'm going to get."

"I don't blame you one bit, sir," I said, opening the cab door on my side. Mr. Clemens and I got out, and Roosevelt went on to his own hotel while we stumbled up to bed.

I felt totally exhausted. Having assisted Mr. Clemens in several previous murder investigations, I had no illusion that the next few days would allow me any better rest than the few unsatisfactory hours I had already gotten tonight. But, as Mr. Clemens's mention of my night in the New Orleans jail reminded me, I'd gone through worse before. I had every reason to believe I would survive it this time.

As it turned out, I overslept. It was nearly eight o'clock when Mr. Clemens came knocking on my door to call, leaving me just enough time to dress and drink a large mug of watered-down coffee before we rushed out to see if we could secure Tom Blankenship's release.

Mr. Roosevelt met us in front of the magistrate's court, a modest brick building adjacent to the jail. "Good morning, fellows," he said, louder than I thought necessary. He did look a good bit more alert than I felt. I wondered if he'd gotten better sleep than I or whether he had a more resilient constitution—he certainly looked healthy enough. Or, I decided, just possibly he'd gotten more coffee than I had.

Mr. Clemens looked around. "What's the lay of the land?" he said. "Is there a set schedule or anything?"

"Not that I've been able to learn," said Roosevelt. "But I've only been here five minutes, and so far the only person I've seen is some sort of clerk who told me to wait until they're open. I tried to pump him a bit, but the rascal just went straight in and locked the door behind him."

"And when do they open?" asked Mr. Clemens. He

looked at the front of the building, but there was no sign there to answer his question.

"When they feel like it, as far as I can discover," grumbled Roosevelt. "Things are quite a bit less regular out here than back east, I'm afraid. In New York—"

"This is Montana, mister. We don't care how you do it in New York," said a new voice. I turned to see a long-faced man with a fringe of grey beard in the style of Abraham Lincoln. He was wearing a broad-brimmed hat and a woolen frock coat, which struck me as likely to be uncomfortable once the day warmed up.

"Good morning, are you the judge?" asked my employer.

"That's right, and you look like Mark Twain," said the newcomer, looking Mr. Clemens up and down. He raised an eyebrow, then added in the same flat tone, "The missus and I saw your show the other night."

"I hope you enjoyed it," said my employer.

The judge pulled a large key from his pocket and noisily opened the courthouse door. Then he turned to Mr. Clemens and said dryly, "Well, *she* did, anyway."

Before any of us could get in another word, he ducked through the door and pulled it firmly shut. Another loud metallic clack informed us that he'd locked it behind him.

Mr. Clemens looked at Roosevelt. "Maybe this isn't going to be as easy as you thought," he said, rubbing his chin. "I'm afraid there's more going on than we know about, Roosevelt. It worries me that Tom won't tell me where he was between the shooting and when they found him . . ."

"Well, he can't be very worried, then, can he?" Roosevelt boomed. "If Blankenship thought he was really going to face a murder prosecution, he'd be telling you every last detail that might exonerate him. He's innocent as a babe . . ."

"That's no lie," said Mr. Clemens, pacing in a little circle. "And that's exactly what worries me. Tom has always had less real sense of danger than almost anybody

I know. Not that he's some kind of daredevil—just the opposite. But you saw him when we came into his cell: more interested in catching up on his sleep than in what might be about to happen to him. I'm afraid he's going to leave all the work of defending himself to me, and I can't think of a more foolhardy way for a man in his situation to act."

"You underestimate yourself, Clemens," said Mr. Roosevelt. "Any man of reasonable intellectual capacity ought to be able to grasp the broad points of the law. You're a good bit ahead of the pack in that regard."

"It ain't the lack of intellectual capacity that disqualifies me from being a lawyer, it's the possession of common decency," said Mr. Clemens with a snort.

Mr. Roosevelt was about to reply to this when the courthouse door flew open and a clean-shaven man in a brown suit peered out at the three of us. "Court's in session," he said. "If'n you got any business to bring a-fore Judge McCoy, now's the time or forever hold your peace."

"What the hell's going on here, a trial or a wedding?" said Mr. Clemens, but Mr. Roosevelt shushed him and we all went through the door into the courthouse.

This was a modestly appointed room, wooden-paneled with a row of benches facing a large but plain desk upon a dais, flanked by an American flag and another that I assumed must be the state flag of Montana. To one side was a railing marking off a jury box, and next to the desk was a smaller witness box. Off to the other side, and to the rear, sat a sullen-looking band of prisoners, flanked by the two deputies we'd seen in the jailhouse. I noticed that Tom Blankenship was not among them; perhaps because of the more serious nature of his alleged offense, he was being kept more closely confined until his case was called.

Mr. Roosevelt marched us up to the front row, and we sat behind a folding table that I assumed was meant for the lawyers. Behind us a handful of locals straggled in, whether as interested parties or as spectators I had no idea.

"Ever'body stand for the honorable Joseph McCoy!" barked the clerk, and as we rose to our feet, the judge emerged from one of a pair of doors behind the desk. He was now wearing a plain black robe, not much different from the ones I'd seen some church choirs wearing. He went to the desk, took a seat, and nodded.

The audience seated itself, and the judge turned to the clerk. "First case?" he asked.

"Billy McBride, drunk and disorderly," said the clerk. "Rode his horse into Mike Thompson's saloon."

"Billy, stand forth," said the judge, and a lanky fellow with straggly red hair hanging below a battered broad-brimmed hat shuffled out of the group of prisoners to stand unsteadily in front of the bench. "How do you plead?" said the judge.

"Joe, I can't deny bein' drunk," said the defendant. "Fellow needs a taste every now and then. But I sure the hell wasn't disorderly. I rode that horse straight in the door and up to the bar and didn't so much as brush nobody on the way."

"That damned horse dumped a pile on my barroom floor!" came a voice from behind me. I turned to see a brawny, bald-headed fellow with a luxuriant handlebar mustache standing and pointing at the defendant.

"Well, maybe the horse was disorderly, then," responded the defendant. "Ain't no fault of mine, Mike. 'Sides, cleanin' up after a horse ain't such a big deal. You got a broom and a shovel, don't you?"

"That ain't the point," shouted the bartender. "You can't come into my place and act like an ign'ant cowboy. These ain't the frontier days anymore."

"He *is* an ign'ant cowboy," came a stage whisper from the back of the courtroom. "How else is he gonna act?"

The judge rapped his gavel on the desk. "Tony Allison, you shut up or I'll have Terry throw you out," he said. He turned to the defendant. "Billy McBride, this isn't the

first time you've been in here, so I can't just let you off.
You've been warned before, and you promised you'd be-
have yourself."

"I know, Joe," said the defendant, hanging his head
now. "I swear I won't do it again."

"You swore the last time, and I let you off," said Judge
McCoy. "Now here you are again, and this time I'm going to have to give you something to help you remember
what you promise. Court finds the defendant guilty. Five
dollars fine or two days in jail. Next case!"

The next case was another drunk and disorderly cowboy, as were the next five defendants, all of whom re-
ceived similar light sentences. Most of them seemed to
be familiar local characters who were harassed by a constant stream of banter from their peers in the audience,
whom the judge perfunctorily gaveled down when they
got too raucous. They were followed by the first actual
criminal case: a tramp who'd apparently been in town
only a few days. One of the deputies had caught him
breaking into the back door of a drugstore. He stared
defiantly around as the sheriff presented the evidence
against him; the judge set bail at $100 and ordered him
to be held for a more formal trial. The gallery was silent
as the sheriff led the would-be burglar away.

That exhausted the list of lesser offenders, and then
the clerk looked at his list and called out, "Thomas Blankenship, suspected of gunning down Jed Harrington last
night."

Judge McCoy turned to look as the door behind him
opened and the sheriff led in Blankenship; a buzz of talk
came from the spectators, causing the judge to turn and
give a baleful stare at the courtroom. He raised his gavel
threateningly, and the buzz subsided as Blankenship was
led to the front of the desk.

"Thomas Blankenship, you stand accused of a serious
crime," said the judge. "Are you represented by council?"

"Yes sir, your honor," said Blankenship. He turned to
look back at us over his shoulder and added, "That's my

lawyer over there—my good friend Sam Clemens."

"Sam Clemens?" The judge's eyebrows raised. "Do you mean you're picking Mark Twain to plead your case?"

"That's correct, your honor," said my employer, rising to his feet. "Tom has asked me to help clear him of these charges, and while the press of other business made me reluctant at first, in light of our long friendship I've agreed to do it."

The judge frowned and turned back to Blankenship. "I'm going to remind you again that you are charged with a very serious crime—one for which you could be hanged. *Hanged*, Mr. Blankenship. Do you really want to put your fate in the hands of a traveling comedian?"

"Well, Judge McCoy, I admit I was a mite worried about Sam's traveling," said Blankenship in a conversational tone. "But he says he'll be here in Missoula a few more days, and I reckon that'll be plenty of time for him to set things straight."

"You reckon so, do you?" said the judge, plainly puzzled. "And what gives you the notion that a man who's never practiced law in his life can do you any good in contesting a capital case?"

"Oh, I've seen lots of lawyers at work," said Blankenship. "Mostly they're men who'll say whatever somebody's paid 'em to say, which is a polite way of saying they're liars."

At this, the audience broke into loud guffaws, until the judge rapped his gavel sharply on the desk. Unperturbed, Blankenship went on: "Now, Sam's a pretty fair liar when he puts his mind to it, but he knows how to tell the truth when it'll serve. And the truth is, I didn't kill Jed Harrington, and that's where I mean to take my stand. So I expect Sam can argue the case for me without straining his capacities."

"We'll see about that," said the judge, whose expression had come to resemble that of a man who finds an insect on his dinner plate. He turned to Sheriff Williams.

"Henry, what makes you think this man's the one who killed Jed Harrington?"

The sheriff cleared his throat. "My deputies found him on Third Street a couple of blocks away from the shooting, making tracks away from it. He was carrying these," he said, holding up a rifle that to my eyes looked much like the one Blankenship had been carrying the night before, and a large revolver.

"Which one of those is the murder weapon?" asked the judge.

"We don't know for sure, your honor," said the sheriff. "We do know the victim was shot, and the witness says there was nobody close enough for anything but a rifle shot. And one of my men saw Blankenship draw on the victim just a few nights before, in a barroom fight."

"That wasn't a fight, that was preventing a fight," said Mr. Clemens, rising and stepping around the table. "That Harrington rascal had blindsided my secretary with a bottle, and was about to do some more damage to him when Tom stepped in and showed him the gun to quiet him down. Harrington took the hint and that was the end of it."

"Until last night, that is," said Judge McCoy. "Then he ran across him on a dark street with nobody to back him up, and he decided to get rid of the rotten apple once and for all."

"Who says so?" said Mr. Clemens. "Where's the witness who told you that? We have a right to hear him say it."

The judge turned to the sheriff. "Mr. Twain's got a point," he said. "Where's your witness?"

"Well, Joe, I reckon he's sleepin' it off this morning," said the sheriff. "He was one of those roughnecks Harrington used to go around with. Anyways, he said in so many words it was this here Tom Blankenship that shot Harrington. When we go to trial, we'll bring him in."

"Very well," said the judge. "The witness identifies

Mr. Blankenship as the shooter. That's all the grounds we need . . ."

"That ain't so," said Blankenship. "Judge, you're supposed to make the sheriff produce his witness, not just take his word for what the fellow said. That's hearsay evidence, and you're supposed to ignore that."

"You seem to know a lot about what a judge is supposed to do," said Judge McCoy with a sneer.

"I guess I do," said Tom Blankenship. "Back home—"

"Ah, so you're not from Missoula?" asked the judge.

"Oh no, I'm just here to visit Sam . . ."

The judge leaned forward over his desk and peered at Blankenship. "Do you have any friends or relatives in these parts?"

"Tom . . ." said Mr. Clemens in a warning tone.

"Just Sam," said Blankenship. "I came here special to see him."

"I see," said the judge. "No roots in the community. No fixed abode, either, I take it?"

"Not hereabouts," said Blankenship. "You see, I live 'bout a hundred miles south . . ."

"I *see*," said Judge McCoy, grinning evilly. He raised his voice and continued, "Based on the sheriff's testimony and the serious nature of the charges, I hereby deny bail. Prisoner is to be held in the county jail pending trial. Next case!" He banged the gavel on the desk, and before Mr. Clemens could say a word, the sheriff had whisked Tom Blankenship out the door and taken him back to jail. My employer stood to protest, but the judge glared at him and said, "Next case!" And so ended Blankenship's day in court.

"All right, what did we do wrong?" asked Mr. Clemens. "It can't have been anything I did—I barely got a chance to open my mouth."

"That seems to be happening a good bit hereabouts," I said, remembering the story-telling contest where none of the locals had let my employer get a word in edgewise.

We sat drinking coffee in a small cafe about a block from the courthouse where Judge McCoy had ordered Tom Blankenship held without bail for the murder of Jed Harrington. The third seat at our table was occupied by Theodore Roosevelt, who had accompanied us to the hearing.

"I'm afraid the locals are rather prejudiced against easterners," said Roosevelt. "I saw a bit of that when I first came west. Until you can prove you're one of them, they look on you as an ignorant outsider. I suspect that when the judge saw three easterners sitting at the defense table, he took it as an affront—not that he'd ever admit to anything so blatant."

"I guess I understand that," said Mr. Clemens. "I had the same thing happen to me when I first went to Nevada. But hell, most of the people out here are probably outsiders if you go back a little bit. It's just like California—I'd be surprised if one Montanan in ten is actually a native."

"Maybe more than that by now," said Roosevelt. He picked up his coffee cup, took a large sip, then continued. "Still, I think your friend Blankenship did more to damage his own cause than any of us did. Once he started lecturing the judge about what his job was, he forfeited the right to bail on the spot. He'd have had more luck telling a bunch of cowboys how to saddle horses. You'd think he'd know better, being a magistrate himself."

Mr. Clemens shook his head. "Tom's always been a law unto himself. I suspect the way he runs a courtroom would throw most of the law professors at Harvard into conniptions. So maybe he *does* know better, but that don't mean he's going to bite his tongue when he runs across a self-important ass like McCoy. I had a mind to favor that judge with a few choice words myself."

"It's a good thing you didn't," I said, looking around to make sure the man in question wasn't one of the small crowd of customers in the cafe. "He'd probably clap you in jail for contempt of court."

"I've got plenty of contempt for *his* court," growled my employer. He looked at Mr. Roosevelt and raised his brows. "You don't suppose there's another court we could appeal to?"

"Nothing close enough to be much use to us, I wouldn't think," said Roosevelt, rubbing the ends of his mustache with his thumb and forefinger. He leaned back in his chair and said, "Better to work on clearing your friend directly. If we can establish an open and shut case against someone else, the sheriff will have no choice but to let Blankenship go free, whatever the judge thinks of him—or of his friends."

"Meaning me in particular, I guess," said Mr. Clemens. He stared into his coffee cup for a long moment. Then he straightened up and looked me in the eye. "I guess we've got our work cut out for us, Wentworth," he said. "We've done it before, and we can do it again. Are you game to catch another murderer?"

"Yes, sir." It was the only possible answer, of course. In fact, much to my surprise, I was actually excited at the prospect of investigating a new murder case—although I knew full well how much hard work and anxiety there was likely to be before it was over. A few short months ago, I would have run screaming from the prospect.

"Good," said my employer. "How about you, Roosevelt? Will you help us get Tom off the hook?"

"I'd never be able to look at myself in the mirror if I backed out now," said Roosevelt, clapping Mr. Clemens on the shoulder. "You know I'm not one to shirk my duty, and there's no higher duty than helping a friend in need. We'll get to the bottom of this, don't you doubt it."

"Good, then let's figure out where we start," said Mr. Clemens. "Normally I'd try to find an alibi for Tom, but as you both saw, he's keeping mum on that score. If worse comes to worst, I'll see if I can convince him to change his tune. But first let's figure out who the other suspects ought to be. A man like Harrington had to have had more than one enemy."

"I'd be surprised if most of the town isn't on that list," I said. "The minute I laid eyes on him, there were people telling me to watch out for him. I doubt he had many friends, if you want my opinion."

"Well, maybe we should start with his friends, then," said Mr. Clemens, nodding. "After all, one or the other of them seems to be the witness the sheriff didn't bother to produce in court today. Do either of you have any idea where he and his two pals were staying before he got shot?"

"We don't know for certain they were staying together," said Mr. Roosevelt. "But if he's from out of town, odds are he stayed in one of the hotels or rooming houses. There aren't that many in a town this size. I say we split up the list among us and go inquire."

"Fine," said Mr. Clemens. "I already know they're not in the Florence, and you'd have seen them if they were in the Missoula. So what's left?"

"I don't think we have to worry about that," I said, standing up suddenly. "The answer just walked past us."

"What the hell?" said Mr. Clemens. But I was already on my way out the cafe's door, in pursuit of the two men I'd seen pass by the front window.

≈ 10

Zach'ry and C. D. were still in sight, walking slowly side by side, as I came out onto the street. "Say, you fellows! Hold up a moment, will you?" I cried, heading toward them.

They turned around quickly, and suspicion grew across their faces as they recognized me. "It's that city boy," said C. D., scowling. He put his hands on his hips, and his partner aped the movement. "What do you want with us, dude? You're after a hard lickin', you come to the right parties."

"All I want is to find out who killed your friend," I said, holding my hands up in a conciliatory gesture. "If you'll come back to the cafe and talk for a few minutes, the coffee's on me."

"That skunk Tom Blankenship killed him," said Zach'ry, and he spat into the street. "Don't need no damn coffee to tell you that. We aim to tell Judge McCoy everything we know, and we'd be purely pleased to stick around for the hanging."

"Maybe you're right," I said. "If you are, that's all there is to it. But if you're not, the real killer might get away. My friends and I mean to find him, whoever he is. So we're on the same side as you. Will you come talk to us?"

Zach'ry and C. D. looked at each other and shrugged. Then C. D. looked at me and said, "What the hell. I wouldn't mind a cup of coffee, and talk's free in this country, last I heard. Lead the way, mister."

"Good," I said, nodding. "Come on, then." I turned back toward the cafe.

I quickly learned that I had made a mistake. I had taken perhaps two steps when a strong pair of arms crushed me in a bear hug from behind, pinioning my arms and pulling me off balance. As I struggled to free myself, Zach'ry jumped in front of me, threw down his cigarette, and began firing punches at my unprotected face. "Take that, you slick son of a bitch," he shouted.

Desperate, I kicked backward, barking C. D.'s shin, then brought my heel down hard upon his instep. He yelped, and his grip on me loosened enough for me to get my right arm free. Zach'ry was still aiming blows toward my face, although with less effect than perhaps he realized. Still, if I remained a sitting duck much longer, there was no doubt I would take a serious beating. I jabbed my elbow into C. D.'s belly, and that took the wind out of him. His arms came free, and I stepped back to the wall of a nearby building and put up my fists. Now that both my attackers were in front of me, I had a better chance to defend myself.

But while I had no doubt I could handle either of the cowboys head-to-head, they had no intention of giving me fair odds. Zach'ry and C. D. drew back a step and whispered to one another, then stepped apart and began to close in on me from opposite sides. It wasn't hard to guess what they were planning; one would harass me from one side, and while I was occupied with him, the other would try to land a telling blow. Worse, they had the advantage of being able to break off hostilities at will, whereas I was trapped between them and would have both of them on top of me if I tried to escape.

Luckily, I had an answer to that. "Roosevelt!" I shouted at the top of my lungs.

Zach'ry stopped in his tracks, but C. D. kept edging closer; I turned slightly to face him, without letting his partner slip entirely out of my field of vision. Even if help came quickly, one of the cowboys might manage to land a telling blow while they still had me pinned against the wall. I had made it so far without serious damage; now was no time to let down my guard.

But a loud bellow made C. D. turn to look over his shoulder, and I saw that Mr. Roosevelt had emerged from the cafe and was charging to join the fray with all the enthusiasm of an angry bull moose. C. D. and Zach'ry needed only a glance to decide they wanted no part of this new opponent, and as if with a single mind they turned to flee.

I had other ideas. I'd come out here to get them to talk, and I wasn't going to abandon that goal so quickly. As they turned their backs, I leapt into action and was on C. D.'s back before he'd taken more than a couple of steps. I brought him down with a tackle around the thighs, and I heard the breath go out of him as he landed on the hard-packed dirt street. I scrambled up to pin his arms, and almost before I completed the action, Roosevelt was standing over us. "That was a bully tackle, Cabot," he said. He reached down and slapped me on the back. "You do your *alma mater* proud."

"This isn't football, for God's sake," I said, panting from my exertion. I pulled one of C. D.'s arms up in a hammerlock, then continued. "If we aren't careful, this fellow's partner will be back—with a gun, for all I know. Help me convince him we're not going to hurt him. If he'll talk to us—"

"I ain't talkin' to nobody," said the cowboy. "You let me go before I call the deputy."

"There's nothing the deputy's interested in here," said Mr. Roosevelt, squatting down to look C. D. in the face.

"Unless it's two men attacking one, and I doubt Cabot did anything to provoke you. If anyone ought to call the deputy, he's the one."

"All right, then, just let go my arm," said C. D., twisting his head around to look over his shoulder at me. "I'll call it quits if you will."

"I asked you and your friend to talk to me," I said, not relaxing my grip. "That invitation still stands. Listen to what we have to say, and if you want to walk away then, I won't say another word. But I think you owe us five minutes to hear us out. And I'll still buy you that cup of coffee."

"A beer would be more like it," muttered C. D. Then he added, in a higher register, "Hey, do I have to say 'uncle'? Could you slack off the arm a little?"

"Sorry, I wasn't trying to hurt you," I said, not sure even as I said it just how true it was. I wasn't quite ready to forget that C. D. had been doing his level best to hurt *me* only a few minutes before. I continued, "I don't know whether I want a beer this early in the day, but if it'll take beer to convince you to talk to us, I guess I can buy it for you. Let's go tell my boss what's going on so he can join us."

I released my grip on his arm and we both got to our feet; Roosevelt rested a monitory hand lightly on C. D.'s shoulder as the cowboy stood up. We walked in a group back to the cafe, where I could see Mr. Clemens standing in the doorway, holding his coffee cup while he observed. Across the street a small pack of schoolboys watched with excitement on their faces—I supposed a fight between grown men might be a rare treat to them. Or perhaps not so rare; from what I'd seen of the west, it was still a good bit wilder than the eastern half of the country, and likely to stay that way.

Mr. Clemens nodded when C. D. repeated his request for something stronger than coffee to drink, and said, "What the hell, this cafe's a little too public, anyway—at least after you boys decided to get rough. You know someplace close where we can get drinks and talk without too many people listening?"

"Sure," said the cowboy. "Benny's place is just around the corner. Anybody there this time of day, he's likely to be too drunk to pay us any attention."

I didn't like that description at all, but my employer said, "All right, show us the way. I could use a shot of whiskey myself, if they've got the real stuff."

"Don't know what you call real," said C. D., "but if you mean the kind of stuff that makes you want to jump up on the table and whoop, they got it."

I liked the sound of that even less, but Mr. Clemens wasn't looking to me for advice, and so Roosevelt and I had no choice but to trail along—unless we wanted to leave my employer in the company of drunken cowboys, at least one of whom had already shown a penchant for violence. In my case, at least, that was no choice at all.

The establishment in question was on a slightly shabby side street, next to a boarded-up building that, from the sign, had previously been a hardware store. Across the street, a striped pole indicated a barber shop; the proprietor (clean-shaven but bald as an egg) leaned in the doorway in his apron, smoking a pipe. He eyed Mr. Clemens's full head of white hair speculatively, but made no effort to solicit his business.

Inside Benny's saloon, the floor was covered by sawdust, with spittoons scattered at random intervals, and the half-dozen tables were more or less clean. The lights were gas, and turned low, since enough sun came through the front window that the place was adequately lit. In the far corner was a cowboy, apparently fast asleep, with his hat pulled down over his eyes and his boots propped up on a table. Two other cowboys leaned against the bar, conversing in low voices. They turned to look at us as we entered, then (evidently deciding we were of no immediate interest) nodded and turned back to their talk. All in all, I was relieved. While hardly a respectable establishment, it was nowhere near as rough as I'd feared.

"I'm buying," said Mr. Clemens. "You fellows tell me what you want and grab a table. I'll go fetch the drinks."

"Beer's fine with me," said C. D. He strolled over to a table by the window.

"Coffee if they have it," I said, peering suspiciously at the rather spartan row of bottles behind the bar. "If not, I'll have a plain soda water."

"Coffee sounds good," agreed Roosevelt. "If they've got any decent brandy, have them put a touch of that in it."

"All right, I'll see what they've got," said Mr. Clemens, and he went over to the bar while Roosevelt and I joined C. D. at the table.

The first chair I tried had one wobbly leg, but I found a better one at the next table and sat down. Roosevelt and I had taken chairs flanking the cowboy, tacitly deciding to stay between him and my employer.

C. D. leaned back in his chair and looked at me. "You know, you was putting up a pretty good fight all by yourself," he said. "No telling what kind of fun we might have had if you hadn't called four-eyes in." He accompanied this last remark with a gesture at Roosevelt.

Roosevelt chuckled. "This fellow was a fine football player in his time," he said. "That doesn't necessarily mean anything in a real fight, but now that I've seen him at work, I'd give him full points for pluck. And for common sense—I've seen more than one fellow take an unnecessary beating by being too proud to call for help when he was outnumbered."

"Well, I can't fault a fellow for playing a hole card when he's got it," said C. D. He turned to me and continued, "Long as you don't hold a grudge. I mean, me and Zach'ry was just doin' what we thought was right, since poor old Jeb got shot down without any show."

"We need to talk about that," I said. "But let's wait till we've got our drinks—Mr. Clemens will want to hear what you have to say about it."

"I ain't got much to say," said C. D. "But I don't mind

who hears it, 'cause every word of it's true." He rapped his fist lightly on the table for emphasis, then leaned back again.

"Here you are," said Mr. Clemens, setting down a glass of beer in front of C. D. and a whiskey at the vacant place opposite the cowboy. He sat down and took off his cap, then turned to me and Roosevelt. "The bartender says he'll make some coffee if you want to wait a little while," he said, "or he can give you soda water now. And after a look at the bottle, I don't know if I'd mess with the brandy."

"I'll take your advice on that," said Roosevelt, chuckling. "Just the coffee, then." I murmured my agreement as well. Mr. Clemens turned and gave the bartender a thumbs-up signal and sat down at the table.

He took a sip of his drink and made a face. He stared wide-eyed at the glass, then turned to C. D. "You weren't lying about the whiskey here. I think the last time I had this kind of poison was damn near thirty years ago, when it was all you could get in the mining camps."

"Don't drink the stuff myself," said C. D., shrugging. "My money goes a lot farther if I stick to the suds."

"Smart man," said Mr. Clemens. "I guess the money will be a lot tighter now that Jed Harrington's gone, won't it?"

"I guess it will," said C. D., frowning. "Jed used to give me and Zach'ry a lot of work, one kind or another. But I guess we're on our own, now. Won't be the same."

"No, it won't," said Mr. Clemens quietly. He swirled his glass and looked warily at it, as if trying to decide whether to drink more of the whiskey. After a moment, he put it back down and looked C. D. in the eye, saying, "Jed didn't deserve to be shot down like that. Nobody does. Were you there when it happened?"

C. D. nodded. "Near as close to him as I am to you," he said. He took a small pouch of "makings" from his pocket and began to roll a cigarette before adding, "The bullet must've gone right past me."

Mr. Clemens leaned forward, putting his elbows on the table. "Now, this is important," he said. "Think before you answer. Did you see who shot him?"

"Hell, it was that no-count Judge Blankenship," said C. D. vehemently.

Mr. Clemens cut him off with an abrupt gesture. "But did you *see* him?"

C. D. licked the cigarette paper and folded it over with his thumbs, then looked at my employer. He shook his head. "No, not right then. It was dark out, and he didn't exactly walk right up to Jed. Too yellow to give a man a show . . ."

Mr. Clemens picked up the whiskey glass, sniffed the contents with a distasteful expression, and put it back down. "All right, then," he said. "Let's go back a step. Tell me all about the time before the shooting. Where were you, what were you doing?"

C. D. drained his beer glass and set it on the table. "That's a mighty long story. A fellow might get dry tellin' it all at once," he drawled.

"We can do something about that," said Mr. Clemens. "Wentworth, go get him another beer. And while you're at it, order me a coffee. Maybe it'll make this godawful whiskey drinkable, if I mix 'em together."

"Yes, sir," I said, and walked over to the bar to place the order. I came back with the beer a couple of minutes later. "The bartender says the coffee will be just a little longer," I reported.

"That's all right, we've got all the time in the world," said Mr. Clemens. "C. D. was telling us how the boys were painting the town last night."

"It was one hellacious time, all right," said C. D. admiringly. By now, the cigarette was in his mouth and burning. "You never *seen* such a ruckus. We was in one place, a fellow rode his horse right into the saloon. Ain't seen that done since I was a little pup. Brought back some old memories, that's for sure."

"There's the western character in its native glory," said

Roosevelt with a toothy grin. "I saw a good bit of that kind of prank when I first came out here."

"Times have changed, and not for the best," said C. D. "But anyway, round about eleven o'clock, Zach'ry disappeared. I figured he'd either passed out somewheres, or he'd found him a girl and didn't want no disturbance. But Jed wanted to go looking for him, and so we went out to see what other bars was open. I didn't mind, since I figured if we didn't find him, we'd just have another drink wherever we ended up, and Zach'ry would show up in the morning one way or t'other."

"That's often the way of it," said Mr. Clemens. "What did you find?"

The cowboy took another sip of beer and continued. "Well, we went one place and no sign of him. We had a couple drinks and moved on, although Jed got in a bit of a face-off with some sergeant from the fort before we did."

"What happened there?" asked Roosevelt. "Just words, or did it go further?"

"Oh, nothin' but words," said C. D. "The soldier called Jed a bad name and Jed called him a worse one back, and they traded a couple more rounds of that. I thought it was going to get thick for a minute or two, but then the soldier walked away, and we drank up and went looking for the next place."

"No chance the soldier followed you out, is there?" asked Mr. Clemens.

"Not a Chinaman's chance," said C. D., scoffing. He was about to continue, but just then the bartender finally arrived carrying three unmatched mugs of coffee and a sugar bowl on a tray. He plopped these on the table with the air of a man unused to that sort of work—which, considering his normal clientele, was probably the truth.

I took a sip of my coffee and immediately reached for the sugar, but Roosevelt grabbed it before I did and proceeded to ladle three heaping spoonfuls into his cup. Mr.

Clemens watched this performance and grimaced. "That bad, huh?"

Roosevelt grinned again. "Back on the cattle drives, the boys used to joke that there were four grades of coffee: town coffee, ranch coffee, stove polish, and trail coffee. But I think this rascal's invented a fifth."

"I thought English coffee was bad," I said, adding sugar to my own cup. "This . . ." I could think of no adequate way to complete the sentence.

Mr. Clemens looked at his coffee cup, then at the still nearly full glass of whiskey. "What the hell, how bad can it be?" he said and poured off two inches of coffee into a spittoon. He topped up the cup with whiskey and took a cautious sip. His brows rose about an inch and his lips puckered. Then he solemnly picked up the cup and poured the rest of it into the spittoon. "Just so I don't get tempted," he said with a sad look.

"Now you know why I stick to beer," said C. D., grinning. Then his expression turned serious, and he continued. "But like I was saying, after the argument with the soldier, we went to another place, but it was so full we could hardly get up to the bar. If Zach'ry was there, we'd have had to pry him out with a crowbar. So we went out again, thinking we'd look for him back where we started. We was halfway there when I stopped under a street light to roll a smoke. Jed stood there with me, and just as I was lickin' the paper, *bam!* A gun went off somewhere behind me and Jed was down and done for."

"So you never saw the shooter," said Roosevelt. "No idea what kind of gun it was, how close he was?"

"A big gun—forty-four or forty-five, I'd say," C. D. said. "I could tell that by the way the shot knocked him back. Your little popguns won't do that."

"What did you do next?" said Mr. Clemens.

C. D. was aghast. "Do? Hell, I ducked behind the first cover I could find. Somebody starts shootin' people, you don't want to stand in the way. Maybe he's done his business, maybe not—don't want to find *that* out the hard way. I waited a bit, but there weren't no other shots, and then I went to see if there was any help for Jed. But he was already gone."

"That's a hard thing to have to go through," said Clemens. "What did you do when you realized he was dead? Did you call the cops, or did they come by themselves?"

"I took his gun out'n his holster, in case the shooter come back looking for me. But the deputies must have heard the shot because they were there almost as soon as I stood up," said the cowboy. "Tell the truth, I'd like to have skedaddled if they hadn't come right away, 'cause you don't want to be the first person they find when there's been trouble. But once I showed 'em it was Jed's gun I was holdin', and it still had all six bullets in it, they went pretty easy on me."

"Do you usually pack a gun in town?" I asked.

"I used to all the time, but not these days," said C. D. "It's been so long since I had to use it, it just seems like there ain't much advantage to it. You get in a tussle with somebody, you can settle it fair and square with just your fists. Out in the country, things are different—but that's neither here nor there. Now, Jed, he always carried his— reckon he'd've took it to church, if he went there. But it didn't help him none that night."

"I guess not," said Mr. Clemens. "Well, I'm mighty sorry. I don't think Jed and I would ever have been friends, but he still deserved better."

He paused for a moment, rubbing his chin, then said, "One last question. Let's say Blankenship can somehow prove he didn't shoot Harrington. Can you think of anybody else who might have been nursing a grudge against him?"

C. D. set down his beer glass—it was empty again— and looked Mr. Clemens straight in the eye. "Nope," he said. "Ol' Jed didn't have an enemy in the whole wide world. Not a single one."

●　　●　　●

"*Not an enemy in the world*," said Mr. Clemens. There was disbelief written all over his face. "That C. D. is either the biggest liar I've met this year, or he has a mighty peculiar definition of 'enemy'."

"Yes, I can think of any number of crucial questions his story leaves entirely unanswered," said Theodore Roosevelt. "For example, where were they when Cabot met their boss outside the hotel?"

"Here's another," said Mr. Clemens. "Where was that fellow Zach'ry all night? They lost him a couple of hours before the shooting. Maybe Harrington did something to make him mad—they were all three drunk as coots, as far as I can tell—and he went off and got his gun and came back to pot Harrington."

"My thought exactly," said Roosevelt. "I don't give C. D. any credit for either observation or judgment, although I suppose we have to accept the bare bones of his story as the best account we have of their doings that night—even though it leaves us with as many questions as answers. If necessary, we can try to retrace their steps and corroborate the key details."

"Jesus, I hope not," said Mr. Clemens. "The one fact I'm sure of without even looking past the face of it is that every damn witness we're likely to find was either dead drunk or well on the way there—well, maybe not all the bartenders. It's going to be one hell of a job trying to figure out whether a single word of it is true. There's got to be some shortcut to where we're going."

"We'll do it if we have to," I said. We'd returned to the hotel, where (after I'd changed clothes and cleaned up from my scuffle with the cowboys) we'd finally found some decent coffee in the barroom. The world was looking considerably brighter and more rational than it had an hour or so earlier. "But I agree, it'd be better to find some quicker way to verify C. D.'s story, and to check on the unanswered questions. We certainly need to find out what we can about Zach'ry's whereabouts when the shooting took place."

"I'd like to know more about exactly what kind of gun killed Harrington," said Mr. Clemens. "It sounds to me as if it had to be a rifle because C. D. says he never saw the shooter. I can't claim to be any kind of expert, but I don't think very many people could nail a man with a pistol from any long distance at nighttime."

"It wouldn't be easy," said Roosevelt, leaning back in his chair. "But there are more people than you'd think who could do it"—he gestured expansively—"and, as it happens, you'll find a fair number of them right here in Missoula, or not far off. I'd bet Bill Cody has five or six pistol experts working for him, and I bet you'll find as many more out at the fort. Which reminds me—I'd like to have a few words with that sergeant this fellow claims Harrington argued with."

"Good luck finding him," said Mr. Clemens. "He's not likely to walk up and volunteer to tell you his story. And unless there were a raft of witnesses, we'll be lucky to get even any kind of description more exact than *a big guy, wearing an Army uniform*. We don't even know for sure he was a sergeant."

"No, but it's a place to start looking," said Roosevelt. "And we do have to start somewhere, if Blankenship's going to be exonerated. That's what we want in the end, isn't it?"

"I reckon so," said my employer. He took his pipe out and began scraping at it with his pocket knife, a routine that I had learned usually meant he was gathering his thoughts before saying anything. People who didn't know him sometimes took his habitually slow speech as a sign of slow wits. I had plenty of evidence to the contrary. So I wondered what train of thought that apparently simple question had set off. Was it possible that he thought Blankenship might actually be guilty? Or was he examining some other, yet unmentioned, trail of evidence?

Finally he tapped the pipe on his palm, blew away the residue, and said, "Seeing as how I'm scheduled to be on a westbound train by the end of the week, we need to get moving fast if we're going to get to the bottom of this. Maybe we need to split up so we can cover more territory. Roosevelt, you say you're friends with a lot of the officers at the fort. Why don't you go see if you can learn what's behind C. D.'s story of Harrington arguing with a sergeant? Wentworth, I'd like you to go to as many of the local saloons as you can. Find out who was working there last night, and see if they remember anything out of the ordinary having to do with Harrington."

"Bully," said Roosevelt, rubbing his hands together. "And what are you going to investigate?"

"I reckon I'll try to find out about the gun," he said. "Somebody must have taken the bullet out of him, and maybe they can tell what kind of weapon fired it. Can't hurt to ask, and maybe it'll narrow down the territory we've got to cover."

"A good plan," said Roosevelt. "Well, I'll get packing out to the fort then. Where shall we meet again?"

"Let's all have dinner here," said Mr. Clemens. "We can compare notes then, and figure out what we need to do next. And just maybe, afterwards, you can get to hear my daughter play piano."

≈ 11

Missoula had no shortage of saloons. Indeed, the number of such establishments along its main and side streets would in my opinion have sufficed to serve a town much larger. Still, I had adequate time for my investigation. If I did my work efficiently, I would be able to cover the majority of them before I had to report to Mr. Clemens at supper time.

I decided to make Mike Thompson's establishment my first stop. C. D. had mentioned being in a place where a cowboy rode his horse into the barroom, and I remembered hearing the proprietor of Thompson's testify that such an incident had occurred in his saloon the previous night. Unless riding horses into bars was more common than I thought, that would be one of the places that Harrington and his two cronies had visited on the fatal night.

Asking directions to Mike Thompson's at the hotel desk got me only a blank stare, but when I asked a cab driver in front of the hotel, he said, "Hop in, boss, I'll take you right there." And sure enough, in less than five minutes, he dropped me off in front of the place I sought—one of three on the same block of Hazel Street.

The fare was ten cents, and I added on another dime as a tip. Good cabbies are useful in a strange town, and making myself appear a desirable fare could reap dividends somewhere down the road.

I went through the swinging doors and found a place not much different from others I had visited: a large, dimly lit room furnished with plain round tables that looked as if they could use a good cleaning. The bare floors were sprinkled with sawdust. At the back of the room was a long bar made of some dark wood, with two rows of bottles behind it. Through the smoky atmosphere I recognized the bald-headed man behind the bar; it was the same one who'd come to court to testify against the cowboy who'd ridden his horse into the saloon.

I walked over to the bar, ignoring the stares of the few patrons who'd noticed my arrival. I suspected they'd paid little more attention to their friend on horseback. From the condition of the furniture I suspected that an entire cavalry troop could have come through the doors without doing enough damage for most of the regular customers to notice. Certainly, the small crowd here at this hour of the afternoon seemed unlikely to care much. Still, I could understand how the bartender might on general principles oppose such shenanigans. If nothing else, it must have made him stop selling drinks long enough to sweep the floor.

I leaned on the bar and caught the bartender's eye. He ambled over and drawled, "What'll you have, stranger?"

"Give me a glass of your best beer," I said, remembering C. D.'s advice at the place we'd been in earlier. Some of the liquor bottles behind the bar bore familiar labels, but that didn't necessarily reflect the nature of the contents—or so I gathered from Mr. Clemens's earlier experience. He surely wouldn't have ordered an unfamiliar brand of whiskey.

The bartender drew a tankard, placed it on the bar in front of me, and scooped up the quarter dollar I'd put down. "Keep the change," I said, and a grin spread across his face.

Then he looked closer at me and said, "I saw you earlier. You were in court this morning."

"That's right," I said. I took a long sip of the beer and nodded. "Good beer," I added.

"You asked for the best," he said. Then, looking at my suit, he asked, "You a lawyer or something?"

"Hardly," I said. "My father's one, back east, and I saw too much of what he has to put up with to want to do it myself."

He nodded. "I could tell you were from back east. What brings you to Montana?"

"I work for a man who's passing through. Maybe you've heard of Mark Twain."

"Sure," said the bartender, his face lighting up. He slapped his hand on the wooden counter. "I thought I saw him there in court, too. Don't tell me *he's* in trouble with the law."

"No, but one of his friends is," I said. "My boss was there to see if he could help."

"Uh-huh," said the bartender. He waited to see whether I had anything else to say.

I took another sip of the beer, sensing that it wouldn't be good to rush things. Then I said, "They claim his friend shot a man. Jed Harrington."

Now the bartender slapped his hand on the counter. "If his friend shot that son of a bitch, he can drink free in my place anytime he's in town."

"I'll tell him that," I said. "The only problem is, if he did shoot Harrington, I doubt he'll have much chance to drink here. From what the witnesses say, the killer used a rifle, from some distance away."

"So it ain't self defense," said the bartender. "Or maybe it was, except the shooter wanted to make sure he got the job done without Harrington objectin' too firmly."

"I didn't think of that," I said. "But from what you

say, there are a lot of people who had reason to dislike Harrington."

"That's putting it politely," said the bartender. "He came to these parts about a year ago, and started to come in here and pick fights, mostly with somebody he figured didn't have the spunk to fight back. If they did, his buddies would wade in, and that was that."

"Yes, I got to see their routine in person," I said. "Harrington tried to pick a fight with me, but before things got as far as fisticuffs, my boss's friend showed a pistol, and Harrington backed down. Later, we learned they'd clashed before. That's why he was the one they arrested."

"If the friend didn't do it, he'll get off," said the bartender matter-of-factly.

"We hope so, but we'd like to make sure," I said. I reached in my pocket and pulled out another coin and put it on the counter. "Do you remember if Harrington was in here last night? And if he was, did he run afoul of anybody?" I rested my finger lightly on the half-eagle.

The bartender glanced down at the little golden coin, then his gaze moved back up to my face. "Yeah, he was in here," he said. "Him and his two sidekicks." His expression made clear his low opinion of the parties in question.

"I thought so," I said. "And did they start any trouble that you saw?"

"I couldn't tell you," said the bartender. "The whole place seemed like it was crazy that night. Hey, you were there in court—I guess you heard what was going on in here. But I'd be surprised if Harrington and his boys weren't twisting somebody's tail. Wouldn't be like 'em not to." He took a dirty towel from under the bar and swiped it across a wet spot, then said, "Lil might be able to tell you something, though."

"Lil?" I asked. I hadn't noticed any women in the bar when I arrived.

"Yeah, she works nights," said the bartender. "She'll

probably be here after eight or so. Might be worth your while to talk to her."

"Thanks," I said. Then, remembering that my evening was already planned, I asked, "Do you happen to know where I can reach her during the afternoon?"

"Nope," said the bartender. "Best you try here tonight. She'll be here."

"All right, thanks for the tip," I said. I pushed the gold coin toward him and finished my beer. "I'll probably see you this evening, then. Tell Lil I'm interested in talking to her."

"You and half the town," said the bartender, pocketing the half-eagle. I set down my glass and headed out the door. There were two more bars on this block. Maybe one of them would have more useful information. If not, I'd come back and look for Lil.

I managed to visit half a dozen other bars in the time remaining to me before our dinner engagement. By the time I'd finished, I knew very little more than what I'd already learned from Mike Thompson. All the bartenders knew Harrington, and to a man they considered him a troublemaker. But on the fatal night, he'd apparently kept his nose more or less clean.

One other bartender remembered Harrington and one or two of his cronies—the witness wasn't sure how many—coming in and knocking back a couple of drinks before moving on. If they'd caused any trouble, the bartender hadn't noticed. I took that with a grain of salt. It was evident from the whole tone of his establishment that it would have taken something on the order of a full-blown riot to distract the fellow from selling drinks.

I was feeling fairly tipsy as I paid for my last beer— I'd had one in each of the places I'd visited, that being a necessity if I wanted to find out anything from the bartender. And while the beer was distinctly watery in some of those cowboy bars, the effect of seven schooners was impossible to overlook. Coming out of Bud Call-

away's Canteen, located in the most run-down section I
had seen in Missoula, I managed to discover one of the
uneven boards in the ill-repaired sidewalk and stumbled
as if I'd stepped into a foot-deep hole. I took two staggering paces forward before regaining my balance against
a hitching post. I took a deep breath and turned back
toward the Florence House, several blocks away in the
better part of town. *Better get a cup of coffee before
dinner,* I told myself, and quickened my pace, hoping the
exercise might help burn off the drinks.

If I had been thinking clearly, I almost certainly would
not have decided to take a shortcut through an alley. I
had just passed between one family's weed-infested back
garden plot and their neighbors' chicken coop when a
scrawny arm came over my left shoulder and around my
throat, cutting off my wind, and another hand went grop-
ing in the vicinity of my wallet. I knew at once that
someone had followed me—and was trying to rob me!

I jabbed backward with an elbow and my attacker let
out a grunt, but the chokehold did not loosen. Instead,
the robber stepped backward, pulling me off-balance and
taking his feet out of range of my heels, robbing me of
my second defense tactic. Unless I somehow broke loose
in the next few seconds, I was going to be helpless—and
I knew that I'd be lucky if my wallet was all I lost, after
that. I chided myself for having displayed too many gold
pieces in the disreputable saloons I'd been in all afternoon. Now I was likely to pay in coin far harder to replace.

As a last desperate measure, I flung myself directly
backward, snapping the rear of my skull into my assailant's nose. There was a satisfying crunch, and at last his
grip around my throat slackened. By sheer strength I
twisted around and threw a punch directly into his mid-
section. He staggered back, and for a moment I thought
his hand was reaching for a weapon. A moment of panic
overcame me; what if I had escaped a choking only to
be shot, or stabbed?

I had two choices—charge or flee—and instinctively I took the former. I suppose it was my football training. In any case, I hit him with a block directly in the mid-section, and the air went out of him. He fell on his back, and I stood over him, fists at the ready. Now, for the first time, I got a look at his face. The lower half was covered with blood streaming from his injured nose, but I knew him well enough. It was Jed Harrington's friend Zach'ry—the very man we'd been trying to find!

If I'd been completely sober, I think I'd have moved faster, and the events of the next few days would have come out differently. But out of surprise, I hesitated a moment, and in that very moment he managed to pick up a handful of dust and throw it in my face. Blinded and coughing, I stepped back a pace, and before I could react, he had scrambled to his feet and started running away.

I gave pursuit, and I thought I had a good chance to catch him. Not only was I younger and faster, but he was encumbered with high-heeled boots. But luck was against me. My foot landed in something soft and skidded out from under me, and I went down hard on my back. By the time I scrambled to my feet again, Zach'ry was out of sight. I ran to the end of the alley and looked both ways, but there was no sign of him, and after a moment I shook my head and decided the cards were stacked against me. I dusted myself off, scraped off my shoe, and headed back to the Florence House. All things considered, I was happy to get there without further mishap.

"Zach'ry, eh? I reckon we just found a pretty good suspect to give the sheriff instead of Tom," said Mr. Clemens. I was sitting in the lobby with him and Mr. Roosevelt, over drinks. We were soon to join Mrs. Clemens and Clara for dinner, so this seemed the best time to get our main business out of the way. In my case, in particular, the details of my day's experience were not appropriate fare for dinner-table conversation.

I had bathed and changed my clothes upon my arrival back at the hotel, and gotten a short nap, to boot. Now I was drinking strong black coffee, with a double spoonful of sugar, instead of the whiskey the other two men were having. I was beginning to think that, with a good meal in my belly and a good night's rest, I might actually feel myself again. But at present we had business to tend to.

Mr. Roosevelt grimaced. "I have to differ, Clemens," he said. "That Zach'ry is undoubtedly rotten to the core—he ran when I came to help Cabot this morning, rather than stand and fight fair. I'd love to see the rascal in jail, and I suspect the sheriff would love to have him behind bars, too. But trying to rob Cabot doesn't make this rascal a killer—not without some more particular evidence. That's what you need to prove if you're going to free Blankenship."

Mr. Clemens took a puff off his cigar and slowly blew out a cloud of smoke before answering. "I hate to admit it, but you're right, Roosevelt. But my problem is, I'd be a lot happier if Zach'ry was somewhere behind bars so he won't go running off while we're trying to prove he's the killer. Damn! I wish you'd caught him, Wentworth!"

"It certainly wasn't for lack of trying," I said. "He only got away because I slipped and fell. Next time—and I think there will be a next time—I won't let him out of my clutches."

"You be careful," said Mr. Clemens. "He wasn't carrying a weapon this time, but that don't mean he'll be unarmed next time you meet."

"Right-o," said Mr. Roosevelt. "In fact, this might prompt him to obtain a weapon. Your best policy is probably to report the attempted robbery to the police and let them do their job. I'd steer clear of him, if I were you."

"I suppose you're right," I said. I took a sip of coffee. "I don't know if I'll be able to resist the temptation to lay hands on him if our paths cross again, though."

"Don't be too eager to mess with him," argued my employer. "Hell, Wentworth, this is a cold-blooded murderer we're talking about—assuming this cowboy is the man who gunned Harrington down from the bushes. If he didn't give Harrington any show, why would he do it for you?"

"Take it one step further, while you're at it," said Mr. Roosevelt. "Even if you're wrong about this Zach'ry, the real killer is somewhere out there—unless he's left town, in which case we're probably wasting our time hunting for him. But whoever it is, if he gets the idea you're closing in on him, he won't balk at setting an ambush for you. And I mean both of you. Leave this to the police and you'll be safest. The world can't afford to lose Mark Twain because of some back country murder."

Mr. Clemens had picked up his whiskey glass, and was about to take a sip. At Roosevelt's words, he stopped the motion with the glass halfway to his mouth and glared at the other man. "And what makes you think it can afford to lose Tom Blankenship? I won't be so arrogant as to pretend I don't value my own hide. But if Mark Twain stands for anything, it's the principle that somebody like Tom is worth saving even if it means I have to go through some personal inconvenience, and danger."

He took a sip of the whiskey, then glared at the two of us again. "If you two feel otherwise, I won't blame you. But I'm the only one who's going to decide whether or not to risk my own mangy skin to save the oldest friend I have. Is that clear?"

"Yes, sir!" I said at the same time as Roosevelt expressed his own concurrence.

"Good," said Mr. Clemens. "Now, does either one of you have any idea how we're going to go about finding this murdering bastard—whoever he turns out to be—before he takes it in his mind to shoot somebody else?"

12 ≈

That question—though it remained unspoken—occupied my mind all through dinner. Granted, it did not entirely distract me from the fine food, one of the best cuts of beefsteak I have ever seen on a platter, cooked to perfection, with all the trimmings. But I could not escape the disturbing notion that somewhere outside the comfortable dining room was a sharpshooter who had already murdered one man in cold blood, and who might well be ready to gun down another if our investigation drew too close to him.

For their parts, Mr. Clemens and Mr. Roosevelt seemed to have put it far from their minds—at least to judge by their conversation. They regaled us with a number of stories about their experiences in the west, many of which I might have believed had they come from someone other than my employer. But Clara Clemens, next to whom I was seated, invariably took a skeptical view of her father's anecdotes. Her dry commentary at last made him stop and say in mock exasperation, "Miss Sass-pot, I wish I'd taught you to respect your elders better. A fellow tries to tell a plain factual story, and there you sit, taking pains to point out every time he makes the slightest rhetorical flourish in hopes of entertaining the audience."

"Father, your rhetorical flourishes may be entertaining," said Clara. "But I hope you don't expect anyone here—except perhaps poor Wentworth—to believe that any of the things you've been saying are at all *factual*."

Everyone at the table laughed, I as much as anyone. Coming from anyone else, I might have taken her comment on me as a slight on my credulity, but I knew her far too well to make anything of it. She would say whatever came into her head, and she shared her father's dislike of sham and pretense. It made her extremely entertaining company.

As far as Mr. Roosevelt's stories, the gusto with which he set forth his narrative might have suggested the same kind of exaggeration that was my employer's habitual mode of expression. But the incidents themselves, while colorful, were rarely such as to inspire disbelief. I saw that Miss Clemens listened to him with obvious respect, and so I decided the stories must be more or less accurate. Certainly, his portrayal of the cowboy's lack of respect for easterners who hadn't proved themselves matched my experience to date.

Finally, dessert was served—fresh ice cream with strawberries, a summer treat I hadn't realized I had missed until I came home from Europe and was served a bowlful here in Montana. I ordered a cup of good hot coffee instead of the liquor my two older male companions were drinking—still feeling the effects of my afternoon expedition to the saloons of Missoula—and sat back with a sigh. The dinner had been almost good enough to make me forget the near-strangling I had endured only a few hours before. For a little while longer, I thought, I would be able to ignore the fact that Mr. Clemens and I were once again chasing a murderer.

Mr. Clemens had just lit his pipe when his wife returned to the dining room and put a hand on his shoulder.

She said, "Youth, if you and the other gentlemen will
come into the parlor, I believe that Clara is ready to perform for us. I have saved seats for you all."

"Thank you, Livy," said Mr. Clemens. "Gentlemen,
would you like to hear my daughter play the piano?"

"I wouldn't miss it," said Mr. Roosevelt, standing. I
added my agreement; I had heard Miss Clemens play
before, and knew already what a fine musician she was.
We filed out of the dining room into the parlor, where
Clara was seated at the hotel's grand piano. There was a
row of chairs to one side, affording a good view of the
player's hands, and we settled into them, I at one end of
the row. She looked at us and smiled, and when we were
all seated she looked down at the keyboard, took a breath,
and began to play.

She had chosen a Chopin nocturne, a piece I had heard
her practicing more than once during our stays in England and in Italy. It began with quiet arpeggios in the
left hand, over which the right hand played at first mysterious chords, then shifted to a minor-key melody that
evoked peaceful, though melancholy, thoughts. The rich
sound of the piano drifted through the room, and every
listener fell quiet.

As the music swelled gradually, I began to notice other
hotel guests quietly stealing into the room, finding seats
as near the instrument as they could manage or standing
at a respectful distance to listen. The music moved into
a livelier passage, and I could see heads nodding among
the listeners; then it slowed down again, grew melancholy, and ended on a somber sustained chord. Miss
Clemens sat with her head down, letting the final notes
fade out into the quiet evening. At last she lifted her
hands and raised her head. A flurry of applause broke
out from all directions, and suddenly realizing how many
people were listening to her, she blushed, and stood looking at the crowd that had quietly gathered while she was
absorbed in her music.

"Play another one," said her father, quietly, and for

once she did not talk back to him. She smiled, nodded, and sat back down at the keyboard. The next piece was by Schumann, and again the crowded hotel parlor fell into silence. It was an utterly magical performance, and I would not have missed it for the world.

Clara Clemens's impromptu piano recital had lasted perhaps an hour, at which point her mother had announced in a quiet but firm voice that the time was growing late. I don't think I was the only listener who was disappointed to see Miss Clemens stand up from the piano stool and say, "Thank you all for listening so politely. I hope I haven't bored you too terribly with my playing," before following her mother up the stairs from the lobby.

I stood and stretched; aside from a bit of stiffness, I thought I had recovered reasonably well from my unfortunate experiences of the afternoon. And my decision to avoid the plentiful wine and brandy at the dinner table appeared to have been well-founded, as well. My head was clear, and my senses were alert. Granted, an early retirement and a good night's sleep would have put me in even better fettle. But rest was a luxury I could ill afford at the moment. There would be plenty of time to rest once Mr. Clemens and I were on a train headed west. What I had to do now was make certain that I had done everything within my power to earn that rest.

Mr. Clemens and Mr. Roosevelt had also gotten up when the music ended. The two of them came over to me and stood in front of me. "You plan on going out?" asked Mr. Clemens in a low voice.

"Yes, I have some business to finish up," I said.

"Right," said Roosevelt. "Back at one of those saloons, no doubt."

"As a matter of fact, yes," I said. "The bartender told me about somebody who might know something about the night of the murder."

"Are you sure you're not going looking for that thiev-

ing polecat Zach'ry?" said Mr. Clemens. "Because if I
were you, I wouldn't." He took his pipe out of his pocket
and began stuffing it with tobacco from a small pouch.

"Exactly what I was thinking," said Mr. Roosevelt. "At
least, not without some help."

I hadn't really thought that question through. Odds
were, I might well find Zach'ry in one of the saloons in
Missoula this evening—possibly even the one I was
headed for. What then? Was I ready to capture him and
take him to the sheriff? What if he resisted—possibly
with a weapon, or with a friend or two on his side of the
argument? I'd already taken my share of damage today.

I shook my head. "I plan to steer clear of him."

"A good plan," said Mr. Clemens. He tamped the tobacco down with his thumb, then looked at me and asked,
"What if he don't want to steer clear of you, though? He
bushwhacked you once already, and ganged up on you
with C. D. before that. Do you want more of that kind
of medicine?"

"I can do without it," I said with a wry grin. "I don't
think he'll be out on the town tonight. He must know the
deputies are looking for him."

"If he knows that, he knows more than they do," said
Mr. Roosevelt. "What makes you think the deputies care
about him? The sheriff and the judge are convinced that
Blankenship's their man. Zach'ry's just another rough
cowboy, not much different from the average. Besides,
have you even complained to anyone about that attempted robbery? Except for us, I mean. I certainly
haven't reported it. Have you, Clemens?"

"Didn't have the time," said Mr. Clemens. He had
taken out a match and lit his pipe, and now it was loosing
fragrant clouds of smoke into the room. "Roosevelt's
right, anyway. You can't go out to those saloons tonight
unless you're ready for whatever kind of trouble turns
up."

"You're being too cautious," I said. "Remember,
there's a man's life depending on this—or have you for-

gotten why we're involved in this business to begin with?"

"I haven't forgotten," said Mr. Clemens. "But I don't want you going out and getting killed because of it, either. You or anybody else. Let's all three sit down and figure out how to get what we need without that happening."

"Yes, that does make sense," I said. "Shall we go someplace private?"

"We don't have any great secrets to discuss," said Mr. Roosevelt. "The point is, if you're going back into that saloon, you need to take a pistol."

"That's not likely," I said. "I've next to no experience with them, and if push came to shove, I doubt I could use it. It's likely to get me into trouble rather than out of it."

"He's right, Roosevelt," said Mr. Clemens. "There's nothing more dangerous than a tenderfoot with a gun—dangerous to himself, I mean. I saw proof of that enough times back in my newspaper days."

Roosevelt sighed. "Then I'll have to go with you," he said, turning to me.

"That's all right with me," I said. "If Zach'ry does show his face, perhaps two of us can capture him where one couldn't. But I'm wondering if we aren't about to put all our eggs in one basket."

"That's the smart way to do things," said Mr. Clemens. "Put all your eggs in one basket, and *watch that basket*."

"Yes, you've told me that before," I said. "But this afternoon when we split up, you two were going to investigate your own angles of this case. Before we bet everything we have on catching Zach'ry, I'd like to know what you've found."

"Oh. Right-o," said Mr. Roosevelt, surprised. "Well, to tell you the truth, I was completely stymied out at the fort. Quite a few of the soldiers admitted to being in town last night, but they buttoned up their lips when they realized I was looking for a murder witness. And once the word got around, they wouldn't even tell me whether they'd been in town. I didn't get to talk to everyone, of course, but the results so far are nil."

"I see," I said. "How about you, Mr. Clemens? Did you learn anything more about the gun that killed Harrington?"

He frowned. "The sheriff claims they haven't got the bullet out yet—the coroner's out of town. And when I told him there's a way to tell what gun fired the bullet that killed somebody, he about laughed his fool head off. Didn't want to hear about the French professor that figured it out. No big rush, anyway, as far as he's concerned. Harrington ain't going anywhere, and neither is Tom. It doesn't seem to bother him that *we're* leaving town on Saturday's train."

"The man's methods are all wrong," said Roosevelt, frowning. "Once he has his suspect, he ought to get every shred of evidence he can, to make the case rock-solid. If he's wrong, the real killer could be slipping away without a worry in the world. He needs to be sure he's right before it's too late."

"*You* go tell him that," said Mr. Clemens. "He figures he's got his man, and that's that. So we've either got to give Tom a foolproof alibi, or we've got to prove somebody else did it. I say you go find that Zach'ry, and we'll see what his story is—and how it holds up."

"That seems to be our only choice, doesn't it?" I said. "Well, come along, Mr. Roosevelt—we'll see whether we can catch him. But first off, we need to go talk to a young lady named Lil."

"Young lady?" said Mr. Clemens. "Are you going to see her to help get Tom out of jail, or just to see her?"

"I've never laid eyes on her," I said. "With any luck, we'll find her tonight. I'll tell you what she looks like— and what she says—when we get back."

"This is the place," I said to Mr. Roosevelt as our driver stopped his rig outside Mike Thompson's Saloon.

Roosevelt leaned forward and peered past me at the outside of the saloon. "More or less what I expected, from what we saw of the owner," he said. "Caters mostly to cowboys and other working men, am I right?"

"As far as I could tell from what I saw this afternoon," I said. I pulled out a dollar and gave it to our driver, Jack Briscoe.

"Thanks, boss," said Briscoe, pocketing the coin. "You want me to wait for you? This ain't a part of town I'd like to be walking around after dark, and you're not going to get another driver once I leave."

"And you're not likely to get another fare, either," said Roosevelt, with a chuckle. "Why not? We can afford the waiting time."

"Ahh, no extra charge for that," said Briscoe with a wave of his hand. "I figure I'll get my proper share of amusement just watching what goes on here, and like you say, there won't be a lot of other fares anywhere else, this time of night."

"Very well," I said. "We shall try to be amusing."

"But not *that* amusing, I hope," said Roosevelt. He made a sweeping gesture with his arm, and we strode side by side through the door into Thompson's place.

Inside, it was more crowded, and noisy. There was a little orchestra—a banjo, two violins, and an out-of-tune piano—playing "Golden Slippers," raggedly but loud. Nobody was dancing or paying the musicians much attention, as far as I could see through the cloud of smoke. Off in a back corner there was a knot of men gathered around what might have been a fight, but it was too far off to make out clearly.

Thompson was still behind the bar, with a couple of assistants now that the place was full. We made our way carefully through the crowd toward him. I had no desire accidentally to jostle someone and attract unwanted attention. Roosevelt and I were likely to get enough of that simply on account of our dress, which was several degrees more formal than that of the rest of the crowd:

cowboys, railroad workers, and others whose work clothes and Sunday best were apparently one and the same. I knew that Roosevelt, at least, had clothing more in keeping with the atmosphere, but there had seemed no point in his taking the time to change, since I had nothing to put on that would not proclaim my eastern origins.

We found an open spot at the bar, in front of one of the assistants, who came over to take our orders. "Two beers," I said, plopping down a dollar, "and a word with Mr. Thompson."

"You got the beers, anyway," said the bartender, a freckle-faced fellow with red hair parted in the middle and a full beard. "I'll see if the boss wants to talk to you."

He went off to draw the beers, and I saw him nudge Mike Thompson and point in our direction, speaking out of the side of his mouth. Thompson peered along the bar, wrinkling his brow, and then obviously he recognized me. He said something to the other man, who nodded and went back to taking orders. In a few moments, Thompson was in front of us with two mugs of beer. "Evening," he said. "I see you came back."

"That's right," I said. "You suggested earlier that I talk to a lady named Lil. Is she here tonight?"

"I guess so," said Thompson, craning his neck. "That's Miss Lil over there in the corner, in the red dress. But if I was in your shoes, I'd wait a piece before I went asking for her—I believe that fight was about her, and those two fellows just might take it wrong if somebody waltzed up and took her away while they was still rasslin' each other."

"Good idea," said Roosevelt, grinning. He took a dollar out of his pocket and put it on the bar. "We'll just bide our time, then, till the boys sort it out."

"All right," said Thompson, picking up the coin. "You let me or Andy know if you need those mugs filled up." He winked and went back to serving his customers.

I took a sip of my beer and surveyed the situation. "I

don't like this," I said. "We need to talk to that woman, but we can't do it if every cowboy in the place is going to take offense when we approach her."

"You're a smart young fellow," said Roosevelt, slapping me on the back. "I can see why Clemens hired you. What we need is a way to distract them, so we can do our business uninterrupted. I have a notion that might work . . ."

Before I could ask what he meant, Roosevelt jumped up on the bar and pulled a fistful of banknotes out of his pocket. He shouted at the top of his lungs, "Listen up, boys! My stingy old dad finally kicked the bucket, and I'm a free man! I'm buying drinks for the house—no rotgut, only the good stuff! Come and get it!"

There was a universal roar of approval, and every man in the place rushed toward the bar. Roosevelt grinned from ear to ear and leaned over to me. He said quietly, "All right, Cabot, now's your chance. Go talk to Miss Lil, and I'll handle the crowd."

"Consider it done," I said, and made my way against the tide of thirsty customers toward the woman in the bright red dress.

Lil was blonde, and she looked older up close than she had at a distance; something like thirty-five, I guessed. Her dress was tight, and cut a bit lower than modesty would suggest. When I reached her, she was pouting, hands on her hips; evidently both the swains who had fought for her attentions had abandoned her for Roosevelt's offer of free drinks. "Excuse me, miss," I said. "Is there someplace private we can talk?"

She looked me up and down, then smiled. "Why, I do believe there is," she said. Then, as if by rote, she added, "But why don't you buy me a drink first?"

"That'd be a bit difficult, just now," I said. Indeed, it would have been a challenge to get within ten feet of the bar. Even the musicians had laid down their instruments to take advantage of Mr. Roosevelt's generosity. I continued, "Suppose I give you enough to buy your own later, and we go talk? I think you might be able to answer a couple of questions I have."

She frowned again. "You're not a Pinkerton, are you? I can tell you're from out of town."

"Not a Pinkerton, no," I said. "I have a friend who's in a lot of trouble, and Mike Thompson thinks you may know something that can help him get out of it. Now, did you say there was someplace we can talk?"

"Upstairs," she said, pointing to one side of the room where there was a doorway I hadn't noticed before. I followed her through a beaded curtain and we went up a dimly lit flight of stairs. There was a hallway at the top of the stairs with four doors. She took me to one of them and led me into a small room furnished with a rumpled bed and one straight-backed chair. On a small table at the head of the bed was a pile of white washcloths. The curtain was drawn.

She closed the door behind her and turned to face me, leaning back against it. She fluttered her lashes and said, "Now, mister, what did you want to talk about? Or did you have something else in mind? I can do all sorts of things . . ."

"Talk is all I want," I said. "Last night—"

"It'll still cost you," she said. She took a step toward me, her hands clasped behind her. "Why not get your money's worth?"

I did my best to keep my eyes on her face. "If you know something that'll get our friend out of jail, that'll be worth my money. How much do you need?"

She looked me up and down and licked her lips. "Two dollars."

"Here's five," I said, taking a greenback out of my pocket and holding it where she could see it. "That'll cover your time and buy you that drink you asked for. Now, do you know a man named Jed Harrington? Or his two friends?"

"C. D. and Zach'ry," she said, her face sober now. "Jed got shot, I hear tell."

"Yes, I understand they were in here last night."

"Yeah, they were," she said, looking at the five dollar bill. "What about it?"

"C. D. told us that they lost Zach'ry somewhere," I said. I kept my eyes on her face, trying to judge whether she was telling the truth. "They were looking for him when Jeb was killed. Do you have any idea where he might have been?"

She took her eyes off the banknote and looked into my face. "He was with me, some of the time," she said.

"So, the scoundrel has an alibi, after all," said Mr. Clemens. He had waited up for Roosevelt and me in the hotel bar, where we found him at a corner table smoking one of his corncob pipes and sipping a whiskey and soda while he read the new novel by Howells he had mentioned to me.

"So it would appear," I said. "The woman says he was with her for part of the night, then passed out. She put him in her bed and left him to sleep off the liquor—he was there as late as midnight. But she can't swear to exactly when he left. So there is one loophole."

"But no evidence of an argument or a falling out with the victim, either," Mr. Roosevelt pointed out. "Even if he had the opportunity, there's no clearcut motive."

"Well, there's motives enough to go around," said Mr. Clemens. "Half the people I know in this town would've been happy to do the old buzzard in, or at least they'd have applauded when somebody else did it. And a fair number of 'em are good enough shots to pot him from any reasonable distance, day or night."

"True enough, although we really don't know what distance the shot was from," said Roosevelt. "It could have been twenty feet or half a mile, as far as anyone can tell. If it was from close enough, we don't even need to assume that the person who fired it was a particularly good shot. That would unfortunately widen the pool of suspects, I'm afraid."

"It's a shame the only witness was drunk," I said. "The chance of putting together any coherent story of what happened seems slighter every time we turn around."

"It's even slighter with Tom playing mum," growled my employer. "He acts as if he's going to get let out of jail as soon as he tells the judge figures out he really is a magistrate up in wherever it is . . ."

"Dillon," I said. "It's south of here." I sipped from my beer mug. I was beginning to feel the effect of the long hard day, but I needed to stay up just a little longer until Mr. Clemens was satisfied he'd wrung every last bit of significance from the evidence on hand. Given how little hard evidence we actually had, I thought the process was taking an annoyingly long time.

"Right, Dillon," said Mr. Clemens. "What Tom's forgetting is that, with all the evidence piling up against him and his best hope for a defense scheduled to leave town before he comes to trial, he doesn't have the luxury of sitting on his tail end. He has to tell me what exactly he was up to that night. That story about carrying along a rifle because he used to hunt when he was a boy back in Missouri stinks to high heaven."

Roosevelt drummed his fingers on the table. "I think we need to go down to the jail again tomorrow and persuade Blankenship to take a more active part in his own defense," he said.

"Damn right we do," said Mr. Clemens. "We'll go down there first thing in the morning. If Tom won't trust me, he's going to have to find another lawyer."

"In the interest of linguistic exactness, I should point out that he can't find another lawyer," said Roosevelt. He waited a beat while Mr. Clemens scowled at him, then added, "If he engages a lawyer it'll be his first, since you've never passed the bar."

"I've passed hundreds of 'em, and had a drink at more than one," said Mr. Clemens. "But now that I think about

it, I'm going to excuse you from joining us at the jailhouse."

"You are?" Roosevelt asked. "Very well. May I ask
why?"

"Two things," said Mr. Clemens. "First of all, it may
look as if Zach'ry's got an alibi. But that doesn't mean
he might not know something useful about the case. I'd
like you to see if you can run him to earth for us. He
seems to have a grudge against Wentworth . . ."

"Nothing compared to the one I have against him," I
said. I felt a yawn coming on and sat up straighter. I had
to keep my eyes open a little longer.

"Yes, there's that problem, too," said Mr. Clemens.
"Maybe you can bring him in alive, Roosevelt. Meanwhile, I'll go see if Tom wants to talk to me—and just
maybe he'll talk freer if there's not as many strangers
around."

"Very well," said Roosevelt, standing and putting on
his hat. "In that case, we should meet at luncheon and
trade whatever we learn. How about at my hotel, for a
change?"

"Fine," said Mr. Clemens. "And now, I reckon Wentworth needs some sleep, and I wouldn't mind some myself. Goodnight, Roosevelt."

"Goodnight, gentlemen," he said, and left the bar. I
was not very far behind him, and made my way wearily
upstairs. I think it was only by sheer force of habit that
I managed to get myself undressed before falling into bed
and going directly to sleep. Between then and sunup the
next morning, the Army could have refought all the Indian wars across my bedroom and I doubt I would have
lifted my head from the pillow long enough to see a
single cavalry charge.

13 ⌒

Mr. Clemens and I arrived at jail right after breakfast the next morning. I had been ravenous when I awoke, and proceeded to devour three fried eggs, several rashers of bacon, four or five pieces of toast with gooseberry jam, a serving of fried potatoes, and the better part of a pot of coffee. For his part, Mr. Clemens had his usual beefsteak and eggs. So I felt a rather guilty twinge to see that Tom Blankenship was eating a meager jailhouse breakfast off a flimsy tin plate: burnt toast, thin coffee, and dry-looking scrambled eggs with a distinct greenish hue.

"Good morning, Sam," he said as the deputy ushered us into the cell. "How are you doing?"

"Not as well as I'd like," said Mr. Clemens, standing stiffly with his hands in his pockets. "We thought we had a real live suspect, but the son of a bitch turns out to have an alibi."

"It's not suspects we need," said Blankenship, shoveling the eggs into his mouth with his remaining piece of toast. "The sheriff already has one of those, and he don't appear to be fishing for more."

"Well, he ought to be," said my employer. "If you didn't do it, then somebody else did. And unless the sheriff starts to look for him, the missing suspect's got a good chance to get away with murder."

Blankenship wiped off his mouth with the back of his shirt sleeve. "You know how I figure it, Sam? As far as I can tell, nobody hereabouts is particularly upset about Jed Harrington getting shot—except maybe them two owlhoot friends of his, I reckon. It's a mighty mean man that don't have any friends at all."

"Well, if you want to know the truth, it was one of those two that was our suspect," said Clemens. "The one called Zach'ry. He got in a fight with Cabot yesterday morning, then tried to rob him later that afternoon. But it looks like he was passed out drunk when the killing happened."

"That would tend to make it hard for him to shoot somebody," said Blankenship. "But anyways, I reckon the sheriff kind of figures whoever shot Jed Harrington done the city a favor. If they can pin it on me, fine they'll be happy to have the case solved with nobody local at fault. And if it ain't me, they'll sort of scratch their heads and figure out what to do next. But nobody's in much of a hurry to do it."

"Except for me, since I've got to be on the westbound train come Saturday," said Mr. Clemens. "And that's likely to leave you hanging . . ."

"I sure hope not," said Blankenship with a shudder. It was the first I'd seen his composure waver, and I wondered if his time in jail might have eroded his stoicism. He put down his tin plate, stood up, and paced a few steps before saying, "You understand, Sam, I didn't like Jed Harrington—he's the kind of man that makes life unpleasant for everybody around him. But he didn't deserve to be shot down like a mad dog in the middle of the street, either—though I'd've done it if that was the only way to stop him hurting somebody else."

"It might have come to that," said Mr. Clemens somberly. "But you're right, even he deserved better."

"That's what I've learned," said Blankenship. "You sit in a magistrate's court, almost everything comes through some time or another: a lot of it just foolishness, some of it enough to make you laugh. And other things will make you feel like crying, or make you want to grab somebody by the nape of their neck and learn 'em how to act right. But you learn pretty soon that you just can't fix it all. And you can't fix none of it by killing somebody."

"That's how I feel about it, too," said Mr. Clemens. "Which is why I don't want to see anybody putting a rope around *your* neck. I'd be agin it, even if you weren't my old friend. But look here, Tom—if we're going to make sure that doesn't happen, I'm going to need some help from you."

"I reckon I can lend a hand, Sam," said Blankenship. "But if it's some fine point of law or evidence, now, you might do just as good looking in a lawbook as asking me. I always just go by my own two eyes and common sense, on account of the way they write down the laws; they ain't always so clear and plain that a regular fellow can figure out what they mean. And sometimes when you do figure it out, it don't make much sense. But seein' as how we're going to be in somebody else's court, you'd better know just what it says in the books."

Mr. Clemens shook his head. "That's not the problem, Tom."

"Good," said Blankenship, " 'cause that's just the kind of mess you could get in over your head on if you don't know what it's all about. And from what I've seen, half your real lawyers don't understand it, neither. So what was it you needed me to help on, Sam?"

Mr. Clemens put on his sternest expression. "Tom, I've got to know the truth about what you were doing the night Harrington was killed. The whole truth."

Blankenship looked at me, and it was as if a door had been closed and locked behind his face. "Sam, I can't tell you," he said, with an expression that left not an iota of doubt.

"Tom, it may make the difference whether or not I can help you at all," said Mr. Clemens, his eyebrows raised. He spoke so slowly that there was a perceptible pause between words, as if he were explaining the matter to a stubborn child.

"It don't matter, Sam," said Blankenship, his face unreadable. "If not telling means they hang me, then I'll hang. That's what the old slave always said was going to happen to me, anyhow—I reckon maybe he was right, after all."

"Damnation!" said Mr. Clemens, stomping across the cell. He stopped by the door, looking through the little barred window out into the hall. He turned around abruptly and faced his old friend. "Why won't you tell me?" he barked.

"'Cause it ain't your business," said Blankenship calmly.

Mr. Clemens leaned over close to his friend, looking him directly in the face. "Tom, I'm your lawyer—at least, that's what you said you wanted me to be. You're supposed to trust me with your secrets. That's what lawyers are for."

"Well, you see, there's one problem," said Blankenship, with another glance at me.

"Is that the problem, Tom?" said Mr. Clemens. He pointed at me. "What if I send Cabot away? Will you tell me if he isn't here to overhear it?"

Blankenship stared at the wall for a few moments. I was beginning to think he wasn't going to reply when he looked up at me and said, "Nothing personal, son. But I know Sam all my life, and I just met you a few days ago. Do you mind going outside while my old friend and I talk a mite?"

"Mr. Blankenship, if it will help us save you, I don't mind in the least," I said. That wasn't entirely true; I was itching with curiosity.

Mr. Clemens patted me on the shoulder. "Good man, Cabot. Wait out front; I'll be out shortly, I hope."

"Yes, sir," I said. We called for the guard; when he came, the other two men watched me in silence as I left the cell, and then the door shut behind me. I wondered what deep secret I was about to miss, and whether I would ever learn it.

I stood in the sheriff's outer office and watched two of the deputies play checkers for ten minutes while Mr. Clemens pried the secret out of Mr. Blankenship. One of them clearly thought himself a much better player than the other, and directed a running string of taunts at his outmatched partner, who plugged away like an old plow horse and kept the game close. I myself had never learned the fine points of the game, but thought I could probably give either of them a match.

Finally Mr. Clemens emerged with an expression that would have piqued my curiosity even if I hadn't known what he and his old friend had been talking about. "Well, we're done here for today," he said to me. "Come along and let's see what else we can figure out before we have to meet with Roosevelt."

Out on the street I turned to him and said, "What can you tell me?"

"Not much," he said. "Tom's always had his own way of looking at things, and what he thinks is important isn't always the same as what you and I think. One thing, though—if he promises something, he'll do his damnedest to keep that promise, and expects you to do the same. I don't know whether what he told me can get him off or not, but I can't use it without his say-so, and that'll take some powerful convincing. I think the damn fool really *would* go hang rather than let this out of the bag."

"Is there a woman involved?"

Mr. Clemens chuckled. "You're not getting it out of me that easily, Wentworth. I'd advise you to forget about it. I'll tell you what it's about when Tom gives me the go-ahead, and not before. He takes confidences seriously, and however corrupted I may be by my years in eastern society, I won't betray my oldest friend when he wants a secret kept. Don't waste your time guessing—I'm not talking. Let's go get a cup of coffee and plan what we're doing next."

That, of course, was guaranteed to make me worry the question like a bulldog with a marrowbone. But since Mr. Clemens had made it clear that he wouldn't respond to guesses, I had to keep my speculations to myself. I still thought my idea of a woman's being involved was the most likely explanation. Why else would he be out late at night, and refuse to say where or why? Of course, that left unanswered the question of his carrying a rifle . . .

We went back to the same little cafe where we'd talked with Roosevelt before our encounter with C. D. and Zach'ry just the morning before. The pretty blonde girl behind the counter seemed to recognize us, and smiled as she brought us our coffee. I thought she must have seen one of the posters for Mr. Clemens's lecture; I didn't remember her being there on our previous visit. But I had gotten used to having random strangers on the street greet me when I was in my employer's company, and so I thought nothing of it.

"All right, here's where we stand," said Mr. Clemens, once we were more or less alone. "If Roosevelt finds Zach'ry, we can still try to find out whether his alibi jibes with the other things we've been told. That girl Lil may feel obligated to protect her customers. Or she may just like the thieving snake, I don't know. Either way, it's worth getting his side of the story."

"Yes," I said. "I confess, I'd be pleased to discover a few discrepancies in his alibi. But I suppose I shouldn't let my personal dislike enter into the question."

"Oh, don't dismiss personal dislike all that quickly," said Mr. Clemens. "You've got a pretty good eye for character—it's one of the reasons I keep you on, you know. Maybe you err on the side of liking people—especially pretty girls—who aren't as respectable as you think they are. But I've never yet seen you take a dislike to somebody who didn't turn out to deserve it. Even if Zach'ry didn't shoot Harrington, he's a skunk. And he's still one of the main suspects, in my book. We just can't bet the house on him."

I looked at my employer over the rim of my coffee cup. "One of the main suspects, you say? I didn't know we had any others worth considering."

"Sure we do," he said. "C. D., for one—we already know he was right there when it happened. And Tom told us he saw him with a gun right after the shooting—although the deputies said it hadn't been fired. But what if C. D. shot Harrington and then reloaded the gun before the deputies arrived?"

"I suppose it could have happened," I said. "Isn't there some way they can tell if a gun's been fired?"

Mr. Clemens scowled. "Smelling it for smoke's usually good enough. If there's anything fancier, I'll guarantee you it ain't common knowledge in Montana. I'm surprised the sheriff's office even has a telephone."

"Well, if he shot Harrington, why would he stay around to begin with? Why not just escape while he had the chance?"

Mr. Clemens put down his coffee cup and tapped the table with a pointed finger. "Because he'd been seen with Harrington earlier that evening," he said. "If anybody started asking questions, they'd learn that pretty fast. He'd be the first one the police came looking for. Smarter for him to pretend he'd been a witness."

That made sense to me. "Yes," I said, "and if his gun had a couple of empty shells in it when the deputies arrived, I doubt they'd have gone looking for another suspect. So he must have reloaded it. Can we prove that?"

"Maybe," said Mr. Clemens. "Even he's smart enough

to figure that one out. He could have hid the empty shells somewhere and gone back and got 'em before somebody else found them and connected it to him."

"All right, you've convinced me to put him on the list," I said. "You suggested there were other suspects. Who are they?"

He leaned back in his chair. "That sergeant C. D. mentioned hasn't shown up, but that doesn't mean he's not real. Harrington *did* attack a soldier that same day, remember? And we know for a fact that soldiers are pretty handy with guns."

"I can't convince myself that's going to lead anywhere useful," I said. "Mr. Roosevelt ought to have been able to find somebody who knew about it, but he came up empty-handed. And it seems out of character for a soldier to assassinate a private citizen."

"That's the problem with you youngsters," said Mr. Clemens. He shook his head, then went on. "If you'd been around during the war, you'd have a more realistic notion of soldiers. Sure, they're supposed to protect the citizens. But when some outsider stirs 'em up, they're like hornets—pick on one, and the whole nest is like to come down on you. It wouldn't surprise me a bit to hear that some sergeant decided to get rid of somebody that was attacking his men—and to hell with what the civilians think. And I'd be even less surprised if everybody who knew about it kept their mouths shut."

"Hmmm," I said, staring into my coffee cup. "If that's so, it won't be easy to prove. Which makes it difficult to exonerate Mr. Blankenship."

"Not necessarily," said Mr. Clemens. "I was hoping maybe Roosevelt would find out enough to convince the sheriff to spring Tom loose without giving him enough detail to finger the real killer. So far, no luck on that front—but I'm not ruling it out, yet."

"I see," I said. "What other suspects are you watching?"

"Half the town," he said. "Half the people we know, in fact. Harrington had no shortage of enemies; I doubt he ever met anybody who didn't particularly hate him after the first few minutes of acquaintance, except maybe C. D. and Zach'ry. And that's not even much of an exception, since both those boys are suspects, too. Two of many."

I frowned. "You keep saying that. Who else would you include?"

"Oh, let's see," he said. "Some of those bartenders whose places he used to tear up. The deputies, if they thought they could get away with it. Any of the blacks or Indians he used to single out for harassment. Roosevelt, Cody, Annie Oakley . . ."

"Now you're pulling my leg," I said. "Why those last?"

"All three of them took an instant dislike to him, just as you did. When they saw him mistreat that soldier, two of them were ready to whip him on the spot, if he'd given them an opening—again, pretty much as you did. And all three are expert rifle shots. That's about the only serious qualification *you're* lacking, if you want to know the truth. If I thought you could shoot worth a damn, I'd put you on the list, too."

"I'm not sure whether to be flattered or not," I said. "Though I certainly hope the police don't decide to take your advice on whom to put in jail. I've done my share of that, and more."

"You don't have a thing to worry about, Wentworth," said Mr. Clemens. "The next time the police take my advice on anything, it'll be the first."

Having failed to reduce the list of suspects to a manageable size, Mr. Clemens and I found ourselves with the better half of the morning to kill before our lunchtime meeting with Mr. Roosevelt. My first thought was to return to the hotel and catch up with my correspondence—I

was seriously behind in writing to my parents, whom I
had sent only two brief letters since our departure for the
west.

But Mr. Clemens had another idea. "I'd like to get a
look at the site of the murder," he said. "I know it won't
be quite the same in daylight, but we can at least get
some notion of where the killer must have fired from."

"That's an excellent idea," I said, "except that I have
only the vaguest notion where Harrington was killed."

"Well, I'm ahead of you on that, then," said Mr. Clemens. "I asked Tom where it was. If he's telling the truth,
and I reckon he is, he got there right after the shooting
took place. It's about three blocks from here; we can go
look it over, then either head back to our hotel or over
to Roosevelt's."

"Fine, let's go see it, then," I said, and we set out at
an easy pace along the sidewalk.

We were already out of the best part of town, and the
area we headed toward was distinctly less elegant still.
In fact, as I pointed out to my employer, the area where
Harrington and his cronies had been drinking on the night
of the killing was only a short distance from the alleyway
where Zach'ry had nearly robbed me. Needless to say, it
was with a certain degree of trepidation that I entered
that neighborhood again.

For his part, Mr. Clemens might have been walking
down the most elegant boulevard in one of the capitals
of Europe. He was rarely in a hurry, and this was not
one of those times. Instead, he loafed along, clearly enjoying the chance to see a bit of the back streets of Missoula. That left it to me to keep an eye open for possible
trouble—for, as I had learned less than twenty-four hours
ago, not even broad daylight would deter someone who
had his mind bent upon mischief.

After a couple of blocks, Mr. Clemens paused outside
a particularly dingy corner saloon and looked both ways.
"Let's see," he said. "Tom said it was on this street, but

I can't remember whether it's right or left. There are street lights both ways . . ."

"What are you looking for, white men?" rasped a menacing voice almost directly behind me.

I must have jumped two feet straight up and made a perfect half-circle in mid-air before coming down. I was ready to fight a bear, if need be.

But instead, I found in front of me the Indian scout we had met out at Fort Missoula—Joe Fox, his name was. He nodded, as if in approval of my athletic feat, then looked at Mr. Clemens and said, "You must be lost, Mark Twain. There are no hotels for rich people in this part of town."

I could see Mr. Clemens biting back a sharp reply. Instead, he said, "I'm glad we ran into you, Joe Fox. I'm looking for a place where a man was killed two nights ago. Maybe you could help me find it."

"Why would I know where a white man was killed?" asked the Indian. "Do you think I was the one who did it? Do you think I keep track of all the white men in Missoula?"

"How do you know it was a white man?" asked Mr. Clemens.

"Because you say it was a man who was killed," replied Joe Fox. "If it was not a white man, you would have said it was an Indian—or a soldier, if he was black."

"You're right," said Mr. Clemens, surprised. "I never realized I said it that way, but you're right."

"Being an Indian may make me poor, and it does make white men hate me," said Joe Fox. "It does not make me stupid. Or bad, like the Indian in your book."

"I've written more than one book, but I know the one you mean," said Mr. Clemens. "That's one character in one book. There are plenty of bad white men in my books, too—and lots of stupid ones. Nobody has a monopoly on being virtuous or smart."

"That's true," said Joe Fox. "Maybe I should read

more of your books, if there are stupid white men in them. I would not mind reading about that."

"I reckon you don't need to read books to find out about that," said Mr. Clemens. "There are lots of them in this town—including the one who got shot. Did you ever have any trouble with a man named Jed Harrington?"

The Indian looked as if he had bitten into a green persimmon. "Jed Harrington," he said. "That man is no friend to Indians. Not to soldiers, either."

"No friend to anybody," agreed Mr. Clemens. "Especially not now. He's the one who was shot—shot dead in the street like a mad dog."

Joe Fox nodded slowly. "Like a mad dog. That is the kind of man he was," he said. Then he looked my employer straight in the eye. He asked, "Why do you want to find the place where this man was killed?"

"Because a friend of mine is in jail for it," said Mr. Clemens. "He says he didn't kill Harrington, and I believe him. We want to look at the place it happened to see if we can learn anything about how it was done. Maybe I can find something to help my friend get out of jail."

"When you told me just now, it was the first I heard about Jed Harrington being shot," said Joe Fox. "But I can tell you who will know what happened. Go to that house, the second from the corner, and talk to old Jenny Larson. She's a widow lady that takes in sewing and washing, and she knows what goes on around here better than anybody. If she don't want to talk to you about it, either it didn't happen or it's not worth talking about."

"All right, that's a worthwhile tip," said Mr. Clemens. "Thank you, Joe Fox."

"You are welcome, Mark Twain," said the Indian scout. "Thank you for telling me you write books about stupid white men. Maybe I will buy one to read when I need to laugh."

"Everybody needs to laugh, sometimes," said Mr. Clemens. He added, under his breath, "I wouldn't mind a little dose of that myself, right about now." And we walked across the street to meet Jenny Larson.

⇌ 14

I think Jenny Larson was the tallest woman I have ever seen. When she came to the door of her dilapidated home, she was eye to eye with me, and a good half a head taller than Mr. Clemens. It was only when I looked down to see that the floor was nearly level with the sidewalk where I stood that I realized that she must be over six feet tall.

"You got washing for me?" she said in a voice with a strong accent that sounded either Swedish or Norwegian to my ears. Her hair was long and blonde-going-gray, done up in long braids, and her eyes were a piercing blue, surrounded by a network of fine wrinkles. I guessed she must be close to Mr. Clemens's age, and I thought to myself that she must have been stunningly beautiful in her youth.

"No, ma'am," said Mr. Clemens, taking off his pilot's cap. "We're trying to find out about a shooting that went on near here the other night, and we wondered if you could tell us where it happened."

"Oh, yeah," she said. She shaded her eyes against the bright sunlight with one hand and pointed down the street to the left. "It happened just down there, right under the light. I heard the shot."

Just as she said this, a small black and white kitten came bouncing out the door, mewing as if it were being deprived of all the joys of life. Mr. Clemens bent down and scooped it up, his face breaking into a smile. "Hey, you can't get away that easily," he said. The kitten looked at him and mewed again, then made as if to bite him with its little teeth. He laughed, and said, "You're a little devil, you are. You'll never get fed if you try to bite your friends."

"He don't know you yet," said the woman, with a hint of a smile. "He just wants a little taste to find out if he likes you."

"I probably taste terrible, but cats don't seem to mind," said Mr. Clemens, holding the little creature up and looking in its face. "Do you have a name, huh?" The kitten mewed again.

"I call him Oscar," said Jenny Larson, smiling. "You want to come inside? I got work to do, but I can talk while I do it."

"If you don't mind—Mrs. Larson, is it?" He handed her the kitten, which she put up against her shoulder so it looked out over her back.

"Yeah, that's right," she said. "Your face looks familiar, but I don't think I know you . . ."

"Sam Clemens is the name," said my employer. "I write books under the name Mark Twain. And this is my secretary, Wentworth Cabot. I appreciate your taking the time to talk to us."

"OK, now I know where I heard of you," she said. "Come on inside and we can talk."

We followed the woman into the house, where she closed the door and set Oscar the kitten down to run free. The house was sparsely furnished, but clean. There was an ironing board set up on one side of the room and a basket of clean laundry on the floor next to it. A couple of flatirons sat on a nearby wood stove, which was burning low even though the weather outside was warm. On a shelf behind us were several bundles of clothing, evidently finished laundry waiting to be picked up.

"I'm sorry, there ain't a lot of room to sit down," she said. "I don't get much company . . ."

"That's fine, we can stand," said Mr. Clemens. "And we won't take up a lot of your time."

"It's all right," she said. "It's good to have somebody to talk to while I work." She bent over and picked a man's shirt out of the laundry basket and put it on the ironing board. Her figure was no longer girlish, but she was obviously supple—and I suspected there was a good degree of strength in her arms and shoulders. She took one of the irons off the stove and began running it over the back of the shirt. Then she looked up at Mr. Clemens and said, "What you need to know?"

The kitten had come over to Mr. Clemens and begun to rub its back against his shins. He leaned over and picked it up again, then turned to Mrs. Larson. "Well, originally we just wanted to know where it happened so we could try to reconstruct events and decide where the shooter had been. But since you actually heard the shots, you may know more than we could figure out ourselves. What do you remember from that night?"

"It was late," she said. "I was already in bed, but I wasn't asleep yet. This part of town is pretty quiet, except when a train comes through, but that don't happen much at night. Anyhow, all of a sudden there was a loud *bang*—I thought it was right outside my door."

Mr. Clemens looked up from the kitten, which looked as if it was about to doze off in his arms. "Did you know it was a gun when you heard it?"

"Oh, yeah," said Mrs. Larson. "I've heard guns before. Sometimes, when the cowboys get drunk, they shoot their pistols in the air. But when that happens, I usually hear 'em whoop and holler, and they shoot five or six times. This was just one shot, and there wasn't nobody hollering."

"What did you do then?"

"I got up and went to look out the front window," she said. "Near the light down the street, where I told you before, there was a man bending over what looked like a bundle on the ground. I had a pretty good idea what it was, though."

Mr. Clemens was rubbing his knuckle under the kitten's chin. He looked up and asked, "Did you see or hear anybody else, besides the man—the two men—down by the light? Did anybody run away, or go toward them?"

"I didn't stay with my head out the window," said Mrs. Larson. "All I can say is, I didn't see or hear anybody right then. I decided there wasn't anything else to see, so I went back to bed. Somebody could have come by before or after, and I wouldn't have seen them."

"So you don't have any idea where the shot came from?"

"I think it was close to my place," said Mrs. Larson. She picked up the shirt and rearranged it on the board so she could work on one sleeve. "You know what I mean—the shot sounded closer to me than to the place the man who was shot fell down. Maybe the shooter was on the cross street out here."

"But you didn't hear anybody yell, or run away?"

"Nope, nobody at all," she said, not looking up from her ironing. She flipped the shirt over and began working on the other sleeve.

"All right, I can't think of anything else to ask," said Mr. Clemens. "Unless you can think of something you haven't told me that I ought to know?"

She thought for a long moment, then looked up from the ironing board and shook her head. "No, that's all I heard that night," she said. "I didn't find out anything more until the next day. Then everybody was talking about it."

Mr. Clemens looked up from the kitten again. "They were, were they? Did anybody say they'd seen the shooting, or was it all just second-hand?"

Mrs. Larson thought again, then said, "The woman next door said she heard the shot, too. Nobody said they saw it. A lot of people talked like they knew all about it, but they all had different stories, so I think they lied—or somebody lied to them and they believed it. Me, I don't pay attention to that kind of talk."

"Probably just as well," said Mr. Clemens, nodding. Then he asked, "Will you take a dollar for this kitten?"

Mrs. Larson's eyes opened wide. "A dollar for Oscar? Are you crazy, mister? I know people that will give *you* a dollar to take *all* their cats away."

"Sure, but I like this one," said Mr. Clemens. "I'm on a long trip, and I think it'd be good to have a cat with me. Then I could introduce it as the cat who'd been all around the world."

"I don't think so," said Mrs. Larson. "You want a cat, you go down to Lew Heller's grocery store—he got a mama cat just had five kittens. I bet he'll give you the whole litter for a dollar. Maybe even for nothing."

"You sure? I'll make it two dollars for Oscar."

"No, thank you," said Mrs. Larson firmly. She set the iron back on the stove and folded her arms over her chest. She looked at Mr. Clemens a moment, as if sizing him up, then said, "The reason I got him is to get rid of my rats. His ma's a good ratter, so I hope he'll be one, too, when he grows up a bit. You want to know anything else? I got work to do . . ."

"No, I think not," said Mr. Clemens. He handed the kitten back to the woman. "Thanks for your help, Mrs. Larson. And when Oscar grows up, be sure to tell him how he missed his chance for a trip around the world with Mark Twain."

Outside on the sidewalk, Mr. Clemens looked down the street. We had knocked on the neighbor's door, but apparently nobody was home. My employer said, "If Jenny and her neighbor both heard the shot, it must have been fired from close by. How far do you think it is from here to that street light?"

I tried to imagine a football field. "Forty yards; maybe fifty," I said. Then, "Were you serious about buying that kitten?"

"Sure, though partly I was just teasing her," said my employer. "I didn't really think she'd sell. Once somebody names an animal, they're usually pretty much attached to it."

"Why'd you keep trying, then?"

"It was sort of a test," he said. "I think she passed."

This puzzled me. "Do you mean if she'd sold you the cat, you'd doubt her word?"

"I'm not sure it's that simple," said Mr. Clemens. "I'm not even sure how much it means. But if I figure out how to explain it, I'll let you know. Let's go over and see if we can see anything near that street light."

To double-check my estimate of the distance, I counted as we walked down the street: It was fifty-five paces from Jenny Larson's doorway to the light pole. That was only partly helpful, since I didn't know the exact length of my stride except that it was undoubtedly short of a full yard. But since we had only a rough notion of where the shot had been fired from or where the victim had been standing, we would have only an approximate measurement in any case.

Mr. Clemens nodded when I told him my estimate. "About what you guessed, then. Not a very long shot for anybody brought up in the country. But to kill a man with just one shot, and after dark at that . . . I don't think most ordinary gunners could do it with a six-shooter. It must have been a rifle."

"The killer must have been hunting for Harrington," I said, looking back toward the corner. "It seems unlikely he would have just run across him by accident—especially with a rifle in hand."

"Well, I won't claim to know that much about guns," said Mr. Clemens. "Roosevelt's done a fair bit of hunting; he may be able to tell us whether a fifty-yard bull's-eye is a garden variety pistol shot or a freak shot only an expert can pull off."

"If it's the latter, things look even blacker for Mr. Blankenship," I said. "Pistols seem to be commonplace hereabouts, but I can't remember seeing anyone but him carrying a rifle in town."

"Well, that's why we need to talk to somebody who knows his stuff," said my employer. "Roosevelt knows guns, and so does Cody. Let's see what they think before we start building too many complicated theories."

"I agree," I said. "Although Colonel Cody might exaggerate the difficulty of some of his tricks in order to make them seem more impressive to the layman."

"That's why we ask Roosevelt," said Mr. Clemens. "And maybe a couple of Army officers, too. That way we don't depend on just one man's opinion."

He turned and looked around at the street and sidewalk, then asked, "Do you see anything out of the ordinary here? I mean, anything that'd tell you there'd been a man shot to death here?"

I looked for a minute or so, then said, "No, but I really don't know what to look for. I suppose if we knew where the body fell, we might look for blood stains there. If it was out in the street, I'd be surprised if the dirt didn't soak up any stains, and then the dust and footprints of the passersby would probably have covered any other traces."

Mr. Clemens nodded and reached in his pocket for a cigar. "This is where the detectives in stories always have the advantage. They've just managed to study up exactly the stuff they need to know to identify the killer. If that stuck-up idiot Sherlock Holmes were standing here, he'd pick up some piece of trash off the street and know it came from one particular place in Egypt, or maybe China, and that would prove that the one person in town who'd been there last week was the only possible murderer."

I laughed. "If he could do something like that, I hardly think that would make him an idiot. Quite the opposite."

"Maybe not him, then," growled my employer, clipping the end off his cigar. "But anybody who believes he can do it is the purest idiot in America. With the possible exception of me."

"Why you?" I asked. "If nothing else, you're sensible enough to hire me as your secretary." I ventured a smile, but Mr. Clemens chose to ignore my joke.

He struck a match and lit the cigar, then said, "I'm damn fool enough to take on Tom Blankenship's case when he won't lift a finger to clear himself. If any more of my old Missouri friends ever get themselves arrested for murder, remind me to let them hang. It'll save the world a heap of trouble."

"It would have saved us a heap of trouble if the victim had written his killer's name in the dust with his finger," I said. "Lacking that, we'll just have to find our man the hard way."

Mr. Clemens looked around at the street again, puffing on his cigar. At last he said, "If anybody wrote anything in this dust, it's long since scratched out. Well, I reckon you're right; we've got to do what we can, while there's still time. Let's go see Roosevelt and have some lunch."

"Fifty yards, you say?" Mr. Roosevelt looked up from his plate of pork chops, the light reflecting off his round glasses. "In those conditions, it's a moderately difficult pistol shot for a steady hand and a good eye—and a well-made weapon. Most of the fellows you'll meet on the street might have trouble hitting a barn door at that range. But for any half-decent rifleman, it's child's play. Annie Oakley could probably do it blindfolded."

"I was afraid you'd say something like that," said Mr. Clemens. "That leaves Tom the prime suspect, unless we can dig up somebody else who was walking the streets with a rifle that night. I wish we could find some witness besides Harrington's sidekick—somebody sober, preferably. I've found a woman who heard the shot, and she says her neighbor heard it, too. But neither of them saw who fired it."

"Speaking of Harrington's sidekicks, I think I finally have a lead on that scoundrel Zach'ry," said Roosevelt. "He usually stays in a cheap working men's rooming house out by the railroad yards—not much more than a place to sleep and to stow some of his belongings. Nobody admits seeing him recently, but odds are, if we keep an eye on the place, we can catch him."

"What's the point to that?" I asked. "He already has what looks like a pretty good alibi for the time of the murder. And I doubt we can come up with any convincing motive; after all, the victim was his friend."

"More people are killed by their supposed friends than by strangers," said Roosevelt, wiping off his mustache with a linen napkin. "Sometimes it's an accident, sometimes there's an argument that gets out of hand, and sometimes their friend turns against them. If Zach'ry's alibi falls through, I wouldn't be so hasty to eliminate him. For that matter, if we could punch a hole in C. D.'s story, I'd consider him a prime suspect—he's the only one who admits to being with the victim at the time."

"Yes, I'd love to see his story fall through," said Mr. Clemens. "But there's that little problem of the shot being fired from fifty yards off—if it really was. I suppose he could have lagged behind, plugged Harrington from a distance, and then run up to act as if he'd been standing next to him all along. But according to the sheriff, the gun hadn't been fired—no smell of powder, no empty cartridges in the cylinder."

"And supposedly Zach'ry had already had more than his share to drink," I pointed out. "Possibly that wouldn't have affected his marksmanship, but I seriously doubt it would improve it."

"It rarely does," said Mr. Roosevelt. "But I'd like to point out an avenue we haven't really explored properly. Little as I like to cast suspicion on our men in uniform, it does appear as if that incident we saw that afternoon, where Harrington knocked down the soldier on the bicycle, was not an isolated case. From what I've learned, Jed Harrington was well known to the Army authorities as a trouble-maker. In particular, he seems to have had it in for the colored soldiers—and for the Indian scouts, when they came into town."

"Just today, we ran into Joe Fox in the neighborhood where Harrington was shot," I said. "I wonder what he was doing there."

"The criminal returns to the scene of his crime," said Roosevelt smugly.

"Hell, Wentworth and I were there, too," said Mr. Clemens. "By that kind of logic, you should put us on the suspect list, too, Roosevelt."

"Actually, any rigorous investigation ought to have taken a closer look at Cabot's doings," said Roosevelt. "He had an altercation with the victim a short while before, and he admits to having been out on the street that night, but he wasn't even questioned. I'm quite sure he'd have been cleared. But I can promise you, Clemens, once I'm Police Commissioner in New York, I'll hold my criminal investigation officers to a much higher standard than we're seeing here."

"Promise all you want," said my employer. "When you're in New York, you can try to keep those promises. Right now, we're dealing with Montana, and we've already found out they do things their own way around here. But maybe we *should* try to find out whether Joe Fox might have done it. From the way he talked about Jed Harrington today, I got the idea those two had butted heads some time or another. Did any of the people you talked to out at the fort say anything about that?"

"Not really," said Roosevelt. "They were very much on their guard against saying anything that might implicate a soldier in the murder. I can't say the question of Joe Fox ever came up. They were pretty incensed about Harrington having wrecked that soldier's bicycle, but since I'd seen that with my own eyes, they couldn't very well pretend it hadn't happened."

"I'd almost forgotten about him," said Mr. Clemens. "I hope Harrington didn't do him any lasting injury."

"When I went to the fort, I saw him back on duty, with a new bicycle," said Roosevelt. "So that, at least, has turned out well."

"And that's about all that has, so far," said Mr. Clemens. He rested his chin in the palm of his hand and continued. "To tell the truth, I'm not sure what we ought to be doing next. One of us should probably try laying for Zach'ry out by that rooming house you found. And I guess it's worth finding out where Joe Fox was at the time of the killing. But there are too damn many loose ends—and dead ends—for me to put together a coherent plan."

"Well, there are two lines we can explore," said Mr. Roosevelt. "I should probably lie in wait for Zach'ry, since he and Cabot haven't hit it off well. And unless you have some other use for him, perhaps Cabot can look into Joe Fox's doings, in view of his obvious antipathy to the victim—not that I didn't feel plenty of antipathy myself."

"All right, that makes sense to me," said my employer. "And while you two are off on those errands, I reckon I'll wander over to the jailhouse again. Maybe I can get the deputies who arrested Tom to tell me what they saw that night—they're the only witnesses I haven't really heard from yet. And if they aren't there, I can at least spend a little more time jawing with Tom."

"As good a plan as any," said Roosevelt. "Frankly, I wonder whether any of this will do poor Blankenship much good. Unless we find some irrefutable proof that someone else killed Harrington, I'm afraid your friend's best chance is going to be to convince a jury of reasonable doubt. And that's not a chance I'd want to risk my neck on."

"All the more reason to find what we can, then," said

Mr. Clemens. "Just do your best—even a blind hog finds a 'tater every now and then." He paused. " 'Course, he's more likely to find something a good bit stronger smelling. Which is about all we've turned up so far."

And on that cheerful note we parted company.

realized, when I came out to the sidewalk in front of the hotel, that I had no plan for finding Joe Fox. He worked as a scout for the Army, so one of my choices was to visit Fort Missoula to look for him. On the other hand, Mr. Clemens and I had seen him in town only an hour or so before lunch, so it might be better to search for him in that neighborhood, which was also very close to the scene of the shooting. That might not be entirely accidental, I thought.

A few moments' thought convinced me to start my search here in town. If I went all the way out to the fort to discover that the scout was still away, I would have to decide between waiting for his return and coming back to town to look for him. Starting here in Missoula, if I didn't track him down fairly quickly, there ought to be plenty of time to ride out to the fort and ask for him there.

The only thing that worried me was that trouble seemed to be chronic in that part of town. Not only was it where Harrington had been shot, it was only a short distance from where I had nearly been robbed and from where Harrington's two cronies had attacked me when I tried to get them to talk about the murder. On the other hand, at least two of those three incidents had involved Zach'ry, who had made himself scarce of late. If I avoided running into him, I might be as safe as if I were sitting on the front porch of the hotel, sipping lemonade and reading a novel.

For all it thought of itself as a city, Missoula remained a small town in actual extent. A ten minutes' brisk walk brought me to the corner on Second Street where Mr. Clemens and I had encountered Joe Fox. When we had been there before, the streets had been nearly empty. Now there was a bit more life. A little corner grocery store was open directly across from me, and two women stood in the shade of the awning, talking. Down the block to my left, a couple of horses were hitched, suggesting that the owners were nearby. And on the right, a barber leaned against the doorway outside his shop, whistling. He cast a longing eye in my direction, clearly hoping I might be in need of his services.

I've always preferred to shave myself, but I hadn't had my hair cut since we had left New York. Now it occurred to me that one of the most reliable sources of gossip in any small town was the local barber. While it seemed unlikely that an Indian would be among his customers, it was probably worth the price of a haircut to find out what he knew about the shooting, which must have been a topic of conversation among his customers. Even if all he knew was hearsay, his customers might have told him something worth my time to listen to. I smiled at him and called out, "How much for a trim?"

"Fifteen cents for a haircut," he said. He was a little curly-haired fellow with a prominent nose and a well-waxed mustache. "If you want, I'll wash it and trim it for thirty."

"Not this time," I said. "But I do need the trim."

Inside the shop, I was greeted with the familiar smells of shaving soap, hair tonic, and tobacco. There was a single chair, evidently well used; there were signs of rubbing on the leather of the seat and arms. The gilt sign on his window—spelling out "Otis's Barber Shop" in three-inch letters—was chipped and faded. I hung up my coat and sat down, and he fastened a bib around my neck. "Haven't seen you in these parts before," he said as he ran a comb through my hair.

"Just passing through," I said, truthfully enough. "My boss and I have a couple of days' layover on the way out to Seattle."

"That so," he said, inspecting my head like a sculptor with a new block of marble. "You sound like you're from back east."

"Connecticut," I said. "It's my first time in these parts. It's a good bit different from back home."

"I guess so," he said, picking up his scissors. "A lot more country, and a lot less people. Most folks out here like it that way."

"I won't argue about the country," I said. "But I'd think a businessman like you wouldn't mind having a few more regular customers."

"Oh, business ain't that bad," he said. "You get too many people, like in the big cities, you start getting a lot of the wrong element. I wouldn't live in New York if I was making a hundred dollars a week. Those people will rob you and cut your throat before you can say *no thanks*."

"Well, I guess that's so," I said. "The first time I was in New York, a man was stabbed to death just down the street from our hotel." (That was only a slight exaggeration.) "But they don't seem to have any patent on murder: If what I hear is true, there was a man shot dead right here in Missoula, just a couple of nights ago."

The scissors went *snip snip* behind my left ear, and he stood back to survey his work before answering me. "Yeah, it was right down the street from here, they tell me. Happened at night, so I didn't see it; I live down on the south side of town. But from what they say, the fellow had it coming. A no-good roughneck, knock you down as soon as look at you."

"Really!" I said. "Did anybody see it happen?"

"The man had one of his friends with him," said the barber, working around my right ear now. "But they'd both been drinking, or so Al says—he's the deputy that arrested the shooter. He was in here the next day for his reg'lar haircut."

"Well, I'm glad to hear they arrested the shooter," I said. "I'd be worried if he were still running loose."

The barber chuckled. "We don't worry about that kind of thing here in . . ."

I didn't hear how he intended to finish the sentence because halfway through it, I leapt out of his chair and went running out onto the street.

There were probably a fair number of Indians who frequented Missoula, but Joe Fox was unmistakable. It was a glimpse of him passing by the front of Otis's barber shop that sent me flying out the door in pursuit of him. "Joe Fox!" I shouted. "Wait a minute! I need to talk to you!"

He stopped and turned around slowly, looking me up and down. I must have been a sight with my hair half cut and the barber's bib over my clothes. "You don't like the way a white man cuts your hair, so you want me to do the job?" he said, with just the faintest trace of a smile.

"No, no, I need to talk with you," I said. "Can you wait for me while the barber finishes? This is important— a matter of life and death." I could see, out of the corner of my eye, the barber staring down the street at me, his mouth open.

"I'm not hurrying nowhere," said the Indian scout. "When Joe Fox is in a hurry, you don't catch me so easy. But I need to buy some tobacco. You go back in the barber shop and I come back and see what you want. I'll wait on the corner. That barber don't want me around his place—I scare off the customers."

"I doubt it," I said, although I suspected he knew better than I what the barber was likely to think of Indians. "But all right—go get your tobacco and come on back. I'll be done in just a few minutes."

I walked back to the barber's, wondering if I had made a mistake in letting Joe Fox go so easily. He might well have an idea that I wanted to talk about the murder, and if he were in fact the guilty party, I might just have given him the chance to escape before suspicion turned to him.

"What the dickens was all that about?" said the barber as I settled back into his chair. "What does a Connecticut man have to do with a redskin?"

"He owes me money," I said, blurting out the first explanation that came to mind. "I lent him a dollar for a meal when I first came to town, and I was hoping to get him to pay me back."

"More likely he spent it on firewater," said the barber, with disapproval obvious in his voice. "Indians can't handle their liquor, no sir. Givin' 'em money is like throwing it down a rathole. You ask anybody 'round these parts."

"Well, I guess I'd rather risk losing the dollar than risk letting a man go hungry," I said. "Anyway, he says he'll come back and pay me as soon as my haircut's finished."

"Hope you didn't tell him to come in my shop," sniffed the barber.

"No, he says he'll meet me on the corner," I said.

"Last you'll see of him," said the barber smugly. He returned to trimming and clipping, and in a few more minutes he seemed to be satisfied. "Here, take a look," he said, twirling the chair around so I could see the results in his mirror.

"That's fine," I said, lying through my teeth. I was suddenly sorry that I'd put myself at the mercy of an unknown barber in a poor section of a small western town. My hair would grow out, but I suspected Mr. Clemens would have more than one merry comment to make at my expense before it did. Too embarrassed to complain, I gave Mr. Otis two dimes and said, "Keep the change."

"Sure enough," he said, smiling now. "Any of your Connecticut friends need a shave or haircut while they're in town, be sure to send 'em to Tony Otis."

"If they ask, I'll be sure to tell them who cut my hair," I said. I adjusted my jacket, and, sadder but wiser, went out on the street to look for Joe Fox.

At first, I thought the barber was right, and that the Indian had given me the slip. But then I saw him come out of a store a few doors down and turn in my direction. He nodded as he spotted me, and we both walked ahead to meet at the corner.

"OK, what you want to talk about?" he asked when I reached him. I could see the telltale bulge of a chaw of tobacco in his cheek.

"This morning we were talking about Jed Harrington's being shot," I said. "I wanted to ask you a couple of questions about that."

"You think I did it?" he said, frowning.

"If you did it, I don't think you would've come back to talk to me when you had a chance to get away," I said, not quite certain whether I believed myself. "But I think you might be able to help me and my boss figure out who *did* do it."

"If I knew, why should I tell you?" said Joe Fox. "The man who shot Jed Harrington did Indians a favor. What makes you think I want to see him punished?"

"You may not want that," I said, "but do you want an innocent man to be punished in his place? That's what Mr. Clemens and I are trying to prevent."

"He said that to me before," said the Indian, his face emotionless. "He said that the man in jail is his friend. But that doesn't mean he is a good man, or that he is my friend. Why do you think I want to help this white man that I have never met, who has never done anything for me?"

I took a deep breath. I hadn't expected convincing Fox to be easy, but I hadn't expected him to make so much trouble, either. "I think if you knew this man you would want to help him," I said. "The day before the shooting, Harrington attacked a colored soldier and damaged his bicycle. Mr. Clemens's friend, Tom Blankenship, made Harrington stop badgering the soldier. He made him pay the soldier to replace the bicycle. If he did that for a colored soldier he didn't know, I think he would have done it for an Indian who was in trouble, too. He would have done it for anyone who was in trouble and needed help."

Joe Fox nodded gravely. "You make him sound like a good man," he said. "But white men have a way of making things sound better than they are. Just because you say he is a good man, that does not make it so."

"You don't have to take my word for it," I said. I was getting angry now; I didn't like having my word doubted just on account of my color. "Go back to the fort, and look for the soldier whose bicycle was broken," I said. "Ask him to tell you what happened that day in town."

"Maybe I will," he said slowly. He switched the chaw of tobacco to his other cheek, then said, "If he tells me that your story about Harrington and this other man is true, maybe I will try to help your boss's friend. I don't promise anything."

"You don't seem to understand," I said. "This is a matter of life and death. Mr. Clemens and I have to leave town at the end of this week. If we haven't found a way to help Mr. Blankenship before then, he may not have anyone to help him. We can't wait for somebody to make up their mind."

Joe Fox shrugged. "If it is a matter of life and death, you would not leave town until this man is safe. Don't ask me to hurry to help you when you are not willing to stay here to help him. I will ask the soldier you say your friend helped, and if I like what he tells me, I will come back and talk to you. But I tell you again, I don't promise anything. And remember this—even if I do decide to help, I may not know anything that makes any difference."

"All we ask is that you try," I said. It looked as if I'd gotten as much commitment from the scout as I was likely to, and I decided to end the conversation while I could do so reasonably graciously. "We're staying at the Florence House hotel. Ask for Samuel Clemens, or Wentworth Cabot—that's me. Or leave a message if we're not in."

He stared at me. "I know how to leave messages," he said. "If I have something to tell you, you will hear it. Now I am going." And without another word, he walked away down the street.

I stood for a moment watching him leave, then turned and made my way back to the hotel. I consoled myself with the thought that at least I had managed to find the man I was looking for—even if it turned out to have been no use at all in clearing Mr. Blankenship of murder charges.

When I walked up to the hotel, Mr. Clemens and his daughter Clara were sitting next to one another in rocking chairs on the porch. As I came into sight, Clara's face took on an appalled expression, which at first puzzled me.

Mr. Clemens wasn't about to let the opportunity escape him, though. "Jesus, Wentworth, when I send you looking for an Indian, I'm not asking you to get scalped," he said. "What the hell did you do to your hair?"

"I made the mistake of going to a local barber," I said. My employer just shook his head. It was not uncommon, when he had a series of public appearances, for him to visit a barber on a daily basis. I considered this fastidiousness about his hair to be barely distinguishable from vanity, but on the other hand I was not the one who had to stand in front of an audience night after night. Still, I did not appreciate being the butt of jokes about my appearance.

"Nonetheless, I did find the Indian," I said, hoping to redirect the conversation by reporting at least a partial success.

"Well, that's more than I managed," said Mr. Clemens. "Did you find out anything useful?"

"I wish I had," I said, and told what had passed between Joe Fox and me. I concluded with the remark, "He seems to hold a grudge against the white race as a whole."

"I reckon you might, too, if you were in his shoes," said Mr. Clemens. "But I hope he doesn't hold back any information that might help Tom just because of what our kind has done to his kind. Unless Tom's changed a lot since I knew him, he's the one man in this territory I'd expect to treat a red man fairly without first figuring out whether there was some particular advantage to himself in doing it."

"That may be true," I said. "But if Joe Fox is disposed to believe otherwise, it won't do Blankenship much good."

Clara Clemens leaned forward and spoke. "And even if Joe Fox decides to help you, he may not know anything useful," she said. "Father, I'm afraid that you and Wentworth are placing too much weight on this one man's evidence. It may be no more than coincidence that he was in that neighborhood today."

"I know that as well as you do," said Mr. Clemens, with some sign of irritation. "Give your father credit for some common sense, young lady. Wentworth and Roosevelt and I have been beating the bushes for ways to clear Tom. The problem is, we don't have any reliable witnesses, and all the evidence seems to point the wrong way. Why that fool had to go walking around the streets carrying a rifle is beyond me."

"Haven't you asked him?" said Clara.

Mr. Clemens grumbled. "Sure I've asked him. His

story is that he's gotten into the habit of carrying it when he walks around the woods back home, so he just naturally took the gun along when he went out for a walk here in town. It sounds so stupid, it's probably true."

Clara frowned and said, "You're going about solving this case the wrong way, Father. You know the old saying: You catch more flies with honey than with vinegar. People will talk to you much more readily if you treat them civilly. The way you've been threatening and badgering them, it's no wonder they don't want to cooperate with you."

Mr. Clemens growled, "Young lady, you don't have any idea what you're talking about. Buttering up a porcupine would be easier than getting these rascals to act civil. Have you forgotten how Jed Harrington treated that soldier the other day?"

"I haven't forgotten that you and your friends confronted him with guns and threats," said Clara stubbornly. "His two friends certainly can't have misunderstood that. Why do you think they fought poor Wentworth when he tried to get them to talk to you? They must have expected the worst from you."

"Miss Clemens, I'm afraid you've greatly misunderstood the situation," I said.

"Perhaps so," she said in a quiet voice. "But I'll ask you to remember back in Italy who it was who got that policeman, Agente Maggio, to help you after he was sent to spy on you. You two would never have gotten a word out of him. Sometimes a gentle touch is the right approach."

Mr. Clemens shook his finger at his daughter. "Clara, I don't know what you're cooking up, but I'm going to tell you right now—stay away from this case. The person we're after shot down a man in cold blood on the streets of Missoula and is willing to let somebody else hang for it. If you think there's any way I'm going to let you stick your nose into that kind of mess, you're sadly mistaken. You hear me? Stay out of it."

"I hear you, Father," said Clara, with a toss of her head. "And I think I have heard all I want of your ordering me around like a child." She stood up and strode away into the hotel.

"Damnation," said Mr. Clemens. "I'm going to have to get Livy to talk to her, now. When Clara gets her back up, she can be as stubborn as a Missouri mule. I don't know where she gets it; her mother is as sweet as they come."

"I can't imagine where she gets it, sir," I said.

Mr. Clemens glared at me for a moment, then saw my attempt to suppress a smile, and chuckled. "Well, maybe that apple fell right by the tree, after all," he said. "Come on, we've just got time for a drink before dinner. And then I'll see if I can make up with my daughter. It shouldn't take more than a couple of weeks to get her calmed down."

I laughed and followed him inside to the bar.

16 ⌒

At dinner in the hotel restaurant that evening, I was very pleased to see that the argument between Clara Clemens and her father appeared to have blown over. She joked with him in very much her usual style, and showed all the signs of having regained the sense of proportion that was one of her distinguishing traits. Indeed, the talk turned away from recent events to the prospects lying ahead of us on our round-the-world journey.

Mr. Clemens was particularly enthusiastic about our plans to visit San Francisco and the Sandwich Islands, two of the places where he had made his first mark as a literary man, as opposed to a mere newspaper writer. "It's been nearly thirty years since I was on the west coast," he said as our dinner plates were being cleared away in preparation for the arrival of dessert. "From every report I've seen, the whole place has grown like Topsy; the population of San Francisco has more than doubled, from what I hear tell, and that's just taking the 1890 census figures. I doubt I'll recognize it."

"It's not likely to recognize you, either, Youth," said

Mrs. Clemens. "You've certainly changed a good deal since I met you—very much for the better, I think."

"For the better? I wonder," said my employer. "If the young rascal that came east in '67 could meet me now, I wonder if he'd think I was even worth talking to. He'd probably look at me as a pathetic old fraud, much too respectable to be any fun at all."

"Such are the rewards of success, Youth," said Mrs. Clemens. "He'd surely envy you your current expedition, even though he'd already been to Europe and the Holy Land, at least by the time I met him. And your having made your living by your pen all these years would have to impress him."

"It impresses me," I said. Then, after a pause, I added, "And I even have an inkling how little work it really is."

"*Et tu, Brute,*" said Mr. Clemens, clutching his chest in feigned injury. "I expect as much from my own flesh and blood, Wentworth, but for you to inflict such a grievous wound—if you keep it up, I may have to put you in my will, just to teach you a lesson."

"I object, Father," said Clara Clemens. "That's cruel and unusual punishment. Poor Wentworth's got enough of a burden to bear just working for you, without your saddling him with straightening out your estate after you're gone. Not even Mama knows what to make of some of the things you've written and never been able to publish."

"Young lady, I'll have you know I can publish anything I want to," said my employer, sitting up straight and putting on a hurt expression. "Why, there are newspapers and magazines all over the world who'd print anything I sent to them, just to have my name in their columns. The only thing that keeps me from sending my work to them is—"

"That they wouldn't pay you enough to cover the postage," said Clara. Then, in a more conciliatory tone, she went on, "On the other hand, I can't complain about some of the benefits of being connected to you. It isn't every girl who gets to go on a trip around the world at my age."

"Or at any age," said Mrs. Clemens. The waiter had returned now with our dessert, warm apple pie with slices of mild cheddar cheese and piping hot freshly brewed coffee. "I am particularly looking forward to seeing the Sandwich Islands, especially after reading your letters and articles on them. They surely must have changed as much as any place on earth in the time since you visited them."

"I'd think so, especially since the United States took 'em over a couple of years ago," said Mr. Clemens in between bites of his pie. "The blasted American missionaries were doing their best to be the ruination of the place even when I was there, and now they've got a free rein to run loose and bamboozle the natives. I expect it'll be a sad remnant of what it was in the old days."

"The old days can't have been that much better," said Mrs. Clemens. "I seem to recall a few passages in your own writings that indicated that the missionaries did a great deal of good, and that the efforts of the American settlers had made the islands a far more pleasant place to live, even for the natives."

"Ah, my own words turned against me," said Mr. Clemens, with a rueful shake of the head. "Take my advice, Wentworth—if you're ever inclined to publish anything, make sure your family don't read it. They're bound to turn it all on its head and make you regret every syllable of it."

"I shall remember that, sir," I said, playing along with him.

"Good," said Clara, with a mischievous grin. "But I hope you're not such a fool as to let it stop you from publishing—or marrying, if anyone will have either your writings or you."

"Oh, Wentworth will do all right," said Mr. Clemens. "Give him another few years working for me, and I suspect he might even begin to cultivate a sense of humor."

"Sir, if I work for you that long, I shall certainly have a need for it," I said. From my employer's expression, he seemed unsure what I meant by that, but Clara and her mother broke out giggling, which indicated that they, at least, knew exactly what I was referring to.

The next morning, Mr. Clemens decided to send me out to ask Colonel Cody about the range at which a good pistol shot could hit a man in the conditions we thought to have obtained at the time of the killing. So I whistled up our cab driver, Jack Briscoe, and he took me on the by now familiar ride out to Cody's Wild West Show's campground.

The colonel was at breakfast when I arrived, putting away a serving of pork chops with fried eggs and potatoes, and a jigger of whiskey next to his coffee cup. At his invitation, I sat down and joined him, and in a few moments the cook brought me a cup of coffee and a fresh basket of piping hot corn bread.

Not surprisingly, he had heard a fair amount about the murder of Harrington. "Live by the sword, die by the sword," he said, shaking his head sadly. "I won't deny I did my share of wild living in my salad days, but sooner or later a fellow's got to grow up. I give the U.S. Army full credit for making a man out of me, young fellow. If you ever get tired of working for Clemens, you could do a lot worse than signing up. I'd make you out for officer material, if you applied yourself."

"Thank you, Colonel," I said. "I hadn't considered that career path, but if I find myself at loose ends I'll certainly remember your recommendation. But Mr. Clemens sent me here to draw on your fund of knowledge this morning." I briefly described the scene of the murder, doing my best to reconstruct the conditions as they must have been that night. "Now, Colonel Cody, in your opinion could an ordinary marksman bring a man down at that distance with a pistol shot?"

"I could do it six shots out of six," he said without

hesitating. "But I'm a cut above the ordinary level, and I've got a fine custom-made weapon, which helps considerably. Still, I think most of the fellows in my show could do it."

"I see," I said. "How common is that level of skill in the general population hereabouts?"

"Not as common as it used to be," he said. He picked up a piece of the corn bread and slathered butter on it. After a bite, he continued. "It would depend on whether we're talking town-bred folks or those who make their livelihood off the land, by hunting and so forth. Almost any country lad can outshoot his city cousins, if only because they've a constant need for accurate shooting."

"A possible exception occurs to me," I said. "Even in the country, I'd think most of the shooting a fellow does would be with a rifle or shotgun. Or are farmers going out to pot a rabbit or a deer with a revolver?"

"Excellent point, young fellow," said Cody. "A revolver's almost entirely a self-defense weapon, and being a good shot with a hunting weapon doesn't necessarily help. You'd be surprised how many fellows can't put a bullet in a three-foot square at ten paces. Especially with some of the cheap guns on the market."

"I believe you," I said truthfully. "I'm afraid I'd be among them since I'm one of those town-bred boys you were speaking of. I doubt I'll ever be much of a shot."

"You could be if you put your mind to it," said the colonel confidently. "A man your age shouldn't have much trouble picking up the rudiments, especially with a good teacher. If you've got a good eye and a steady hand, they'll take you a long way. But of course there's no substitute for firing off a few hundred practice rounds. Little Annie Oakley's got the best eye of anyone you'll ever meet, but even she works hard at her shooting."

"I can understand that," I said. "I can't think of anything worth doing well that doesn't benefit from practice. I doubt I'll get much chance to do it any time soon, though, what with my duties for Mr. Clemens."

"I'd think about it seriously, if I were you," said Colonel Cody. He wiped his mouth with a linen napkin, then looked me right in the face and said, "To put it frankly, young fellow, you and Clemens are headed for parts of the world where a party of travelers that includes a couple of white women might attract unwelcome attention. A wise man would look into making sure he could extricate himself from any dangerous situations that might arise."

"Thank you for the advice, sir," I said. I decided it might be less than diplomatic to point out that the worst danger we had come into so far on this journey had been from Jed Harrington, a white American. Nor did I express my own distaste for firearms, a preference the colonel might consider evidence of soft citified ways. Instead, I added, "Naturally, I'll have to consult my employer's preferences in the matter, but the point seems well taken to me."

"Good, feel free to come to me if you want any advice in picking out a suitable weapon," he said. "It's too bad you won't be in these parts long enough for us to give you some lessons; I have a couple of men who could give you quite a head start on becoming a decent shot. Now, I hope you don't have to hurry back into town; there's something happening today that I think you'll enjoy seeing."

"I can spare a little more time, sir," I said.

"Good, then come on out to our practice field," he said. He stood up from the table and downed his shot of whiskey, and a moment later we were on our way down to the field.

After our conversation, I had thought he might be planning to give me a shooting lesson. Instead, to my surprise, on the field were close to fifty of the colored soldiers from the Army base, in company with Annie Oakley and her husband Frank Butler. "I think you'll find this interesting," said Colonel Cody. "Annie's been practicing shooting from the seat of a moving bike, and when Colonel Burt heard about it, he asked me if she'd be willing to give his fellows some tips. I didn't have to hesitate a second on that one. Annie's a strong supporter of our men in blue, and of course I owe a lot of what I am today to the Army. I told him to send me as many men as he wanted, and so today we got the first contingent."

Annie Oakley was standing by her bicycle and the soldiers were gathered around her, those in the front row sitting so the others could see easily. Behind them, their bicycles were set up in lines that gave meaning to the term "military precision." To one side stood Sergeant Johnson, alert for any sign of inattention on the part of his troops.

"The whole secret of shooting from a bicycle is learning to keep a steady course without touching the handlebars," she said. "You've got to have the same control of your rifle as when you're standing on solid ground, or riding horseback. Can all of you ride without using your hands?"

"Yes, ma'am," said the soldiers, in chorus. The sergeant chuckled. "That's about the third thing we teach 'em, Miss Oakley," he said. "And they already know to stop pedaling and coast just before they take aim, so they can keep a steady bead."

"Oh, then the rest should be a breeze," she said. "Let me show you. I'll be using a shotgun instead of a military carbine, but the idea's just the same." She leaned the gun over her shoulder, with one hand holding the stock, and put the other hand on the handlebars of the bicycle. She put her feet on the pedals, then began riding off down the flat field where the Wild West Show practiced.

Actually, seen up close, the field was not quite as level as it might appear; there were plenty of hoof marks where horsemen had ridden, and ruts from the wheels of the Deadwood Stage. This made it slightly more difficult for her to keep her balance; on the other hand, it was probably a better approximation of the conditions soldiers were likely to meet in the field. She rode off down the field, made a circle, and came back toward us. "Are you ready, Frank?" she called.

"Ready when you are, Annie," her husband replied. He had his hand on the lanyard of a trap to fire clay pigeons.

Annie Oakley came up to the end of the arena, turned again, then took her hands off the handlebars and shouldered her gun. "Pull!" she called. Almost at once, a pair of clay pigeons came swishing out of the trap and down the field. *Bang! Bang!* Two shots rang out in quick succession, and both targets shattered in mid-air. The soldiers broke into enthusiastic applause, whistling and grinning at the display of marksmanship.

Miss Oakley shouldered her weapon again, grasped the handlebar again, and turned back around to coast to a graceful stop in front of the soldiers. "There! You see?" she said, smiling back at them.

"That's very good, Miz Oakley," said Sergeant Johnson. "You make it look easy. I reckon my boys will find out just how hard it is when they get to tryin' it themselves. One question, though. Anybody that's done it knows the biggest problem of shootin' a firearm off a bike is the recoil. What can you tell 'em about keeping the bike steady while they're firing? You hit that bird with your second shot just as clean as you did with the first, so I guess you've figured out some answer."

"Thank you, Sergeant," said Annie Oakley. "For one thing, I'm using a very light load, which does a lot to cut down the recoil, and a shotgun's a whole lot more forgiving than a rifle. Your Army carbines are likely to be a bit harder to manage. But the best thing you can do is brace the gun solidly against your shoulder, and keep your left arm absolutely straight, so it can absorb most of the recoil."

"You hear that, you jaybirds?" said the sergeant. "If this little lady can stay on the bike while she's shooting, I don't want to see any of you falling off. All right now, we're going to practice this by squads . . ."

• • •

Before I left Cody's camp, I wanted to give my regards to Annie Oakley and her husband. She nodded to me to indicate that she had recognized me, but held up a finger to let me know she wanted to finish talking to the soldiers before greeting me. So I waited while she dispensed a few more tips, showing how she kept her balance, reminding the soldiers not to move their legs while aiming, and sharing other esoteric lore that undoubtedly would have made sense to me had I known more about shooting a rifle.

Finally, she told the sergeant, "I think you can turn them loose to practice on their own now." She slipped her shotgun into a fine tooled leather case, closed it up, and came over to me. "Hello, Mr. Cabot! What brings you out our way this morning?"

I greeted her and her husband and told them briefly about the murder, Tom Blankenship's being accused, and the state of our investigation to date. When I mentioned Joe Fox, she said, "I know Joe—he was one of a group of Sioux who came to the Wild West Show after Sitting Bull left us, on his recommendation. Joe traveled with us a couple of seasons before he went back to scouting. If you want, I'll try to get in touch with him—I'm sure he'd talk to me."

"Thank you," I said. "We'd appreciate any help we can get, now. Mr. Clemens's daughter Clara has even threatened to go out questioning witnesses herself—although I think her father has talked her out of it."

Frank Butler laughed. "Don't you be bettin' on it, Mr. Cabot," he said. "For every man who thinks he's talked a lady out of something, there's a lady who knows she's put something over on her man. Even Miss Annie here— sure, and she knows how to get her own way."

Annie Oakley gave him a playful jab in the ribs. "And Frank Butler may have to go learn to cook his own supper," she said. She turned back to me and said, "Really, Mr. Cabot, I hope you'll tell Mr. Clemens that I'll do anything I can to help his friend. I saw what kind of man he was when he stood up to the bully who knocked that poor soldier off his bicycle. I don't know if you noticed, but that man's here today—back on his bike and looking fit for duty."

"Really?" I said, looking back at the men in uniform. It was a bit embarrassing that I hadn't recognized the man Harrington had harassed in front of our hotel the afternoon before the shooting. "I wonder if he has a moment to spare to speak to me. Possibly he could throw some light on a couple of things we haven't been able to sort out."

"Why don't you ask Sergeant Johnson?" said Frank Butler. "I doubt he'll object if you tell him what it's about. Meanwhile, if you'll forgive us, Annie and I have to catch up on our own rifle practice."

"A pleasure seeing you again, Mr. Cabot," said Annie Oakley. "And I won't forget—if I can get word to Joe Fox about your need to talk to him, I will."

I thanked her, and shook hands with Mr. Butler again. They walked away in the direction of the main building, and I turned to the soldiers. "Good morning, Sergeant Johnson," I said. "I don't know if you remember me . . ."

"Sure do," he said. "You work for Mr. Mark Twain, don't you? I didn't know you were friends with Miz Oakley, too."

"Not exactly friends," I admitted. "She's friends with my boss, so I got to meet her. But there's a favor you might be able to do for me . . ." Quickly I began to describe how the incident with his soldier might have precipitated the murder.

"Shoot, I knew some of that, but there's a heap more I didn't know," he said. "I ran across that mean son of a bitch Harrington in town later that night, and I gave him a good piece of my mind."

"You were the sergeant he ran into, then!" I said. "One of his cronies told us that, but we could never verify it. Did it come to anything more than words?"

The sergeant shook his head. "No, I didn't think he'd be worth getting myself thrown out of the bar, which I reckon would have happened if we'd gotten into a tangle. Harrington looked like he was ready to come after me if his two buddies would've backed him. But they looked like they were tryin' to talk him out of it. His kind never wants a fair fight—they'd rather stomp a man that's down. It's a good thing I didn't know he was the one who knocked down Private Green. I'd have torn his damnfool head off and thrown it in the latrine. I didn't learn who'd done it until later, after I heard he was shot."

"Were there any other soldiers in town who might have known?" I asked.

"Maybe," said the sergeant. "I didn't, anyway. But I see what you're gettin' at. Much as some of us might have liked to shoot him down, I can promise you it wasn't nobody from the fort. Regulations—nobody takes a weapon off base without specific orders. A mighty smart rule too, if you ask me; otherwise there'd like to be a heap of dead civilians every Sunday morning. Fist fights to blow off some steam is one thing. Soldiers been doing that since Hannibal was a pup. But we don't want our boys to start shooting the folks we're here to protect."

"Yes, that makes sense to me," I said. In the back of my mind I wasn't quite certain that someone angry enough to kill Jed Harrington might not have been willing to bend a regulation or two in the process, but I didn't voice the question. Instead I asked, "Do you mind if I speak to Private Green for a few minutes?"

"No, not a bit," said the sergeant. "His squad's done with the drill, and he'll just be cleanin' his weapon now. He's with that group over there." He pointed to a knot of men seated on the turf a few yards away.

I thanked the sergeant and approached the group. Sure enough, there sat the man I'd seen knocked down in front of the hotel the afternoon before the murder. "Hello, Private Green," I said, squatting down next to him.

He smiled as he looked up from his work and recog-

nized me. "Hello, mister," he said. "I never did get to
thank you all for comin' to help me—that was a mighty
fine thing you did." His accent was rich and musical,
similar to many I'd heard on my trip down the Mississippi with Mr. Clemens.

"I'm glad to see you're back in trim," I said. "I hope
you've recovered from your fall?"

"Yes, sir," said the private. "It hurt me a lot less than
it did my bike. And the bike's fixed up, too, so everything's fine."

"Good—I'll pass the word along," I said. "The man
who did the most to help you will be especially glad to
hear it, I think. I'm afraid he's in jail, and I hope the
news will cheer him up."

"Jail!" said the soldier. "Not for helpin' me, I hope."

"No, that would be especially unjust," I said. "But you
may have heard—the man who tormented you was killed
later that night, and the sheriff thinks Mr. Blankenship
did it."

"That ain't right at all," said the soldier. "You tell Mr.
Blankenship that if Private Silas Green can do anything
for him, it'll be done. Same for any of the other folks
that came to help me—you say the word, and I'll be
there. You can take that to the bank. And I can promise
you, a whole lot of the other boys will be right there with
me."

"Thank you, Silas," I said. "I'll make sure he knows
that. It's good to see you back on your feet." I shook his
hand, took my leave of Sergeant Johnson, and (since the
day was pleasant) decided to walk back into town. In the
thin mountain air, the sun was comfortably warm, and
ahead of me to the east I could see the tops of the peaks
we had come past on our train ride. About halfway back,
I spooked a jackrabbit—the same one we'd seen a few
nights before?—and laughed as I watched it bound off
into the underbrush. This was a fine part of the country;
perhaps the barber was right that it was only the people

who spoiled it. The jackrabbit would almost certainly agree with him.

I arrived back at our hotel just in time for luncheon, during which (over a platter of cold fried chicken and potato salad, washed down with a cold lager beer) I gave Mr. Clemens a report on my visit to Colonel Cody's.

"Good work, Wentworth," he said. "That's about three birds killed with one stone. If Annie Oakley can get that Indian Joe Fox to work with us, it might save a load of trouble—although I'm starting to think he knows less than we do about the murder. And I'm glad you finally found out about that sergeant Harrington argued with. I reckon we can eliminate him as a suspect, too."

"I'd like to think so, sir," I said. "Still, it'd be good to get independent corroboration for his story. If he *had* killed Jed Harrington and was trying to conceal the fact, I think he'd have told me exactly the same thing he did."

"I won't argue with that," said Mr. Clemens. "In fact, I wouldn't particularly blame him—or most of the other people on the suspect list—for shooting down Jed Harrington, except for the fact that none of us is in much of a position to decide who lives or dies. And as far as I'm concerned, that includes judges and generals as well as ordinary folks. But leaving Tom Blankenship to sit there in jail, and maybe even to hang, for a murder somebody else committed—I couldn't condone that even if Harrington were the most evil man alive. And he wouldn't even get to the starting line in that competition."

"Not even close to it," I agreed. "Still, finding the real killer is our only sure way of clearing Mr. Blankenship. So even if we find ourselves in complete sympathy with the killer's motives, I fear we'll have to turn him in to the sheriff."

"That's the hell of it, ain't it?" said Mr. Clemens. "If I could spring Tom without putting the finger on some-body else, I reckon I'd do it. But I'm not sure I could look myself in the mirror if I knowingly let a killer run loose—maybe next time he'll gun down somebody that *hasn't* been a thorn in the side of everybody decent in the county. So we just have to do the best we can. And I reckon you've done all right for one morning. Why don't you take the afternoon off? This was supposed to be a rest stop, and here you've been working overtime almost every day. Go out and see the sights, or go upstairs and nap—I won't bother you until after supper."

"Thank you, sir," I said. "But if there's anything else that needs doing, especially in regard to Mr. Blankenship, I hope you won't put off calling me. I can get enough rest when we get back on the train."

Still, I felt some relief at being able to call an afternoon my own. I left the dining room and headed for the stairs up to my room. But before I was across the lobby, a familiar voice called out, "Mr. Cabot! Do you have a moment?" It was Clara Clemens.

"Certainly, Miss Clemens," I said. "What can I do for you?"

"Really just a moment of your time," she said. "Father told me you'd gone out to Colonel Cody's camp this morning. Did you see Miss Oakley there?"

"Why, yes, as a matter of fact," I said. "She was teaching some of the soldiers from the fort how to shoot while riding a bicycle, the way she does in her act in the Wild West Show."

"Oh, that must have been fun to watch," she said. "Did she say whether she'd be at home this afternoon?"

"No; the question never came up," I said. "Why? Did you want to see her?"

"The other way around, actually," said Clara. "She and I spoke some after dinner the other night, and I promised to help her choose some music to accompany her act. I thought if she were going to be free today, it might be my last chance to go visit her."

"As far as I know, she and her husband planned to do some target practice today, but I've no idea what else she had on her slate."

"Pooh!" she said. "I suppose I'll just have to ride out there and see if she's free. In any case, it won't take long to give her a few titles to consider. Then she can get the music sent to her and choose. Would you like to come along?"

"Normally, yes," I said. Clara Clemens was always amusing to talk to, and I fancied we understood one another better than many other people our age. "But I've just been out there, and your father's rewarded me with the afternoon off. I think I'm going to take advantage of the chance to get some rest. Thank you for the invitation."

"I'm sorry you can't come along," she said. "I'll just have to get a ride out there myself. I should be back by dinner time, if anyone asks."

"All right," I said, and made my way up to my room. There I spent perhaps half an hour reading before (between the summer heat and a shortage of sleep the last few nights) I found myself nodding off. Giving in to the inevitable, I stretched out on the bed and let myself doze off.

I slept soundly until I was awakened by an insistent knocking on my door, and my employer's voice. "Wentworth! Are you there? Clara's gone, and we can't find her!"

17

"Gone?" I sat up on the edge of my bed and stared at Mr. Clemens. "What do you mean, gone?"

"She's not in her room, not anywhere in the hotel," said Mr. Clemens. "The last time anybody saw her was at lunch, when she told Livy she was going out to see if she could find some piano music she wanted. There is a music store in town—the hotel desk confirmed that—but we have no idea whether she ever got there. They're closed, now, of course."

"That's not what she told me," I said, and told him the story she'd told me about helping Annie Oakley find music for her act. "I suppose she might have been looking for music for Miss Oakley at the store. But even if that's so, she should have been back long before now, or at least have sent word that she was staying late. If she wasn't going to the music store, or out to Cody's, where might she have gone, do you think?"

"That's what worries me," said my employer. He walked into the room and closed the door behind him, then sat down in the chair my trousers were hanging on.

"I think the little fool's got it into her head that she can solve this murder case faster than you and I can, and she's gone off to try. And where that puts her right now, God only knows, but I'm worried, Wentworth. Worried sick."

"I can well imagine," I said. "Does Mrs. Clemens know?"

"Yes, of course," said Mr. Clemens. "She's the one who found out she wasn't in her room when she didn't come down for supper. Livy's very worried, and I'm afraid what it'll do to her if anything's happened to Clara. Her heart isn't strong . . ."

"I know," I said. Fighting against my aching head, I stood up and stretched. "We'll go looking for her. Where do you think we ought to start?"

Mr. Clemens stood up and began pacing, which gave me a chance to get my trousers off the chair. "Damn if I know," he said. "I never expected to have to go chasing after her. She might be almost anywhere—out at the fort, in one of the cowboy saloons . . . down at the hoosegow, for all I know. I suppose we ought to send somebody out to Cody's to ask, not that I expect she's set foot there at all."

"We need to split up," I said, pulling my suspenders over my shoulders. "Have you gotten word to Roosevelt? He'd be glad to help, I'm sure."

"Good thinking," said Mr. Clemens. "When we go down to the lobby, I'll send the bellboy over to his hotel with a message. And I'll get the manager to have his people look for her here in the building, and to keep an eye out in case she comes back while I'm gone."

"I don't know . . ." I said. "You might want to come back every so often yourself, to check on whether Clara's back, and to look in on Mrs. Clemens. She'll want to be kept up to date on the progress of the search."

He stared at me for a long moment, then said, "You're right, she will. Here's my plan, then. I'll go over to the jail and ask the sheriff to have his deputies keep an eye

out for her. While I'm there, I'll talk to Tom a bit, and
then look around that neighborhood to see if anybody's
seen her. I'll stay in this general neighborhood so I can
check back here periodically. So instead of my sending
a boy to get Roosevelt, why don't you go over there and
tell him what's going on, and the boy can go out to
Cody's. Then the two of you can decide how to search
the parts of town farther away from the hotel, and you
two can leave messages for me as you have any news,
either at the sheriff's office or back here."

"All right," I said as I finished tying my shoes. "I'll
get straight to it."

"Good man," said Mr. Clemens. He put his hand on
my shoulder and said, "Don't leave anything to chance,
Wentworth. You know I'm counting on you. Livy and I
both."

"I understand that, sir," I said. "Trust me—if she can
be found, I'll do it."

"I'll tell Livy that," he said. And I followed him out
to begin the search.

I found Roosevelt just finishing up a late dinner, with
a cup of coffee and a snifter of brandy in front of him.
When I told him what the matter was, he pushed aside
the brandy and gulped down the coffee. "Well, Cabot, it
looks as if we've got our work cut out for us," he said.
"How do you think we ought to proceed?"

I had sat down across from him at the table. "First
question is where she's most likely to be," I said. "That
depends on what she's gotten herself into. Odds are,
everything's fine, and she'll come walking into the hotel
and have nothing worse to worry about than a lecture
from her parents. But if she's gotten herself in trouble,
time could be precious."

"Exactly the point," said Roosevelt. "Did she give anyone any clue where she was going?"

"She told people she was going out to visit Miss Oakley. But her father has a notion she's decided to solve

our murder mystery all by herself," I said. "Yesterday afternoon, she was accusing her father of frightening off the witnesses. It was pretty clear she thought that Zach'ry or Joe Fox would respond better to questions from a pretty girl than from a cranky old man."

Roosevelt gave a low whistle. "That's a dubious proposition if ever I heard one," he said. "So you think she went looking for them?"

"That's my best guess," I said. "Mr. Clemens will take the area near the hotel, and he's going to ask the hotel staff and the sheriff's people to help search. I think you and I ought to do a quick sweep through the cowboy saloons, to begin with—I think that's where she'd go looking for C. D. or Zach'ry. What say I take the ones out on the north side of town, and you can take the ones down along Missoula Street. If we don't find her, let's say we meet back at the Florence House at ten o'clock— that ought to be enough time—and decide on the next step. And if one of us *does* find her, we can leave a message for the other at the hotel desk."

"Good plan," said Roosevelt. "Just one refinement: If one of us gets a lead we can't ignore, let's send a message back there for the other—with enough detail to let the other follow our steps, if necessary. That way there won't be two missing persons to worry about."

"Yes, that's something I hadn't thought of," I said. "Fine, let's see if we can turn up Miss Clara. And I hope to God she hasn't come to any harm."

"If she's come to harm, I'd surely hate to be the one who caused it," said Roosevelt. "Clemens may be a peaceful man on general principles, but I think if anyone touched one of his daughters, he'd tear the fellow limb from limb."

"And then he'd really get angry," I agreed. "Let's just make sure it doesn't come to that."

"Hold on a moment," said Roosevelt. "I've got a spare revolver in my room. I think you ought to take it tonight."

"You must be joking," I said. "I have almost no experience with guns. If I were carrying one, I'd be lucky not to kill myself with it."

Roosevelt shook his head. "A shame you haven't learned to use one. Knowing how to shoot well isn't something you need very often—at least, one hopes not. But just as with swimming, when you do need it there's no substitute. I'm tempted to give you the revolver anyway, just in case you get in a pinch there's no other way out of."

"I'm still going to decline," I said. "I'm not sure I could fire it if it came to the crisis, and one thing I've learned is that showing a weapon you aren't ready to use is likely to put you in more danger than if you're unarmed. Our suspects are almost certainly armed, and they're probably not reluctant to use *their* weapons. Better not to give them cause."

"Very well, then," said Roosevelt resignedly. "I don't entirely agree, but I won't insist that you carry one against your better judgment. I'll tell you what, though— if we get a chance, before you leave town, I'll be glad to give you a few shooting lessons. It's not just a useful skill; I think you'd get a good deal of enjoyment from learning to shoot well."

"Possibly," I said. Then I smiled. "I suspect I'd find Annie Oakley a more pleasant instructor," I said. Roosevelt frowned, but I cut him off before he could reply. "Since she hasn't shown the slightest interest in giving me lessons, perhaps I'll take you up on your kind offer, if the opportunity arises. But tonight we have urgent business to attend to. Shall we get started?"

He flashed one of his toothy grins and said, "Yes, let's. *Boot, saddle, to horse, and away!*"

I looked at him. "I hope we won't have to ride," I said. "That's another skill I've never picked up more than the rudiments of."

" 'Ah, don't they teach you poor chaps anything at Yale?' " said Roosevelt. His grin was now mischievous.

"I don't mean riding," he explained. "I was quoting a line of Browning."

"I see," I said. "Well, there, at least, I should hope the cowboys won't have me at a disadvantage. I haven't heard a single one of them quote poetry at me. But we can talk about literature another time—let's go find Miss Clara."

He said nothing more, but slapped me on the back. We strode together out the door into the Montana night.

My first stop was Mike Thompson's saloon, where Lil, the hostess, had supplied Zach'ry with his alibi for the night of the killing. As a known haunt of both the victim and his cohorts, it was a likely place for Clara to go looking for information—assuming she had overheard our previous discussions of the investigation. That, unfortunately, remained an unknown factor; none of us really knew how much information Miss Clemens had on the suspects, or on the case in general.

As before, the place was full of noise and smoke when I walked in. The little orchestra—it seemed to be the same four players as before—was playing an out-of-tune version of "Red Wing" this time, but there were still no dancers in evidence. I stopped for a second to survey the room, but saw no sign of Clara. Dressed as she usually was, she would certainly have been noticeable in this crowd. Satisfied that she wasn't in sight, I went over to the bar to see if anyone there remembered seeing her earlier in the day.

Mike Thompson was not on duty behind the bar, but his red-haired assistant Andy was. I caught the bartender's eye and flashed a silver dollar; he nodded, threw his towel over his shoulder, and sidled over to me. "What'll it be, boss?" he asked.

"Give me a short beer, and keep the change," I said, plunking the dollar on the counter. He grinned and went to draw the beer. When he returned I said, "I'm looking for a young lady."

"Well, let's see," he said. "Lil won't be in until eight, but Connic's here, and—"

"No, I mean a specific young lady," I said. "She'd be about five feet two, maybe twenty years old, dark haired, wearing a full dark skirt, a white blouse with a bow at the throat, and a straw hat . . ." I went on to give the best description I could of Miss Clemens and the outfit she'd been wearing that afternoon.

The bartender shook his head. "She ain't been in here since I come on, about an hour ago," he said. "If she was in here before then, Mike might have seen her. He's out having supper, before the crowd comes in, but he ought to be back directly. You wait a bit and you can ask him when he gets back."

"Thanks, Andy," I said. "I think I will wait."

I turned around and leaned back against the bar, idly surveying the customers. They seemed to be very much the same crowd as on my previous visits, although I didn't recognize individual faces. Or . . . *Wait a minute!*

I stood up straighter and peered through the cloud of tobacco smoke. There, at one of the tables, nursing a beer and holding a hand of cards, was none other than Jed Harrington's partner in crime Zach'ry, who'd been all but invisible ever since the day he tried to rob me in an alleyway. He was facing slightly away from me, his gaze on the other men in the game with him, but it was unmistakably him.

I hadn't come in here looking for Zach'ry, but I could hardly let this unexpected opportunity pass. I took a sip of my beer, trying to decide the best way to handle the situation. He would hardly take kindly to being called away from his game. On the other hand, with finding Clara Clemens as my primary goal, I could ill afford to wait for him to leave the table. Unless the cards went against him and he lost his entire stake, he might well sit at the table all night.

Zach'ry took two cards out of his hand and discarded them. The dealer gave him two more, and I saw a sly grin come over the cowboy's face as he spread the cards to examine them. The other players looked at their cards, and a round of wagering began. From this distance, with all the noise in the room, I couldn't hear the players' comments, but it was clear that Zach'ry thought his hand was a winner. He shoved a bet into the center, and the player to his left—a man with glasses and a dark mustache—immediately threw down his cards with a disgusted expression.

The next player, a big man with long hair and a full beard, scowled at the cards, then shoved his own bet into the pot. Another man, red-faced with an unkempt fringe of gray hair around a balding pate, joined the betting, and two more threw down their cards. Now the betting had come back to Zach'ry, and he shoved another pile of silver—it looked like at least five dollars—into the center. The big man matched him again, and the third player added his share once more, tossing an even bigger handful of coins into the pot. By now, a group of spectators had gathered around the table, sensing what must be a high-stakes game, at least for this workingman's saloon.

Once more, Zach'ry made his bet, and the other two matched it. Now the betting was done; the big man sneered and showed his cards. The red-faced fellow's face fell, and he dropped his hand on the table. But Zach'ry leaned forward and slapped his cards onto the table, face up. With a predatory grin, he began to gather in the money.

The big man let out an enraged bellow I could hear even over the noise in the bar. "You son of a bitch, you cheated me!" He stood up, towering over the table. His fists were balled, and his face was a mask of rage.

Zach'ry leaned back in his chair, looking coolly up at his opponent. Now the saloon had suddenly grown quiet. (Even the musicians cast their gazes toward the disturbance, although they kept plugging away at the dance tune they were attempting to play.) So I could hear

Zach'ry's reply quite clearly. "Larry, this ain't a game for little boys. Don't play if you can't lose like a man." He continued to scoop up the money.

Larry's eyes blazed, and I thought for a moment he was going to attack Zach'ry. But then he snatched up the small pile of money on the table in front of his seat and stomped away with a curse. A sigh of relief—or perhaps of disappointment at not seeing a fight—went through the spectators, and Zach'ry allowed himself a smirk. "There's an empty seat," he said. "Anybody else want to play?"

One of the spectators, a thin man with a beakish nose and an earnest expression, slid into the vacant seat, and the dealer began shuffling again. The moment of tension seemed to have passed, and the murmur of voices in the room returned to its more usual level. The four musicians had shifted into "A Hot Time in the Old Town Tonight," which somehow seemed an appropriate choice.

I still hadn't settled on the best way to approach Zach'ry. He was obviously winning, and would likely resent any interruption of his lucky streak. Worse, he had already shown a decided unwillingness to talk with anyone about Jed Harrington's murder. And while he apparently had an alibi for the time of the killing, it wasn't at all clear how well it might hold up under questioning. To complicate things further, I still had to consider finding Clara my first priority. So whatever action I was going to take, it had to be taken soon.

I beckoned Andy, the bartender, over. The large tip had done its business; he was there in less than a minute. "What's your pleasure, boss?" he asked.

"Is there a public telephone in the neighborhood?" I asked.

"A what?" he asked in the tone he might have used in response to a customer requesting a glass of Chateau D'Yquem. I had been afraid that would be the answer. Had there been a phone within a block or so, I could have tried to call the jail to tell Mr. Clemens that I'd found the cowboy we'd been looking for. I'd seen a phone in the sheriff's offices, although I had no guarantee that Mr. Clemens would still be there.

"Never mind that," I said. "Are there any local boys I can trust to deliver a message for me? I need to send something to my boss, and I'm willing to pay."

He nodded. "Let me see if little Willie's here," he said, and went into the back room behind the bar. A few minutes later, he emerged with an urchin in tow—perhaps a ten-year-old, I estimated. "Willie, this man has a job for you," he said, and left the boy with me while he went to sell more drinks.

"Willie, do you know where the sheriff's office is?" I asked.

"Yeah, I know," he said. I wondered if it was my appearance or something I'd said that made him stare at me.

I took out my pocket notebook and said, "I'm going to write a note, and I want you to take it there and give it to Mr. Clemens." (Here I added a description of my employer.) "If he's not there, he'll be at the Florence House Hotel. Do you know where that is?"

"Yeah," he said, nodding. "It'll cost you a quarter."

"I'll give you a quarter now, and when Mr. Clemens gets the note, he'll give you another," I said. "But it has to be delivered quickly, and you're to put it in his hands only. Do you understand?"

"Sure, I can do that," he said. "For fifty cents, I'd take it all the way to Idaho."

"I'm hoping that won't be necessary," I said. I verified that my pencil had a workable point, and began to think about the wording of the note. But I had barely gotten past "Clemens—Zach'ry playing cards in Thompson's saloon" when some intuition made me turn and look toward the table where the cowboy sat.

To my horror, Larry, the big man who'd accused Zach'ry of cheating, had returned from wherever he'd gone and was standing a short distance behind the cowboy. In his hand was a large hunting knife, apparently invisible to those at the table. Even as I watched, he lifted his hand and began to edge forward.

I leapt into action, not really thinking about the possible consequences. I grabbed the nearest beer stein off the bar behind me, and in three quick steps I was close enough to swing it with all my might at the back of Larry's head. Beer sprayed in every direction as he staggered from the blow, and then I grabbed the hand with the knife and held on for everything I was worth.

"Yee-hah! Ride him, dude!" came a raucous voice from behind me, and then I was in one of the most desperate struggles of my life. Larry must have outweighed me by fifty pounds, and even though much of it was in his gut, I was at a serious disadvantage on account of having to keep the blade from coming into play.

I tried to twist the arm, hoping to make him drop his weapon. He let out a roar and tried to break loose, jerking like a horse with a burr under its saddle. Belatedly, I realized that he was probably a good bit stronger than I was; worse yet, the longer we wrestled, the more likely his greater weight would tip the balance against me. Unless I could settle things quickly, I was likely to regret jumping in.

I let go of his wrist with one hand and drove a punch toward his adam's apple, but he ducked his chin and blocked it, and tried to bull me backwards. I barely managed to keep my balance, slipping on the beer-covered floor, but I did recover my grip on his arm. Now I threw a kick at his kneecap, hoping to bring him down so I could break away without exposing myself to the knife. Again he dodged my attack, and began to exert his strength to overpower me. The knife hand drew upward, against all my efforts to hold it, and I could see that I would soon be forced to devote all my efforts to avoid being slashed.

Then, suddenly, his eyes rolled upward and his arm went limp, sending the knife clattering to the floor. I kept my grip on his wrist and managed to kick the knife away under one of the tables. Then, at last, I let go of his wrist and stepped quickly back as he slumped down, unconscious. Only then did I see the bar owner, Mike Thompson, standing there with a two-foot length of billiard cue. "You want to take up bear rasslin', you ought to start with the little ones," he said with a crooked smile. "Or at least the ones with shorter claws."

"I'll remember that next time," I said. "Unfortunately, this one didn't give me any choice. If I hadn't stopped him, he'd like to have killed a man I need to talk to."

"Who's that?" said Thompson.

"Why, that fellow," I said, turning to point to the seat where Zach'ry had been sitting. But the cowboy I had fought so hard to save from the man with the knife was nowhere to be seen.

18

Naturally, in the excitement of watching my struggle with the knife-wielding Larry, nobody at Mike Thompson's saloon appeared to have noticed when—or in what direction—Zach'ry had made his departure. I suppose I should have been gratified that several of the spectators were ready to buy me a drink as reward for my involuntarily providing part of the night's entertainment, but my search for Clara Clemens prevented me from accepting their hospitality.

Similarly, Mike Thompson, who had come to *my* rescue, had no useful information to contribute to my search. If Clara Clemens had entered the saloon while he was present, he would undoubtedly have noticed her—I got the distinct impression that a respectably dressed young woman's arrival at his establishment without escort was about as common as an appearance of Halley's Comet. So after all my efforts, I had to leave the saloon not only tousled from my fight with Larry, but without accomplishing either of my objectives. Before leaving, I gave a quarter to young Willie, the boy I'd asked to deliver a message to Mr. Clemens. I had the distinct impression he would have considered himself repaid just by watching the fight, which had made his mission superfluous after Zach'ry's disappearance. But promises are important to a boy that age, and I had no compunction about paying.

As I reached the sidewalk in front of the saloon I paused, trying to decide which of the cowboy watering holes to visit next. I couldn't have been there more than a few seconds when a pleasant voice came to my attention. "Hello, big fellow. Come back to see what you missed?" It was Liz, the dancing hostess who'd given Zach'ry his alibi.

"Good evening," I said. "No, I came back looking for a friend—my boss's daughter, in fact."

"And did you find her?" Was there an edge in her voice? There was still light enough to see her face, but her expression told me nothing.

"Not here, no," I said. "I did run across a friend of yours, but he couldn't wait to talk to me."

"What do you mean, mister?" she said a bit sharply. Now I could see she was frowning.

I told her, briefly, about seeing Zach'ry playing cards, about the fight with Larry, and how Zach'ry had disappeared before I could speak to him. She listened impassively, then when I was done, said, "You should've let Larry carve him up. That skunk wasn't worth the saving."

"I'm surprised to hear you say that," I said. "I thought you and he were on good terms."

"I thought so, too," she said, pouting. Suddenly her face looked much younger, and I wondered if I had guessed her age wrong. "But he lied to me, and played a mean trick on me. I don't ever want to see him again."

This sounded interesting. "I'm sorry to hear that. What kind of mean trick did he play?" I asked.

"He got me in trouble, and he cost me money," said Lil. "When I found out about it, and told him I didn't like it, he laughed at me for believing him. He called me names in front of a lot of people. I don't like being made fun of. He's lucky he wasn't still here when I came in, or I'd have done worse to him than Larry did."

"I'm not sure I understand," I said. "How did he get you in trouble?"

She put her hands on her hips and looked up at me. "Why should I tell you? What business is it of yours?"

A pair of cowboys walked by us into the saloon, ogling Lil. "Hey, honey," one of them said. "Don't pay no attention to that dude. Come on inside and have a drink with me."

"I'll be there in a minute, sweetie," said Lil, smiling at the man. "I'm just talking to this fellow for a minute. I'll come looking for you." Then she turned back to me and said, "If I tell you what happened, are you going to laugh at me?"

"Of course I won't laugh at you," I said. "In fact, I think you might be able to help me—and more important than that, you might help an innocent man clear himself of a murder charge."

A skeptical expression came across her face. "I don't know whether to believe that or not," she said. "A lot of people think I'm stupid. They tell me things that aren't true, and laugh at me for believing them."

"It's absolutely true," I said, raising my right hand as if taking an oath. "A man's life might depend on it."

"I don't know," she said, frowning. "It's a long story, and I have to get to work." She looked over her shoulder, through the door where the two cowboys had gone. The tip of her tongue came out between her lips for a brief instant before she turned back and looked at me.

"I know you have to work, and I have to go search for Miss Clemens," I said. "Just tell me what kind of trouble you got in. I promise that nobody will laugh at you."

She looked at me a long moment, doubt in her eyes. Then she said, almost inaudibly, "He acted like he was too drunk to walk, and he passed out in my room. There wasn't anybody to help me move him, and I didn't really want to throw him out on the street. So I had to share a room with another girl, and that meant we both made less money than we were supposed to. The boss didn't like that, and he yelled at me for letting it happen."

"That's too bad," I said. "But do you mean he wasn't really drunk?"

"That's what he told me last night," she said. "He said he just wanted to lay down and rest, and my bed was right handy. And when I told him I'd gotten in trouble, he just laughed at me and called me a stupid whore. If I see him again, I'll scratch his eyes out."

Liz's story was a useful revelation. I wasn't quite certain of its importance—although it did mean that Zach'ry's alibi was even weaker than it had appeared. Now it looked as if he might have been able to sneak out of the saloon while everyone thought he was passed out upstairs. That still didn't mean he had killed Harrington—just that he had a better opportunity than we'd been led to believe. I would have to follow it up once my current mission was complete.

I visited three other saloons but found no one who admitted seeing Clara Clemens in any of them. It seemed unlikely she had been to any of them and gone unnoticed, and less likely still that anybody had reason to say she hadn't been there if she actually had—although I wouldn't have put it beyond her to ask the bartenders to deny having seen her, if she wanted to cover her trail. If she had thought to do that, my task would be all the more difficult.

I emerged from the fourth saloon on my list feeling slightly tipsy, although I had confined myself to short beers, and one only at each of the establishments where I had made my inquiries. My major positive accomplishment was avoiding any more fights, which was not necessarily as easy as it sounds, given my size, my accent, and my citified attire. I took a deep breath—it was good to get a mouthful of air not tainted with tobacco smoke— and looked around, trying to decide where I would go next. I realized that I was only a short distance from where Jed Harrington had been shot. Quite possibly this had been the last bar where they had been drinking before the murder. Where, then, were they likely to have been heading if the way there led them past the spot where the shooting took place?

I tried to recreate a map of the town in my head, but perhaps because of the beers I'd drunk I couldn't quite visualize the neighborhood I was in. Not far from where the shots had been fired were the barber shop where I'd seen Joe Fox walk by and the store where the Indian had bought his tobacco. Then I remembered Mrs. Larson, who lived less than a block from the murder site, and who claimed to have heard the shots. From where I stood, the little house she lived in was around a corner and down the side street. I wondered if perhaps Clara Clemens might have taken it in her head to visit her. Close as I was, I decided that a visit was in order. It was still reasonably light out, so odds were the washerwoman would still be awake unless luck was completely against me tonight.

It was no more than two or three minutes' walk to Mrs. Larson's doorstep. I knocked softly, not wanting to disturb her if she'd already retired. But a moment later, the door opened a crack and she asked, "Who is there?"

"My name is Wentworth Cabot, Mrs. Larson," I said. "Perhaps you remember me—I was here just yesterday, with my employer. Do you have a minute to talk?"

"I remember you," she said, opening the door a bit further. "What do you want, mister?"

"My employer's daughter Clara is missing—a young woman a bit younger than I am." I described Clara as best I could and asked, "Have you by any chance seen her?"

"I saw her," said Mrs. Larson, nodding, and she opened the door further. She stuck her head out and looked down the street both ways, then said, "Come inside, and I tell you."

I stepped into the front room of the little house. Evidently Mrs. Larson had been working late; there was a man's shirt on the ironing board, and two irons on the stove. Or perhaps this was a normal working hour for her; I realized I had no idea what her daily life must be like. She went halfway to the ironing board, then turned and looked at me.

"Tell me where you saw Miss Clemens, and when," I said. "Her mother and father are very worried about her."

"Three or four hours ago, she came here," said Mrs. Larson. "It was before I eat. She wanted to know what I saw and heard that night the man was killed."

"And what did you tell her?"

"The same as I tell you and your boss," she said with a shrug. "It's the truth; what else is there to tell?"

"That's usually enough," I said. "Is that all that happened? You answered her questions and she went away?"

"I answered her questions, yes," said the woman. She walked over to the ironing board and began to fold the shirt, then looked back at me and added, "But she asked some questions you didn't ask. You want to know what they were, and what I told her?"

"Yes, that might help us find her," I said. "What else did she want to know?"

"She asked about a man who comes to this part of town sometimes," she said. "An Indian who scouts for the Army."

"Joe Fox," I said. She was right; Mr. Clemens and I hadn't even thought to ask her about him, although he was the one who had given us her name.

"Yes, that's the one," she said. She pointed to the washtub sitting on the floor nearby. "I wash his clothes sometimes. I don't tell most people that because some of them don't want their clothes washed in the same place as an Indian's. Me, I think dirt is dirt, and money is money. I wash an Indian's, or a colored man's clothes, if he brings them here. I don't mind telling you because you don't live here. You'll go away soon, and won't tell nobody what I say."

"What did Clara want to know about Joe Fox?" I asked. Oscar the cat had come into the room, and he stood looking at me with his big kittenish eyes, then went bouncing across the room to rub against his mistress's ankles.

"She wants to know if I see him the day of the murder," she said, reaching down to pick up the kitten. She rubbed him behind the ears, then said, "I tell her I don't think so, but it's not something I'd remember. He isn't so special that I remember every time I see him. Then she asks whether I know where he lives."

"We didn't even think to ask you that," I said ruefully. "What did you tell her?"

"The truth—I don't know," said Mrs. Larson. "I think he has a place to stay out at the fort, but there's some reason he comes in here, too. Not just for the washing, either; I see him in the stores sometimes, or just walking down the street. Maybe he visits somebody here." She put the kitten down and went back to folding the shirt.

"I see," I said. That was worth knowing, although where it led was far from obvious at present. It *would* be especially useful to know whether he had been in town the day of the shooting. He had already said enough to make it clear that he might nurture a grudge against Jed Harrington. Whether that grudge had grown to the point of murder was impossible to say; but one thing I could do was determine whether anyone had seen him in town that day. That suggested another line of investigation.

"Can you tell me which stores you've seen him in?" I asked. "One of them might remember whether or not he was around here the day of the shooting."

"I see him buy tobacco sometimes in Ed Potter's general store," she said. "That's across the street, that way." She pointed to the right—the direction in which the victim had been standing when he was shot.

"Will he be open this time of night?" I asked. It had finally begun to turn dark outside, and by my best estimate it must be nearly nine o'clock.

"Ed stays open when he wants to and closes when he wants to," said Mrs. Larson. "I think he stays open so he can talk to people. His wife, she died two years ago. Now he just stays in the store a lot. Go see—tell him I sent you, and maybe he tells you things he wouldn't tell some stranger." She put the folded shirt with a pile of others, and took another one out of a basket on the floor. She draped it over the ironing board, then said, "And good luck finding your Miss Clara. She's a smart young lady, that one."

"Thank you, Mrs. Larson," I said. "I appreciate all your help." Oscar tried to follow me out the door, so I picked him up and handed him back to his mistress. He almost immediately began to purr, so loud that I could still hear it when I closed the door behind me.

Ed Potter's store was exactly where Mrs. Larson had said. I never would have noticed the place unless I had specific business there, but there was a light visible through the open front door, which was all the invitation I needed. I walked in to find a cluttered general store not much different from little country stores I had seen in my native New England, and indeed at many other locations around the country.

The single electric bulb showed barrels and baskets strewn around the floor, crackers and candies in glass-lidded bins, shelves lined with everything from soap powder to gunshells to dime novels, and a long counter the whole width of the back of the store. Behind the jars of pickled pigs' feet, boxes of cigars, and canisters of pipe tobacco, a slate on the wall listed the prices of a few choice commodities.

As I was absorbing the barrage of colors and odors, a dry voice to my left asked, "Can I help you, stranger?"

I turned to look for the source of the voice. There I discovered, in an ancient rocking chair, a lean fellow with a long face framed by abundant side whiskers. On his head, in spite of the lingering summer heat, was a battered slouch hat. He had his thumbs tucked underneath his suspenders, and a short-stemmed corncob pipe (which appeared at the present moment to be unlit) in his mouth.

"Mrs. Larson tells me I should talk to Ed Potter," I said. "Are you he?"

"I'm him," said the fellow, mumbling around his pipe. "How's Jenny doin'?"

"Very well, as far as I can see," I said. "She seems to have plenty of work, in any case."

"Well, good for her," said Potter. "Bad for those as'd like to see a bit more of her, but good for her. You don't happen to play checkers, do you?"

I noticed a board set up on top of a salt barrel next to the rocking chair. One of the black pieces had been replaced by a small lump of coal. "I've played some," I said. "It's not really my game—I'm better at chess."

"Chess." He sniffed. "Never could get the hang of that, with all them kings and queens and jacks on the board. Now, checkers, that's a good old American game. Set down and let's play a spell, and we can talk while we play."

"All right," I said. "I'll warn you—it's been years since I've played. You'll probably make short work of me."

"Don't matter," said Potter. "You take the black men and go first."

I sat down on an upended box next to the board and shifted it so I could comfortably reach the pieces. We each took a moment to adjust our pieces on their proper squares, then I slid one of the men in my front row forward to begin the game.

"Huh," he said, squinting at my move. Then he slid forward a piece on the other side of the board, more or less mirroring the move I'd made, and looked up at me. "What's Jenny think I know that she sent you to talk to me?"

"There's a fellow named Joe Fox who shops in here,"

I said. I looked up from the board to judge how he reacted to the name.

His face was neutral. "Injun," he said. "Buys chewin' tobacco, mostly. A little candy now and then."

"Yes, he's an Indian scout for the Army," I said. I pushed forward another man on the checker board, threatening the piece he'd just moved. "Do you remember whether he was in here on Monday?"

Potter looked up from the board. "That the same day Jed Harrington got ventilated?"

"Yes, that same day," I said. "My employer and I are trying to find witnesses to the shooting."

"What you need that for?" asked Potter. He moved a man to back up the piece I was challenging. "You gonna give a medal to the shooter?"

"From what I understand, a lot of people in these parts would support that," I said. "But no. The man they've arrested is a friend, and we're trying to help him build a defense."

"Uh-huh," he said. He thought for a minute, then said, "You think the Injun done it, do you?"

"We don't know who did it," I said. "We're trying to find witnesses, people who might have had a motive, people who had the opportunity to kill him . . ."

"Uh-huh," he said again. Then he pointed at the board. "You can keep playin' while you talk, you know."

"Oh," I said. "Yes." I moved another man, then said, "So, do you remember if Joe Fox was in town that day?"

"Can't rightly say I do," said Potter. "He don't come in the store every time he's in town, so he might've been here without me seeing him—or maybe he was and I just don't recollect it."

"I see," I said. We played a few more moves on the board, although I was starting to regret having begun the game. It would be the height of rudeness to break it off unfinished, but it seemed clear that the storekeeper knew nothing useful.

Thus distracted, I moved one of my men to where it

set up a double jump. Potter removed my pieces, then said, "You can't play right if you don't keep your mind on the game. I reckon that killin' has you worried."

"Yes, it does," I said. "That, and the fact that Mr. Clemens's daughter is missing. I need to go back and report to him—possibly she's come home by now."

"Young dark-haired lady with a straw hat?" he asked.

"Yes," I said. "Did you see her today?" I mentally kicked myself; I had almost forgotten her in the quest for information on the murder.

Potter peered up at me. "Sure, Jenny Larson sent her here, too. Name's Clara, I seem to recall—right sharp little lady." He pointed to the board again. "Your move."

I looked at my pieces and saw a jump for one of my men, so I moved it and took his from the board. "What did you and Clara talk about?" I asked.

"Well, she wanted to know about Joe Fox, too," he said. "And she wanted to know how much of the shootin' I saw and heard."

"Were you here when it happened?" I blurted. That possibility hadn't occurred to me. Of course, by now it was no surprise to me that Clara had gotten there ahead of me, or that she had thought to ask it.

"Sure, I live in the back room," he said. "No point paying rent twice, says I."

"No, of course not," I said. "Did the shooting wake you up?"

"Nope," he said. He made a move blocking one of my men, then added, "Couldn't sleep on account of the heat. So I was settin' out here rockin', and smoking my pipe. Saw them three fellows go by just before the shot."

"Three fellows?"

"That's right," said Potter. "They gone up Second Street together, laughing and staggering like they'd been drinking. Then after a bit, I heard a shot. Went to look out the window, and down by the light was one fellow lying on the ground—that was Jed, I reckon—fat enough, anyway. One of the other fellows was kneeling near him.

After a while, the deputies came, and that was that."

"I see," I said, my mind suddenly far away from the game of checkers. I stared at the board, trying to make sense out of what I'd just heard.

"Your move," he said after a while. Mechanically, I reached down and moved one of my men. It was only when he jumped it that I saw how I'd opened up my position. The rest of the game went rather quickly—and, if I had been at all serious about it, embarrassingly for me. But by that point, I had much more pressing issues to consider.

⤚ **19**

I left Potter's store in a state of confusion. I still couldn't assess the significance of Potter's report of seeing an unknown third person with Harrington and C. D. just before the shooting. Was this the person who had shot Harrington? Or did he leave the group before the shooting? Neither possibility jibed with what C. D. had told Mr. Clemens. In fact, he hadn't mentioned a third party at all, and Potter's inability to supply the person's identity was no help—though I had an idea who it might have been. Still, perhaps Potter had miscounted, or assumed that someone merely going in the same direction as Harrington was part of his group. And, I realized, with all this fresh confusion, I still had no better idea than before where Clara Clemens might have gone.

My most logical course of action at this point was to get back to Mr. Clemens and report what I had learned. Together, we might be able to puzzle out what had happened. By now, Roosevelt might have returned, too. And if luck had decided to favor us, Clara would be home— possibly with clues none of the rest of us had uncovered. At least, I hoped she was home; until we knew that my employer's daughter was safe, it would be difficult to make any real progress in our murder investigation.

Mr. Clemens had promised to meet me either at the sheriff's office or back at the hotel. I was closer to the former, so I headed toward the center of town. And, as it happened, the most direct route took me back past Mike Thompson's saloon. Given my experiences earlier in the evening, I had no particular desire to set foot in the place again. Indeed, considering that I had nearly been robbed in that same neighborhood, avoiding the place entirely might even have been prudent—especially after dark. But I was in a hurry, and had no real desire to lengthen the distance between me and my employer. Walking past the saloon on the opposite side of the street was quite sufficient, as far as I was concerned.

A few doors away from Thompson's I noticed a row of bicycles along the sidewalk in front of another saloon, mingled with a few horses and a buckboard hitched nearby. It was easy enough to deduce that some of the soldiers from the 27th Infantry had come to town for a drink. I wondered briefly how well they'd be able to navigate their bikes in the dark going home, especially with a few drinks under their belts. But then I realized that even with the sun down there was light in the sky, and a peek over my shoulder verified what I had guessed: A nearly full moon was beginning to rise over the eastern edge of town. As long as the clouds stayed away, the soldiers would have reasonable light to find their way home by curfew, whenever that was. Aside from having seen them go through their drill for Mr. Clemens and his family, I had very little idea what sort of discipline these troops were subjected to. For all I knew, they had sneaked away from the fort to have a drink, and planned to return as surreptitiously as they had left.

That thought jogged my memory. C. D. had claimed that, on the night of the murder, Jed Harrington had gotten into some kind of argument with a soldier—a sergeant, he had said. And this morning I'd learned that

Sergeant Johnson was the soldier in question. I'd reported as much to Mr. Clemens and Mr. Roosevelt, but I had the impression they had decided to dismiss it as irrelevant. Still, it might be worth my trouble to follow up that lead; Sergeant Johnson had claimed there'd been nothing more than words exchanged, but there was no guarantee that he was telling the truth. But for now, learning whether Clara had returned safely to the hotel was more important than investigating what might be just another dead end.

A couple of blocks away I nearly collided with Mr. Roosevelt bustling around a corner. He grabbed me and flashed his wide grin. "Hello, old man. Have you had any luck finding Miss Clemens?" he boomed.

"Not really," I said. "From the fact that you're asking, I take it you haven't, either."

"None at all, unless you count finding half a dozen people she talked to," said Roosevelt. "The young lady leaves an impression, I'll say that much."

"One would expect as much," I said, nodding. "Well, let's go see if Mr. Clemens has any better news than we have. Perhaps our efforts have been unnecessary, which would be the best news I could get."

"Yes, I agree entirely," said Roosevelt. "If the young lady's come home on her own, I won't begrudge this evening's work at all."

But when we entered the sheriff's office, one glance at my employer's face was all it took to tell me that if there was any news at all about his daughter Clara, it could not be good.

"I've talked to a good two dozen people, and been back and forth between here and the hotel twice," said Mr. Clemens, looking as worried as I'd ever seen him. "No word from or about Clara. She'd never been to Cody's of course. I don't know what to make of it."

Mr. Roosevelt and I had already told him what we knew, which amounted to the fact that Clara had gone through parts of the saloon district asking questions about the murder. She had also been to the scene of the killing, and had talked to at least two people who had been there at the time of the murder. But where she had gone next, none of us seemed to know. The best bet was that she appeared to be trying to locate Joe Fox, the Indian scout who appeared to live in the same neighborhood as Jenny Larson and Ed Potter.

"Someone at the fort must know where in town Joe Fox stays," said Mr. Roosevelt. "I'd be willing to ride out there. I suspect I can convince whoever's on duty to give me that information, if I tell him what's involved."

"I wish this damned town had more telephones," said Mr. Clemens. He crushed out a cigar; he'd barely smoked a quarter of it. To me, there was no clearer sign of his agitation. "It'd make some of this running back and forth a lot easier," he continued. "A fellow gets used to a certain level of civilization, and it's no easy adjustment to go back to the way things were before."

"True enough," said Roosevelt. "Even when the civilized way is brand new, and everyone else throughout history took the old way for granted. But we just have to make the best of it. Shall I get on my horse or not?"

"You might as well," said Mr. Clemens, standing up. "It would be just like Clara to drive out there herself, if she thought it would show her poor old father that he ain't as smart as he thinks. The only thing I can't understand is why she's taking so long, unless she's run into trouble."

"All right, I'll head straight out there, and come back as soon as I can with any news," said Roosevelt.

"Wait just a moment," I said, remembering something I'd heard. "The sheriff, or his deputies, may know more about Fox than anyone else we've talked to. The barber I talked to the other day said that one of the deputies— I think his name is Al—comes in his shop, so he must know that neighborhood. Let's see if that fellow is on duty tonight. Perhaps we can get an answer right away, and save you a ride."

Al, as it turned out, was out patrolling the streets, most likely in the saloon district, that being the part of town where trouble was most likely to crop up this time of night—or at any other time, if my experience was symptomatic. While there was no guarantee of finding him in any specific place, a search for him was likely to yield an answer to our query more quickly than an expedition out to the fort and back.

In any case, Mr. Clemens was tired. Even if the sheriff had not begun to make it obvious that my employer was an impediment to his business, there was little point in his waiting around the jailhouse any longer. So it was easy enough for Roosevelt and me to convince Mr. Clemens to let us take him back to the hotel for the night; he could supervise the search as easily from there as anywhere. Then Roosevelt and I would go out together in search of the deputy. If we didn't turn him up before midnight, one of us would check back here around then, when Al and his partner were due to come off duty.

"I'm not going to have much luck sleeping," said Mr. Clemens as we stepped out into the moonlit streets. "I wish you boys would let me come along—I'll be a lot happier doing something out on the streets than I will be sitting around the hotel room."

"Undoubtedly," said Roosevelt. "But there's one thing you can do back there that none of us can, which is to stay with your wife and try to calm her down."

Mr. Clemens snorted. "Calm her down? Haven't you noticed I'm about to break out in hives from all the worry?"

"Well, then, the two of you can calm each other down," I said. "You'll know you've got the two of us out working on finding Clara, and the sheriff's office knows she's missing, too. There's not much more you can do beyond enlisting the Army in the search . . ."

"That's not an entirely bad idea," said Roosevelt. "If

we haven't found her by morning, I'll go out to the fort
and see if Colonel Burt can spare some of his men to
help us."

"I hope it doesn't come to that," said Mr. Clemens.
"Maybe she'll be at the hotel. I hope to God she's there.
I'll never forgive myself if anything's happened to her . . .
If I hadn't gone off playing detective again, she'd never
have gotten into trouble. Damn me, this ought to cure
me for good."

"If you weren't playing detective, your oldest friend
would be facing a trumped-up murder charge with nobody to help him clear himself," I pointed out. "It would
be a poor friend who wouldn't help a man in those circumstances. And you had no way of knowing she'd in-
volve herself in the case."

"I suppose you're right," said Mr. Clemens, although
I could see he wasn't entirely convinced. "I reckon . . .
What the hell was *that*?"

Before I could attempt an answer, one was provided
in the form of a buckboard careening around the nearby
corner from the direction of Mike Thompson's saloon. It
was upon us in a flash, and all three of us were forced
to jump to one side to avoid the hooves and wheels. In
that moment, I clearly saw the driver: C. D. held the
reins, driving as if his life depended on it. Right behind
him was another familiar figure: Zach'ry. But what really
riveted my attention was the slender figure whose arm he
held. She was standing up as if about to throw herself
over the side. Her face was turned away, but there could
be no other young woman in Missoula wearing a Paris-
made dress and straw hat. It was Clara Clemens, and she
was in the hands of our two prime murder suspects!

"Stop, you scoundrels!" shouted Mr. Roosevelt. He
had seen it, too. "Damnation, my horse is halfway across
town!"

"There's no time for a horse," I said. I ran quickly
around the corner to the front of the saloons, took the

first Army bicycle I found, and sped off in pursuit. As I passed Roosevelt and Mr. Clemens, both puffing along the street, I shouted, "Tell the soldiers I've borrowed a bike to catch a murderer! And tell the sheriff I'm going to follow them. Follow me and bring help."

I was going too fast and paying too much attention to the buckboard, still visible in the bright moonlight perhaps a hundred yards away, to hear exactly what Mr. Clemens shouted back at me, but I am fairly sure he used the word "crazy" at least once. If I'd had time to reflect, I probably would have agreed with him. Odds were the men I was chasing were armed, and even if they weren't, they had me outnumbered. What I would do if I caught up with them was a question I willingly postponed until I had to deal with it. For now, I had more than enough to worry about, just trying to keep the buckboard in sight.

Luckily for me, C. D. evidently decided there was no particular need for haste once he was beyond the outskirts of town. About a quarter-mile past the campgrounds of Cody's Wild West Show he slowed down to an easy trot, no doubt to spare the horse, and I managed to catch up a bit—although I didn't want to get so close that the cowboys noticed me. I was as good a rider as any of the soldiers, I thought, and the Army had provided its men with an excellent model of bicycle; but if the cowboys in the buckboard decided to outrun me, they almost certainly could.

I didn't even want to think about what would happen if they decided to fire a couple of shots my way. In that case, I could only hope that they were among the majority of pistol owners who, according to Colonel Cody, didn't practice enough to be accurate. On the other hand, if one of the two had killed Jed Harrington from fifty yards away, they might be able to do the same to me from this distance . . . I pedaled forward, eyes on the buckboard, glad for once that I was wearing a dark suit.

By now we were several miles west of town, with woods on both sides of the road. The only sounds were the muffled clip-clop of the horse's hooves, the distant jingling of the harness, and the whirring of my bicycle's chain. There was a slight uphill pitch to the land, but not really enough to make for difficult cycling—for which I was thankful. I knew time was of the essence; otherwise I might have stopped at Cody's and tried to enlist help— a good rifle shot or two might be a useful ally at this stage.

But the chance for that had passed. Eventually the buckboard would turn off the main road, and at that point I would face a choice. I could simply continue my pursuit, but that would leave no way for anyone following me to know which way I'd gone. Or I could try to leave some sort of sign to alert my pursuers; that would have to be done quickly, and at the same time it would have to be clear enough that nobody could miss it, even in the dark. Perhaps I could draw an arrow in the road with a sharp stick, with a brief message . . .

I had to hope that my employer and Mr. Roosevelt were persuasive when they spoke to the sheriff. If help was not reasonably close behind, I was running into trouble—and I could only hope that it wasn't more than I could handle by myself. I'd probably do better using my wits than my fists, I told myself, and that was assuming I could stay close enough to the buckboard to do anything at all. Not for the first time, I found myself glad that I'd taken up bicycling during our stay in Italy. Thanks to riding from Stettignano to Florence and back almost daily, my wind and legs were holding up reasonably well here in Montana.

Ahead of me the buckboard slowed. I picked up my speed so that if it turned off the road, I could hope to follow whatever turns it made. I still hadn't decided what, if anything, I could do to mark my trail for whoever came looking for me. But I crouched low, hoping to make myself as hard as possible to see if the men ahead of me looked back.

The rig turned right, and as soon as it was out of sight,

I put on all the speed I could manage, hoping to have time to leave some mark to show the trail before I took up the pursuit again. At the intersection, I got off the bicycle and quickly picked up a fallen branch that was about a yard long. I broke it off and laid the pieces down in the form of an arrow pointing up the side road. Now I could only hope that anyone coming after would see it and grasp its meaning. There was no time to admire my workmanship; I hopped back on the bike and started after the buckboard again.

The side road was narrower, headed uphill, and the ruts were deeper. It was harder to keep the buckboard in sight, and harder to make much speed. Luckily for me, the buckboard slowed down, too. I stopped twice more to mark the trail. Then, at last, I became aware that the buckboard had stopped. We were in a moderately large clearing—perhaps a former homestead. In the moonlight I could discern the outlines of a cabin in the clearing. The horse was hitched to a sapling in front of it, and as I watched, the warm light of a coal oil lamp came through a window. The chase had reached its end—or so I hoped.

Now I was going to have to answer the question I had so far postponed considering. Having caught up with Clara and her abductors, what was my next step? I was still outnumbered two-to-one—assuming there weren't other accomplices I didn't know of inside the cabin. A moment's reflection convinced me that the two cowboys were probably alone; if someone had been waiting for them here, the light would already have been on, I reasoned.

At the same time, I realized that I couldn't in good conscience wait outside for help to arrive. Unless Mr. Clemens and Mr. Roosevelt had acted with unusual dispatch and gotten instant cooperation, there was likely to be a considerable delay in the arrival of reinforcements. And during that time, Clara would be at the mercy of two men whose character I already knew to be less than exemplary. I would have to expose myself, if only to distract them from her.

I set the bike up where I hoped it would be visible to anyone who came looking for me. Then, after taking a deep breath, I walked up to the cabin and knocked on the door.

There was an anxious wait, during which I attempted (with little success) to make out what was going on inside. At last, the door creaked open to reveal Zach'ry, with a pistol pointed at my face. "I'm not armed," I said quickly, and raised my hands to show him they were empty.

"Get inside," he barked, which I did—making every effort to avoid giving him any excuse to use the gun. There, in the light of the lantern, I saw that I was in a single-room cabin, which appeared to have been uninhabited for quite some time before the last few days, when someone had moved in and put it to use again. Perhaps this was where Jed Harrington had spent his nights. The floor was nothing but packed earth, which probably was just as well, considering how little effort seemed to have been made to keep it clean. Clara Clemens was sitting at the back of the sparsely furnished room, on a three-legged stool by a crude fireplace. Her eyebrows rose as she saw me, but she said nothing.

"It's the city boy! What the blazes are you doing here?" said C. D., who had his own revolver in his hand.

"That's my boss's daughter," I said, nodding in the direction of Miss Clemens. I kept my hands high. "I saw her in the buckboard as you left town, and I decided I'd better find out what was going on. Are you all right, Clara?"

"I'm not hurt," she said quietly. "If I had my choice, I'd rather be back in town with my father and mother, but other than that, I suppose I'm all right."

"You listen to us and you'll stay all right," said C. D. "We don't mean any harm to the young lady, mister. But she showed up and started asking too many questions, and coming up with answers we didn't want her telling people. So we decided to get her away from other people long enough to get ourselves a head start on the law. We didn't plan on nobody else droppin' in on us."

"I'm sorry to spoil your plans," I said. "But I'm afraid she's not the only one who's figured out what went on the night Jed Harrington died. When enough people start putting two and two together, you shouldn't be surprised that they start coming up with the right answers."

"This blows it all to hell, C. D.," said Zach'ry. "There might be a posse comin' after us right now. I say we tie 'em both up and skedaddle before somebody comes lookin' for 'em."

In fact, I fervently hoped there was a posse on the way. But unless I wanted the killers—for that is what I believed these two men were—to escape justice, I had to contrive some way to keep them here a little longer. The only problem was that there would be an element of danger if they were surrounded here while they still held us prisoner. I was willing to take that risk myself, but did I have any right to subject Clara to it?

She saved me the decision by turning to them and asking, "Before you go, I'd appreciate it if you told me just one thing. Everyone thought you two were Jed Harrington's only friends. What happened between you that you had to kill him?"

"Wasn't nothin' between us," said C. D. "More like, it was what was happenin' between him and everybody else. Like when he knocked over that colored soldier, and half the town was ready to horsewhip him. And he was lookin' to us to take his back."

"Right," said Zach'ry. "That's all we needed, to go to war with the goddamn U.S. Army. Maybe Jed was too drunk to care about it, but C. D. and me knew right then he was courtin' more trouble than any three of us could handle. After that mixup with the colored soldier and Judge Blankenship in front of the hotel, he went and cussed us out good and hard for not jumpin' in to help him when we seen he was outnumbered."

"I don't see how he could hold that against you," I said. "There are times when it's smartest to walk away from a fight. But I guess Harrington didn't understand that."

"God, no," said Zach'ry. "The damn fool just went out lookin' for more trouble—found it, too. He told us about layin' for you by the hotel, when Blankenship got the drop on him again. He didn't care; soon as he found us again, he was tryin' to get us to come help him bush-whack the judge."

"That was when me and Zach'ry knew we was out of choices. We had to get rid of Jed, before he got us all killed," said C. D. He rolled a cigarette as he spoke. "He kept up the way he was goin', there wasn't any doubt somebody was goin' to kill *him*. One of them colored boys from the Army, most likely, although there was a lot of other folks didn't have much use for him. In fact, me and Zach'ry had pretty much run out of use for him, too." He licked the crooked cylinder of tobacco and paper and fished for a match.

"Why didn't you just break with him?" I said. "It seems the easiest thing to do. Just walk away and stop associating with him—that way you'd be out of the way of trouble."

"Y'know, we tried that once," said Zach'ry. "Jed wouldn't leave us alone. He come lookin' for us, kept on us until we went out so he could buy us a drink. And sure enough, once I had a few beers in my belly, ol' Jed didn't seem so bad. His little pranks and stuff were down-right funny, in fact. You can't really walk away from a fellow that makes you laugh like that, even if he is like to get you killed—either from a bullet or a rope."

"That's what it would've come to, too," said C. D. "When he knocked down that colored soldier, and you and Judge Blankenship and those other fellows come run-ning to the rescue, it was just that close to Jed pulling out a gun and going for it. I was scared plum silly, I tell you. I knew right then that we'd have to do him in before we got caught in a crossfire. And when he called out that sergeant in one bar, and then had that run-in with Blankenship later that night, we knew it couldn't wait."

Zach'ry spit a stream of tobacco juice and said, "The thing was, we had to find a way to snuff him out so they couldn't pin it on either one of us. We weren't so green as to think the sheriff and his boys would just wink an eye at us for riddin' the country of him, much as it was a sort of favor to 'em."

"An interesting way to look at it," I said. "I might almost sympathize with you, if you hadn't left Mr. Blankenship to rot in jail, accused of the shooting."

"Oh, hell, it served him right," said C. D. "Back in Dillon he persecuted Jed every single chance he got, no doubt about that. And we got our share of the persecution, too. He fined me three or four times, and put me in the can a couple of nights, too. Ol' man Blankenship sure don't have no partic'lar favors comin' to him from *me*."

"A-*men*," said Zach'ry. He leaned forward, his arm around C. D.'s shoulder. "What we hit on was almost an accident. We was in Mike Thompson's place, all three of us right after he told us about Blankenship pulling a rifle on him. I got talking to that little hussy Lil. And durn me if I didn't think it'd be more fun to stay with her awhile than to go out raisin' hell with Jed, the way he was. So I went upstairs with her, and made like I was drinkin' a whole lot more whiskey than I was—I didn't drink hardly any, to tell the truth—and like I passed out on her. She was sort of put out, I could tell, 'cause there I was in the bed she used for business, you know?"

Clara Clemens, who had been following the conversation without saying anything, turned bright red at this remark. Not wishing to expose her to further embarrassment, I decided not to let him linger on that subject. "Then, when nobody was looking, you crept out and followed Jed and C. D., I take it?"

"You take it right," said Zach'ry. "I figured if we took care of our business good and quick, I could sneak back in to Lil's bedroom fast enough that nobody'd know the difference. The idea was C. D. would be able to prove he didn't do it, 'cause his gun hadn't been shot when the deputies found him. And I would have the alibi of bein' passed out back at Lil's, which gave me a witness."

"Well, it obviously worked; you fooled us, and you seem to have fooled the sheriff," I said. Flattery seemed a useful ploy, if only to keep them more or less occupied with bragging rather than worrying about what might be happening outside their hideout. "But which one of you actually shot him? We couldn't figure that out at all."

"That one did it," said a voice from behind them.

Clara Clemens gave a little shriek, and everyone emitted some sound of surprise as all four of us turned to see who had crept into our midst without any of us noticing. "Joe Fox," I said. "How long have you been here?"

The Indian scout was sitting calmly on the windowsill, a rifle cradled in his arms. His face was as placid as if he had been sitting under a pine tree, watching the clouds pass by. "Long enough to hear these men tell their story, and to know that they are telling you the truth—at least, about the part of it I saw."

"You say you saw it?" Zach'ry asked. Then his face turned shrewd and he said, "You gotta be lying, Injun—there weren't nobody on that street but us."

"You think that," said Joe Fox, his voice still level and quiet. "There are many things you think that are not true, and many things you do not think about at all. How long was I here before any of you knew it?"

"Better you ought to ask how much longer you're goin' to be here," said C. D. "There's two of us and only one of you; if me and Zach'ry both go for our guns at once, you can't kill us both before we get you."

"That's where you're wrong again," said the scout. "I don't need to kill anyone, and even if you get me, you aren't safe or free. Look out the window behind me."

Until then, my gaze had been focused on Joe Fox. Now I realized that outside the farmhouse I had been seeing movement for quite some time. Looking directly at the moonlit yard, I saw what I had been missing. There, moving into position outside the little building were men on bicycles—black men in uniform. The 27th Infantry Regiment had set up its picket lines outside the house. We were surrounded by the U.S. Army.

"Where the hell did they come from?" C. D.'s eyes seemed ready to bulge out of their sockets. Zach'ry's mouth was open with surprise, as well. "I didn't hear a thing," C. D. added.

"This is a good thing about the two-wheeled machines," said Joe Fox approvingly. "They are quiet. Many men can ride up close to an enemy without being heard. They are no good in the mud, and they have no souls at all."

"My father would agree with you on that last point," said Clara Clemens. She turned to me and said briskly, "Well, Mr. Cabot, shall we go?"

"And just where do you think you're goin' to?" snarled Zach'ry. I turned to see that he had his revolver in his hand. "You're our only bargaining points, now—you two and the Injun, if anybody wants him. C. D. and me, we aim to get on our horses and ride out of here. And if anybody tries to stop us, you're the ones who'll be the first to pay."

"It won't be that easy," I said. "Those men out there are sharpshooters—they can pick you off like sitting birds before you fire a shot."

"You want to bet your life on that?" asked Zach'ry. "Now, shut up and get over there against the wall, so's I can cover you all at once. And you, Injun, put that rifle down 'fore I lose my temper. I'll plug you soon as look at you."

Clara and I looked at one another and, wordlessly, moved over to where the cowboy had indicated. Meanwhile, Joe Fox shrugged and set the rifle down on the

floor at his feet. C. D. quickly stepped forward and
picked it up while Zach'ry covered him.

Fox spread his now empty hands. "The young white
man speaks truth," he said. "Do you want me to show
you? Make me one of your cigarettes."

"What, give a smoke to a redskin?" snorted C. D.

"Why not?" I said. "If I understand what he's going
to do, I think it'll be worth your while. Besides, the Indians were using tobacco before any white man came to
America. I'd say he's entitled to a little bit of it back."

"What the hell, now I'm curious," said Zach'ry. He
reached in his pocket and tossed a little pouch to Joe
Fox. "Here's the makin's—fix your own."

Joe Fox took papers and tobacco out of the pouch and
quickly made a slim cigarette from them—much slimmer
than usual, I thought. C. D. snorted. "Don't cheat yourself," he said. "Go 'head and make a good fat one."

"That's easy to say when it ain't your 'baccy," said
Zach'ry. "That one looks fine to me."

"It is enough," said Joe Fox, tossing back the pouch.
"This will do. Does one of you have a match?"

"Hell, if you ain't got a match, you won't be needin'
the smoke, will you?" guffawed C. D. But he reached in
his pocket and pulled out a matchbox. "Here." He tossed
it to Joe Fox.

"Very good," said Joe Fox. "Now, I think everyone
should stand away from the window." C. D. and Zach'ry
looked at one another with puzzled expressions, but before they could ask what the Indian meant, he had struck
the match and held it up an inch from the tip of the
cigarette, now in his mouth. I think he held it there for
perhaps two seconds before a sharp report rang out outside and his cigarette was cut in two by a bullet that
thwacked against the back wall of the cabin. The cut end
of the paper had barely fallen to the floor when another
shot clipped off the end of the match, just below the
flame.

"Jesus!" said Zach'ry, as Joe Fox nonchalantly put his

moccasined foot atop the still burning match end and ground it out. "What the hell was that all about?"

"That was to show you what the men outside can do," said Joe Fox. "There are guns pointing at this house right now. Do you still want to get on your horses and ride away from men who can shoot like that? How far do you think you will get? Not all of them can shoot that good—I won't lie to you. But only one of them needs to do it, I think."

"To hell with you, Injun," said Zach'ry. "Better to go down like a man than to swing, says I. With the girl and the dude for shields, we can get to the horses, and then we've got a show. Are you game, C. D.?"

C. D. looked at him and shook his head. "No, sir," he said. "Nobody ever called me a coward to my face, but you're talking about plain suicide, Zach'ry. Might as well have stayed with Jed as try to run away from fifty sharpshooters. I ain't goin' to do it." He took his gun from its holster and put it on the dust-covered table next to him, then stepped back from it. "I ain't getting no more blood on my hands," he said.

Zach'ry said something very foul. "They'll *hang* us, C. D.," he said, a desperate look on his face. "I won't let 'em do it. A bullet's cleaner. Come on, let's make a stand."

"You won't hang if you can prove self-defense," said Clara Clemens calmly.

"Self-defense?" said Zach'ry. "Why would they believe that?"

"Because everyone, from the sheriff to the judge to every saloon keeper in town, knows what kind of walking trouble Jed Harrington was," said Clara. "You've as much as said you were afraid he'd get you killed, and I believe it. Why shouldn't a jury believe it?"

"The girl's makin' a lot of sense, Zach'ry," said C. D. "Jed was a mean man, you know that as well as anybody. You think all those people are goin' to hold it against us for getting rid of him for 'em? They might even vote us a medal, if we play our cards right."

"I just don't know," said Zach'ry, nonplussed. "There ain't no guarantees to it. It's an awful big chance."

"But you still would have a chance," said Clara. Her voice was almost a whisper, but it cut right through the silence around the cabin. "A far better chance than if you make a run for it or try to make a stand against those Army marksmen. If they fire their guns again, I don't think it will be as harmless as the first two shots."

"Miss Clemens is right," I said. "You've already seen how smart she is, tracking you down when none of the rest of us could. Listen to her now. She won't lead you astray." I had no idea how realistic her suggestions might be, but anything that reduced the possibility of gunplay struck me as eminently sensible. The men outside might be sharpshooters one and all, but a single stray shot was all it would take to ruin what had been so far a very convincing rescue.

Zach'ry looked down at the gun in his hand, then over at the cut half-cigarette on the floor. At that moment, Joe Fox held up the inch-long matchstick that the second bullet had cut, saying nothing, but looking him straight in the eye. There was a long moment of silence, then Zach'ry said, "Aw, shucks. Take my gun, somebody. I never thought I'd go down without a fight, but you done convinced me. I'll take my chances with the law."

I took the pistol he handed me, and at the same time Clara picked up the rifle and returned it to Joe Fox. "Thank you," I said. "I think you've made the right decision."

"I just don't know," said Zach'ry, but then the door burst open and half a dozen men in uniform swarmed in to take him and C. D. prisoner. Clara Clemens let out a long sigh. Our ordeal was over, and we were free again.

⇒ 20

Tom Blankenship leaned back in his rocking chair and propped his feet up on the railing of the Florence House's big front porch. He flicked an ash off his cigar and grinned. "Didn't I tell you all along, Sam?" he said. "You was the best lawyer a fellow could ask for."

"I don't know how you get that," grumbled my employer, who sat in an adjacent rocking chair. "I damn near got my daughter and my secretary shot up by a pair of cowboys, and had to send in the U.S. Army—and Theodore Roosevelt and Annie Oakley, too—to rescue 'em and catch the killers. And even then, if C. D. hadn't talked his head off when we got him to the sheriff's office, you might still be behind bars. With that kind of record, I doubt I'll ever get another case."

"But I'm out, ain't I?" said Tom Blankenship. "And everybody's safe. That's what matters, Sam. All's well that ends well, even if you got a bit of a rough ride on the way there."

"I'm the one that had the rough ride," said Roosevelt, who sat on the other side of Blankenship from my employer. "Those bicycles may be the coming thing, but given the choice, I'll stick with horses, thank you very much. I must have jarred every bone in my body trying to keep up with those soldiers." After a moment's thought he added, "It was a bully rescue, though. I'd do it again in an instant."

"Frankly, I think I'd forego the pleasure," said Clara Clemens, who leaned next to me on the railing facing the three seated men. "Not that I'm at all ungrateful, mind you. I'm sure you could find other volunteers to be rescued, and to enjoy all the glory and excitement. But once is quite enough for me, thank you."

"Sam, you got you a smart young lady there," said Blankenship. "Adventures ain't nothin' like what they're cracked up to be, no sir-ee. In point of fact, I don't think they're a bit healthy. Just a-sittin' and a-rockin' is a lot more my style."

"Do you think C. D. and Zach'ry will be hanged?" asked Clara.

"It'll mostly depend on the judge," said Tom Blankenship. "I'd surely hate to be the one to decide it—not that I'd ever get to, in a case where I was so mixed up in it. They *did* murder Jed Harrington, not much doubt about that, seein' as how C. D.'s confessed that he and Zach'ry done it. Not to mention having that Injun Joe Fox come forth as a witness, once he saw how the wind blew. His word'll go a long way, and might mean that Mr. Cabot and Miz Clara don't have to come back for a trial. But Jed Harrington wasn't nobody's favorite, and I s'pose that might make a jury go soft on 'em—maybe just a long time in jail. C. D. may get off easier, since Zach'ry did the shooting. Help 'em a lot if they got a good lawyer, though." He looked at my employer and grinned.

"I'm not available," said Mr. Clemens. "In fact, I'm leaving town for parts west on the train tomorrow morning. Seattle, San Francisco, the Hawaiian islands—it'll be a grand adventure, Tom. I wish you could come along with us."

Blankenship shifted his corncob pipe from one side of his mouth to the other, took a puff, then said, "I reckon I'll pass, Sam. Adventures was always more your style than mine. Besides, I've got a bit of unfinished business hereabouts . . ."

"In the form of a pretty Norwegian widow?" said Mr. Clemens. "I always wondered what kind of girl would catch your eye, Tom. I think you found a good one."

"Aha! So that's the great secret Clemens couldn't tell," said Roosevelt. "But why are you telling us now, when you wouldn't before?"

Blankenship smiled. " 'Cause, while I was settin' there in jail, I got a good chance to think about a lot of things, Mr. Roosevelt. If you put a fellow behind bars, and tell him he's goin' to be put on trial for murder, and maybe end up hangin', it's like to give him a real fine sense of what's important and what ain't. So the first thing I done when the sheriff let me loose was walk over to Jenny Larson's place and ask her if she'd ever thought about havin' another husband, and whether she thought I might be the kind of man she'd have."

"And I take it she agreed to have you?" asked Clara Clemens. She was smiling broadly, and Blankenship's grin grew wider, too. He said nothing, but simply nodded. "Oh, good," said Clara, clapping her hands.

"Well, I sure hope so," said Mr. Blankenship. "There's one little complication, in the shape of another pretty widow down in Dillon—Sally Wakeham by name. She and her husband Ben were my neighbors down there. I used to set and smoke and be sociable with Ben after he lost his leg in that railroad accident back in '87. Then when my poor Abbie took sick, Sally'd come over and help around the house. So we got to know each other right well before her husband died three years back, about two weeks before my wife. And we just kept on seein' each other. 'Fore long, it started feeling right comfortable to be around each other. Her kids was mostly growed up, and I never had any. And after a while, we started thinkin' about gettin' hitched. You know, it gets mighty cold at nights up here." He blushed.

"Were you engaged?" asked Clara Clemens.

"No—not like we had any announcement, or bans read, or like that," said Blankenship. "But Dillon's a small town, and everybody just took it for granted we was a couple, you know?"

"Do you care for her, though?" Clara persisted.

"Well, sure," said Blankenship, looking up at his old friend's daughter. "That's why, when I met Jenny, it was, like . . ." He stammered for a minute, then went on in a quiet voice. "It was like nothin' else that's ever happened. She came down to Dillon on the train, visitin' her sister, and I was like I got hit by lightnin' when I saw her. Here I am, closer to sixty than fifty, and durn if I didn't feel like a young pup again. When she left to come back here, there was something gone from my life."

"And Sally—did you say anything to her?" asked Clara, leaning forward in her chair. I think it pleased her to get a glimpse of the tender side of her father's old friend.

Blankenship sighed. "I told her all about it, and she understood, I think. She was a widow, too. I told her I wouldn't see Jenny again—told her I'd forget her. Well, not seein' her was easy, a hundred miles away. But I couldn't forget her. And when I heard Sam was coming through here . . . I reckon you can figure out the rest."

"She's a mighty fine woman, Tom," said Mr. Clemens quietly.

"Yes, but that ain't the point, Sam," said Blankenship. "When I was arrested, I couldn't let folks back in Dillon know where I'd been—seeing another woman, when they all thought me and Sally were going to get hitched. How could I let her be humiliated all over Dillon?"

"So that's why you refused to tell the judge you were a magistrate back home," I said. "You were afraid they'd call down there to verify your story, and word would get back to her."

"She got wind of it, anyway," said Blankenship. "First thing I found when I went back to my rooming house was a letter from her. She writes a right pretty letter, Sam. She said I ought to follow my heart . . . and that was all the word I needed. 'Cause after I'd spent a few days sittin' in jail and thinkin' about things, I made up my mind that Jenny was right for me. And since she sees it the same way, I'm a happy man."

"My congratulations to you, then," I said. "But I have a question of my own—one that's been bothering me ever since you came and chased away Jed Harrington in front of our hotel a few hours before he was killed. Why were you walking around Missoula with a rifle in your arms that night?"

Mr. Blankenship blushed. "Well, I didn't want to tell this before, on account of I was embarrassed for Miz Jenny about it. You know she lives in a kind of run-down part of town not the worst, mind you, but not the best either. The long and short of it is, there's a whole swarm of rats in that house of hers. She's tried traps, and she's tried poison, and the durn things just keep comin' and comin'. I went and got her a little kitty-cat, but it's goin' to have to grow a heap before it'll be much help in that department. And quality folks, the kind that send her their laundry and ironin', might stop sendin' it if they knew them varmints was running all over her place. So I volunteered to help out a bit."

"I don't follow you," I said.

"I do," said Roosevelt. "I'll bet he was going to go up there and pick off as many rats as dared show their hides. But you couldn't have done it that night, Mr. Blankenship—people would have reported the shots when they were questioned about the shooting. And nobody remembered but the one shot."

"Well, I was goin' to do it the next morning," said Blankenship. He blushed and said, "The idea was I'd stay with Jenny that night, and that's where I was headed when Jed got shot. With me carryin' my gun, and the deputies on the prowl, that sort of messed up my plans. I was headed back to my rooming house when the deputies caught me, and then I didn't want to say nothin' to bring attention to Jenny, you know?"

"Well, it's a good thing Joe Fox finally brought her to our attention," said Mr. Clemens. "And a better thing that she sent Clara, and then Wentworth, to talk to Ed Potter, who was still awake when the shooting happened, and who remembered seeing three people walk down that street together instead of just two."

"That was my first hint that C. D. and Zach'ry might have been the killers," I said. "Well, it's all sorted out now, I suppose. And thank God Miss Clemens is safe— although we ought to be thanking her for finally flushing the guilty parties into the open."

"I was wondering if anyone would notice that," she said with a wry smile. "I consider my little expedition quite a success, in that regard at least."

"Young lady, that's the kind of success we can all do without," said Mr. Clemens. "If you were a bit younger, I'd turn you over my knee . . ."

"Father, if I ever again show any sign of wanting to run off to hunt for murderers, I hope you *will* turn me over your knee," said Clara. "I won't pretend to have enjoyed it. But you brave gentlemen were getting nowhere at all on your own, and so it was high time for a woman's touch. In fact, if I hadn't gone to talk to Lil, as that poor woman calls herself, at Thompson's saloon, I might never have run into C. D. and Zach'ry—and we'd be no further along than before."

"There was a remarkable bit of luck all around," said Mr. Roosevelt. "If there hadn't been soldiers in town, so we could recruit their help . . . if the killers hadn't led us past Cody's camp, where we could enlist Miss Oakley— and Joe Fox, of all people to find there! If Cabot hadn't thought to mark his trail . . ."

"If somebody will pour me another shot of whiskey, I'll be happy enough," said Mr. Clemens. "Tom, as much fun as I've had getting to see you again, I can't say I won't be happy to get out of Montana. There's a whole big world waiting along those railroad tracks, and with any luck, the Madam and Clara and I will get to see it without ever hearing the word 'murder' again. And poor Wentworth won't have to face anybody more dangerous than a theater manager."

"Sir, I'm afraid you've already lost that wish," I said.

"What did you say?" said Mr. Clemens, squinting at me. "What are you talking about, Wentworth?"

"I reckon I can tell you, Sam," said Tom Blankenship, with a chuckle. "Unless he quits his job, he's going to have to deal with you almost every day. And you're the most dangerous man to be around I ever met, Sam."

"Why, Tom, how can you say that?" said Mr. Clemens, with an offended look. "Here you've just been face to face with killers, and like to be hanged for something you never did, and you call me dangerous?"

"I sure do, Sam," said Tom Blankenship. He took a puff on his pipe, smiling quietly, then added, "I ain't had such a week of fun since you and me was tykes, stealin' rides on steamboats and all such nonsense. But I reckon it's time to let things go back to how they usually are. When you're back from your trip around the world, come on by and see me again."

"I will, Tom," said Mr. Clemens. "I promise I will."

"Good," said Blankenship. "Maybe by then I'll be rested up enough to take on another round of adventures. Until then, Miz Jenny Larson ought to be all the excitement I can stand. You done your best by me, even if it did take a couple dozen soldiers, and an Injun, and Miss Annie Oakley, and so forth and so on. I don't know where else I could get that kind of service. You couldn't find another lawyer in Montana that would do the like. But, if I get my choice in things, I mean to carry on so I don't need any more lawyers. I done had my fill."

"I'm glad to hear it, Tom," said Mr. Clemens. "Because I just retired from the lawyer business—forever.

And I reckon the business will be the better for it."

"One thing for sure," said Clara Clemens. "It will never be the same again." She paused and added coyly, "And so much the better for all concerned!"

Mr. Clemens tried his best to frown at that, but in the end even he couldn't help joining in a general round of laughter.

Epilogue

A few weeks later, upon our arrival in San Francisco, the following letter was waiting for Mr. Clemens at our hotel:

Dear Sam,

Well, I was sure glad to see you when you came through here last month, and I reckon it was a good time, all things told. I didn't plan on spending so much of it in jail, but I been there before and they didn't treat me too bad this time.

I thought you'd like to know how everything ended up with the Jed Harrington murder. C. D. and Zach'ry decided to stick with the story Miss Clara told them to use, about killing Jed in self-defense so's they wouldn't get in trouble later. The newspapers here had a ball with it all. Called it the "Mark Twain defense," which Judge Joe Mc-Coy didn't like at all, seeing how you'd made him look like a monkey in his own courtroom.

But a big shot lawyer from Helena, Leon Dirksen, read about it in the newspapers and came out to volunteer to defend 'em. And regular folks was saying as how, "They was really good boys at heart, and they wouldn't of got in such trouble except for bad company, and they done a service to the community when they killed that mean old bully." Dirksen, he mostly encouraged that kind of talk, except he played the soft pedal on that last part.

And then one morning, about two days before the trial was set, they was gone, in spite of the sheriff putting double guards on them and all that. The way everybody figures it, somebody must have snuck a key to the jail in C. D. or Zach'ry's dinner plate, and then made sure the guards didn't pay very good attention when they used the key the way it was supposed to be used. Anyhow, they ain't been seen since.

Dirksen was all down at the mouth on account of he didn't get a chance to defend 'em—folks say he wants to run for Governor, and he thought he could make himself famous. I wouldn't vote for him, but I reckon he can't help bein' a lawyer, and other folks don't seem to mind. And Joe McCoy wanted to bring charges against Dirksen for inciting folks to let 'em loose, but ain't nothing come of that, neither.

I went back home and talked to Sally Wakeham. She's taken up with a farmer name of Phil Morrow, and looks to be ready to marry him, and she don't hold nothing against me. It was a considerable relief to know I hadn't broke her heart after all, and so I went and married Jenny Larson with a clear conscience. We ain't decided whether I ought to move to Missoula or she ought to come down to Dillon yet, but whichever it is I reckon she'll be happy long as she can bring along her little cat Oscar.

I sure do hope you can come back here, and bring your ladies and Mr. Wentworth when you're done going 'round the world, and I hope we don't have no more murders when you do. I had my share of that kind of excitement long since.

> *Your old pal,*
> *Tom Blankenship*

CARROLL LACHNIT

MURDER IN BRIEF   0-425-14790-8/$4.99

For rich, good-looking Bradley Cogburn, law school seemed to be a lark.
Even an accusation of plagiarism didn't faze him: he was sure he could
prove his innocence. But for ex-cop Hannah Barlow, law school was her
last chance. As Bradley's moot-court partner, she was tainted by the same
accusation. Now Bradley Cogburn is dead, and Hannah has to act like a cop
again. This time, it's her own life that's at stake...

A BLESSED DEATH   0-425-15347-9/$5.99

Lawyer Hannah Barlow's connection to the Church is strictly legal. But as
she explores the strange disappearances—and confronts her own spiritual
longings—she finds that crime, too, works in mysterious ways...

AKIN TO DEATH   0-425-16409-8/$6.50

Hannah Barlow's first case is to finalize an adoption. It's a no-brainer that
is supposed to be a formality—until a man bursts into her office, claiming
to be the baby's biological father. So Hannah delves into the mystery—and
what she finds is an elaborate web of deceit...

JANIE'S LAW   0-425-17150-7/$6.50

The day convicted child molester Freddy Roche walks into Hannah
Barlow's law office is the day unwelcome memories of the past come
flooding back to her. But Roche is asking Hannah to help him fight for his
right to start over. It's a controversial case that may cost her her life...